Jones Whitman, Time Traveler

Geared to the Present

Jones Whitman, Time Traveler

Geared to the Present

by

Dana Bennett

TandemWriters

Geared to the Present

Copyright © 2014 by Dana Bennett

This is a work of fiction. Names, character, places, brands, media, and incidents are either the product of the author's imagination or are used fictitiously.

Cover design by Clarissa Yeo
Logo design by Olivia E. Bennett
Edited by Daniel James Johns Kenyon

ISBN: 978-0-61596-812-4 (Trade Paperback)
ISBN: 978-1-63173-515-8 (eBook)

This book is dedicated to my fellow time traveler, Blakely Bennett, my wife and spiritual partner.

ACKNOWLEDGMENTS

I want to acknowledge H. Engle, B. Munroe, B. Lewis, BHop53 and S. Carver for their invaluable support and feedback. Daniel Kenyon, editor, for his excellent contributions to the manuscript and Clarissa Yeo, Yocla Designs, for her magic in designing the cover, and of course, all those who took an interest in the development process as the characters came alive. It meant a great deal to me that you were interested. Thanks to S. Higgins for setting up the cover reveal and Blakely Bennett for her wonderful expertise with book formatting and publishing.

This is a solo endeavor, but as Blakely has already shared with our readers, it never takes place in a vacuum. We tandem write, even on our individual projects, loaning an ear, sharing ideas and being each other's first readers.

Tuesday, 1 September 1891, 3:30 pm

Boston, MA

From above, the Boston Haymarket terminal appeared as a chaotic dance of ricocheting atoms. Black top hats and colorful parasols twirled, morphing into gears that spun in synchronization with the massive steel wheels of a black cast-iron engine that hissed steam as it screeched to a halt. The elevated squealing of steel on steel and loud whistle followed by the cascading echo—like leather trunks slammed shut one by one—heralded their arrival at the Haymarket train station. Two young men, remarkably different in stature and dress, stepped from the train onto the platform and pushed through the throng of commuters.

"Right on time as usual," Jones noted with satisfaction as he pulled a gold-embossed pocket watch from his gray waistcoat. "A prompt arrival gives one a sense of security."

He held the open pocket watch up toward Roark's face and pointed to the massive train station clock above the exit.

" 'at and a small gun," Roark said.

"Ha!" Jones chortled. "An excellent observation. I, however, cannot imagine needing any weapon other than you."

Roark's unwieldy size attracted unsolicited attention wherever they traveled. Dressed in common brown pants, work boots and a linen peasant-shirt, he contrasted to a significant degree with the wiry Jones in his semi-formal apparel. He intended to keep the Irish brute within arm's reach for the sake of both of them.

They arrived at the station storage and retrieved Jones's

1

motorbike from a burly fellow who seemed a bit confused by the contraption. The bike appeared tiny next to Roark while he held it in place for Jones.

"Roark, be a good fellow and carry my satchel will you?" Jones removed his topcoat, waistcoat and floppy bowtie. "And these items as well?" he flashed a smile. "I shall pull my topper down tight for the ride home. I will need my dustcoat and goggles for safety. Oh, and I will take my pocket watch with me to time the trip."

Roark unleashed the gold pocket watch from the buttonhole of the waistcoat and handed it to Jones. He pulled out Jones's dustcoat and goggles from the satchel, hung them on the handlebars, and folded the waistcoat and topcoat, pushing them into the satchel with the tie.

"See ya at home 'en," Roark said with a nod. He turned and started his trek to the Victorian house at number 4 Garden Court Street, half a mile away.

Jones planned to take the long way home as he mounted the saddle, lit the external fire tube and waited. The single stroke engine fired off just as the priest approached.

"You amaze me," Father Carlini called out over the steam engine as he rushed towards Jones causing his black cassock to flow out behind him and his shoulder cape sleeves to flutter. "What'ta exactly do you have against'a God that you cannot'a be satisfied?" he chided while flailing his arms. "Forever exploiting your power and wealth—in spite of the dismay you'a bring to this'a community—with your unseemly spectacle of noise and machinery. You'a heretic and'a rude." Father Carlini leaned in close to Jones and growled, "And if I cannot'a bring you to God, I will, nonetheless, find a way to put'ta you away same as your'a uncle. You Whitman are all alike."

Jones amused himself with the thought that the priest looked like a peacock with the purple sash and buttons running down his robe, but he kept those thoughts to himself. Father Carlini postured in a manner meant to intimidate Jones.

Jones reached out and, in a brazen manner, fingered the cassock sleeves. "Nice material. From China, perhaps?" He stared into the eyes of the priest. "Father Carlini, surely you and the Vatican have much more important endeavors than attempting to find a way to end the transcendentalism movement. Why do you not feed the poor and cure the sick? I do feel certain you think we are competing for the minds and hearts of the common person. Rest assured you have nothing to fear when it comes to your sheep—I mean your flock, as they will follow you without question wherever you may lead."

"You'a believe philosophy will'a bring happiness, but you are sadly mistaken young man." He wagged his finger in Jones's face. "Have'a you no fear of the God Almighty? Soon, I shall see to it that you'a will be contemplating your life from the inside of an asylum cell."

"Your egregious attitude gives me pause. Is it because of my belief in transcendentalism as well as my scientific pursuits?" Jones paused with his hand on his chin. "On the other hand, I suspect a more personal conflict: you resent that Emily has chosen me. Dare I say you are jealous? Be careful, Father. She is a parishioner." Jones adjusted his goggles over his eyes and pulled his top hat down tight over his short dark hair. "In addition, you do not have enough power, including Pope Leo, to change my domicile of choice. Have I made myself clear? *Arrivederci*, Father."

Jones glanced at his watch and released the clutch to

engage the gears attached to the steam piston and waved as he drove away. He motored the loud single stroke engine through the streets down past Boston Harbor at great speed.

"'Yes, yes, yes!" Jones cried out. "This is ultimate freedom." As he slowed for pedestrians, he could not contain his vision of the future. "There will be thousands of these steam driven velocipedes on the road someday."

A toothy grin lit his face as he sped along his usual route to the house, where upon his arrival, he dismounted, made note of his time in a pocket journal and guided the bike up a ramp he had affixed to the front porch. He maneuvered the bike through the front door, coming to rest in the parlor. While his immediate neighbors found his behavior odd, to say the least, they nonetheless tolerated the young man's proclivities because of his status in Boston society.

Jones's uncle, Walt Whitman, the poet, had made a name for himself in the transcendental philosophical movement. Jones had adopted the viewpoint for himself, and coupled with a degree in engineering from Harvard University's Lawrence Scientific School, he determined he could realize anything he had conceived.

Jones shed his goggles and jacket, hung them on the mirror in the hallway, and continued into the kitchen where Roark had set out preparing the evening meal.

"Roark, my travels from the station to home took a mere ten minutes and thirty-seven seconds. It is remarkable. Every time I ride at such great speeds, I feel exhilarated beyond explanation."

"Ya, I can tell 'at about ya."

"What does that mean?"

"I've a feelin' the best is yet to come fer'ya. We should think on what we're doin' this evnin' cause we got a lotta work still wait'n."

"Yes, well. We shall eat our meal and then I will return to the lab to finish my calculations and drawings." Jones took his seat at the table. "I am confident, Roark, by this time next week we will be on the precipice of time travel."

A dainty, modest voice chimed from down the hall.

"Jones," the voice called out. She passed the parlor opening and glanced to her left, "Oh my, why does he insist on keeping that contraption in the parlor? This will just not do."

"In here, Miss Fuller," Jones called out. "You are in time for dinner. Roark set another place for Emily, will you?"

"Oh, no thank you," she said as she made her way down the hall. "I've only stopped by to tell you that we have had the most fortunate luck in reserving the garden chapel for our wedding."

"Oh, how nice for you."

Jones waited at the entrance to the kitchen. Emily strolled down the hallway toward him, stopping to inspect her red coiffed hair as she passed the mirror.

"Do you like my bangs this way?"

She swayed from right to left. Her high-necked dress conformed to her hourglass shape and the ruffled laced sleeves, which stopped just under her elbows, flowed with her movements.

"Alluring as always and there is no doubt in my mind that you sport the finest bangs in Boston."

He embraced her.

"You are such a cad. You would say anything to keep me happy… and quiet."

The light from the kitchen illuminated the paleness of her unblemished skin that blended nearly seamlessly with the off-white of her dress.

"This is far from the truth. I would not compliment you just to keep you quiet." Jones gently pinched her cheeks and smiled. "And as for your assertion, I am indeed a cad, my dear. You and I both know I adore women…" He smiled. "…especially those willing to stand their ground."

"Yes, well, you should have been born earlier and you could have made more of an effort to becharm my Aunt Margaret."

"Your Aunt Margaret could have taught you a couple of life's lessons, I dare say. Anyway … I may be overstepping my bounds."

"I should say so. Your rebuke is a tad offensive and hurts my feelings." Emily pouted, placing her hands on Jones's chest, while staring into his clear blue eyes. "Moreover, if I am to be your lawfully wedded wife, I need your assurances more than your lectures. After all, I am not one of your crony transcendental whatever persons."

She turned her back to Jones.

Jones reached around her waist and drew her in close.

"Correct. I can say, with assurance, you are not. However, in spite of that flaw, I still adore you."

"How very sweet of you," Emily said sweetly. Then, without warning, she broke free of the embrace. "I am off then. Shall we partake of a leisurely bicycle ride tomorrow? Maybe downtown for lunch… or even breakfast?"

"Maybe. I do have several issues I need to take care of before next week. Give me a kiss and then please take your leave before I get too distracted."

Jones bent forward and lifted Emily onto her tiptoes, kissing her more like a lover than a wife-to-be.

"Jones," Roark said. "It's me job to remind ya, we got a

lotta work tonight."

"Alright, I shall let you know concerning the bike ride and will ring you first thing in the morning with my answer. Go and have a wonderful evening."

"Good night, Roark, sweet dreams." Turning back to Jones, Emily batted her long eyelashes and said, "Bye, love." She stroked Jones's cheek one last time and set off. The sound of her heels rapped down the hall, halting at the mirror. After a moment of silence, the tip tap continued until the front door slammed.

Wednesday, 2 September 1891, 8:00 am

J ones retrieved his bicycle and pedaled over to Emily's house, where she was waiting impatiently by the front gate.

"This is far more difficult than the Columbia, I must say." Jones dismounted and greeted Emily with a warm hug.

"Good morning, Mr. Whitman," Emily whispered. She pushed him away and began to twirl. "What do you think of my new bloomers?"

She wore a fitted olive jacket over a white blouse with a large bow at the neck. The green plaid bloomers hung like a skirt, just below her knees, showing off her high tan boots.

"I am impressed. Very striking, I might add." He pulled her back to his embrace and fingered her collar and bowtie while staring into her wide green eyes. "You are remarkably beautiful, soon-to-be Mrs. Whitman."

"I like the sound of that." She kissed his lips. "We are too late for breakfast yet too early for lunch."

"Shall we take coffee at Bailey's Cafe next to the market?"

"That would be fine." She straddled her bike. "That will give me enough time to make my appointment with Father Carlini at ten."

"Concerning this appointment, I would rather remain in the dark, if I may, in an effort to keep the peace between us."

"Nothing important I am sure. Most probably wedding planning. However, I will keep it all to myself."

Emily pushed off in front of Jones.

The two rode in tandem through the sunny side streets of Boston.

"How are you feeling about the wedding?" Emily asked.

"The same way most men feel … left out." He flashed her a look. "But I assure you, I have no problem deferring to your feminine wisdom on such matters."

"You are so lovable. I adore that you allow me to take care of… well, my mother, to take care of everything."

"Your mother is living vicariously through you."

They turned the corner for Bailey's.

"That's not fair. She is only trying to help."

"Your mother would sail with us on the honeymoon were she given the choice."

"That is not true…" She rode a bit further then allowed Jones to catch up. "Well, maybe it is true. Would that be so awful?"

"Yes. Yes *is* the correct answer here."

"You can be such a brute sometimes. I do not see how having my mother and father along would make any difference in the world."

"Perhaps you are right. I shall bring Roark as well."

They rode silently for a short stint.

"Fine, I get your point and I am finished with this conversation."

They rode the rest of the way to the diner and dismounted. After securing their bikes, they entered. In courteous fashion, Jones pulled Emily's chair out for her.

As the server walked away, Jones said, "I am glad we have this time together. I have so much to do this week. I have expectations of a great breakthrough." He shared a broad smile. "Here's to our future. May it always be... timeless."

He raised his cup of coffee.

"Yes. Eternal. Without end." Her attention wandered. For the next hour, they forgot their worries and talked happily of future promises.

Glancing at the clock above the barista, Emily began to gather her personal effects.

"I must be off. I'll see you later, perhaps?"

Jones escorted Emily outside where they shared an unabashed public display of affection before parting ways.

Wednesday, 2 September 1891, 10:00 am

"**E**mily, my child, so good of'a you to meet with me." Father Carlini stood with his neck stretched to give him the appearance of additional height. He wore his usual cassock with a flamboyant purple scarf. He bent forward eyes closed, sniffed the aroma from Emily's hair and kissed her on the forehead.

Emily bristled at his closeness.

"Please, have a seat next to me." He patted the chair. "I'a do so enjoy my little piece of the earth here. Would you'a care for anything?" He reached for his teacup and drew a sip into his mouth.

"Oh, no thank you, Father." Emily assumed her seat aligned right next to the priest. "You have me full of curiosity concerning our meeting. I hope it is nothing unfavorable you have heard pertaining to me in your travels around the city. I assure you they are not true."

"No." He paused to look at her, shook his head dismissively and continued. "I'm'a concerned still with your favor of the young Jones Whitman. Dare I'a say he is not one of my favorite people and I would'a not be doing what I'm'a ordained to do should I not express my concern. He is—"

"Jones is a wonderful person, Father." Emily shifted in her seat to face him. "You really should get to know him. He is intelligent and—"

"He is an evil man and sins against the very God'a whom I serve with great honor and'a fear." His upper body lunged toward her, closing the small gap between them.

"I do not understand why you think Jones evil." Emily shifted farther back in her chair. "We are all sinners, are we not? So should we not take a more lenient view of others who are lost, perhaps?" She did not wait for his answer. "I believe my marriage to Jones will bring him into the flock. He's revered in Boston society and has great potential, I am told, as an inventor. He is wealthy and devilishly handsome." She stopped herself abruptly, and sighed. "Sorry, Father. He is heavenly and I respect him. I know my family is somewhat disappointed in our decision to marry… and I too have some small doubts, until I am in his presence. It is in these moments I know I could not live without him."

"You are'a making a mistake, child. Im'a truly sorry because I do not wish to be so harsh." His words were mild, but he continued to raise his voice with each subsequent statement. "Im'a afraid for you and I would'a not want to see

10

you'a hurt in the end. It is my duty to inform you of my fear that there are dire consequences to be associated with Jones. Are you'a aware he does not'a believe the church has a place in ordinary people's lives? I'm'a sure his philosophy could'a bring him a great deal of negative attention in'a his future. He will not convert to Catholicism and if'a he did, it would'a be a mockery."

Emily blinked her eyes, as she saw the redness in the priest's face.

"I don't much listen to his ramblings on science or philosophy; however, when he speaks people do listen. He has observed that when one believes they have all the answers, they then become content to look no further. To Jones, that is not judicious."

"He doesn't deserve your affection," he growled. Taking a moment to rein in his ardency, he attempted a conciliatory tone, "What'ta I mean to say is … you are'a too good for him." He paused. "Nevertheless, I can'a see I'm'a failing at influencing your decision. However, you'a must make a promise to me that should'a you hear even a single word regarding what'a Jones is up to, you will'a confess those findings to me."

"He is always respectful to me and such a gentleman. Is that not what matters most? In fact, he's taking me for another bike ride tomorrow," she said defiantly.

"I see." He paused, stroking his goatee. "*Scusi,* but when'a was your last confession?"

"It's been a while now," she admitted, sitting forward and adjusting her jacket.

"I have'a time if you would'a like for me to hear your confession today, right now," he said with some insistence. He shared a strained smile and waited for Emily to answer.

11

"Well… um…" she said, searching for a plausible reason to decline. "I am due at another meeting with my mother. Family business before the wedding. Perhaps another time… soon." Emily stood and extended her hand. "I want you to know I do appreciate your concern for me and I will not take it lightly. I plan to consider your request to report on Jones." She waited uncomfortably. "Thank you, Father, for everything. I will see you on Sunday." She attempted to tug her hand away and failed.

Father Carlini had cupped her hand in his and with his eyes closed, lingered over their connection. He rose and gave Emily an awkward hug.

Once released, she retreated to the path, feeling the weight of his stare against her back as she stalked the course to the gate leading onto the street. Outside, she closed the gate, leaned against the wall where she had propped her bicycle and exhaled in relief.

Wednesday, 2 September 1891, 6:45 pm

The makeshift lab, in the turret on the third floor, displayed a wall of tick-tock brass and hardwood clocks, set to different time zones of cities Jones had visited. A small cabinet, distinguished by a series of dark wooden drawers, labeled by number, with smaller compartments at the top, graduating to larger drawers at the bottom, contained various sized gears and screws.

His writing tool and shop drawings covered the largest table in the middle of the room with a floating light hanging over the drafting table. The drawing tool bore a counter weighted cog allowing for ease of movement. The ratcheted elbow allowed Jones to retract the attached ballpoint pen when he needed to examine his drawings. On the opposite end of the workspace sat a rectangular metal frame that held several gyroscopes and a myriad of gears. The gears were synchronized so the chordal pitch allowed the top and bottom landings to mesh in a flawless manner. In theory, this would generate a low vibration in the key of D, without creating friction and heat.

On a long flexible arm, attached by a clamp, a magnifying glass aided in placing the last five cage gears Jones had cast and filed to perfection. Last, a parchment of the newest drawings of the globe hung over the entire back wall. It included the latitudinal and longitudinal meridians he used to calculate where he might time travel with his Atomotron.

"Roark, would you be so kind as to swing the light a little more in this direction, please?"

Roark looked up from the drawings and swung the arm so the light fell right over the last area left to gear on the time travel machine.

Jones whispered, "This is very exciting." He used needle-nosed pliers to place the last gear that was so tiny he had to use the magnifying glass. "I hope these can withstand the revolutions. Roark did you know that the Tibetan monks perform a sound they believe to be the harmonic of the universe. The Om matches the vibration of the turning of the galaxies, which is a significant element used in the Atomotron."

"Jones, ya neva talk about what happens if it don't work."

"It is not in my purview to define my inventions in failing terms."

Jones pushed the magnifying glass away and inspected

13

his work.

"Yeah, I know this 'bout ya. But if it dun't work whatta I do?"

"Well," Jones started, "pull on your Donegal and go for a walk. I have made arrangements to care of everything. My barrister has my full confidence. He will tell you all, when the time is right, should we fail... again... an outcome in which I have no interest."

"Ya ain't listenin' ta me, Jones. You become like famly... and me best friend. I'm not so sure 'bout this as ya are. All yer explanin' barely meant anythin' ta me. I'm not as clever as ya are."

"Roark, dear friend, I am confident not because of me but because of the perfection of mathematics and the science of engineering. This is, at best, a calculated risk. As long as my calculations are correct, there is no risk."

Emily, unsure of her choice to report Jones's activities to Father Carlini, found herself easing into the foyer, stopping at the bottom of the stairs to eavesdrop on the conversation between Jones and Roark. She tiptoed back to the front door and slammed it shut.

"That must be Emily downstairs," Jones said. "Could you escort her to me, my friend? And watch your head."

Roark ducked under the doorframe and left Jones hovering over the time machine, placing the final gears before the first trial. He could feel his body shaking with anticipation when the door flew open and the lilt of Emily's voice filled the room.

"This room is your mistress and I do not much care for it." She paced the room and then turned to Jones. "Besides, what will people think of you? They will believe you to be some kind of mad scientist retreating into this world of...

14

Whatever shall we do with this space after we are married?"

"And what pray tell brings you to me this evening?" he asked, half hearing her words.

"Jones, you bad boy," she said as she approached. "You have been ignoring me and I will have nothing more to do with it. You must leave your silly experiment and take me to the symphony tonight." Emily then resorted to the most powerful weapon in her arsenal, pouty lips. "Please, Jones. I miss you. The Boston Symphony Orchestra is hosting the Hungarian born, Arthur Nikisch this evening to perform Liszt."

She laced her fingers behind his neck.

"I am sure I would be wildly entertained, but I really do have a commitment to make tonight my first trial. This is a long anticipated event. Surely, you can understand."

Emily leaned into him with her hands on his chest.

"I suppose, Jones, but I must tell you there are plenty of young men in Boston who would leap at the chance to spend the evening at the symphony with me." She stared into his eyes.

"I have no doubt. You should go with someone we both know, and trust, so that you do not miss tonight's performance."

"I know… I shall ring Father Carlini." She pirouetted and glided to the doorway, and pivoted back to see Jones's reaction. "I will explain everything to him. I shall tell him how you are ignoring me for your inventions. I am certain he will accompany me and then you will have no need to feel insecure or jealous."

"I am certain I said someone we both trust." Jones paused. "Well, I suppose he is acceptable. He is a priest after all." Jones turned to face Roark. "Do you think she is safe with Carlini?"

"I dunt trust priests, but I'll make sure she's safe." Roark looked down at Emily and smiled. "Tell Father Carlini Roark Fogarty says 'top of the evnin' ta ya.'"

"Very well, it is settled. If Roark is comfortable, then I am comfortable. Give me a kiss."

"No. I do not want to now." Emily raised her gloved hand to her chin and stuck the end of her pointer finger in her mouth. "Oh, all right then." She swanned back over to Jones. "However, you must find time for a ride tomorrow or I shall never forgive you."

"I promise."

Jones took her by her shoulders and kissed her full lips.

She waved as she made her way downstairs, to the hall, stopping at the mirror for a quick glance, then came the inevitable slamming of the door.

"I will have to replace that door once a year after we marry," Jones said to Roark with a chuckle.

Wednesday, 2 September 1891 7:15 pm

After Emily made her exit, Jones retrieved the Atomotron from the drafting table and placed it in a small standing closet used for cleaning materials. He then screwed on a threaded pipe to the steam generator and opened the valve to allow enough pressure to make a short round trip. He stepped inside the closet and began a systematic procedure that he denoted to Roark as a way of tracking his process through the set up and execution.

"Very well, because I am an auditory learner," he said, sticking his head out of the closet, "I will speak loudly so you might hear my thoughts." He returned to the closet. "My theory is this, my friend. Here on the Atomotron." He rotated the brass tumblers. "I shall toggle in the location coordinates so the machine will appear on the table in the center of the room. Once it arrives, I will set the return coordinates for the closet." Jones closed the filling valve connected to the steam furnace. "Pressurized... and I am now disconnecting the filling tube."

"Aint sure I kin watch this, Jones."

"Ah... I failed to mention *you* will be wearing the time machine not I." Jones stared at Roark, maintaining a serious expression on his face for as long as he could. "I am toying with you, Roark. I am not a complete lunatic. The Atomotron will go and return on its own. If and only if this works, will I have the courage to depart this time zone for another. What time is it?"

"8:07..." Roark said looking toward the wall of timekeepers to the largest clock in the center set to local Boston time.

"All is set, Roark. Are you ready?"

"Ho'd on. Why in da closet?"

"Well, should it explode—which I do not believe will occur—the damage will be minimal ... I hope."

Roark rubbed his chin.

"How will ya not lose yer arm or hand when pullin' the lever should it give way?"

"You think of everything and that is why I have you as my assistant. We will use the writing tool arm to reach into the cracked open closet door while we crouch down behind those two chairs. How does that sound?"

"Ya won't actuallay need me. I'll jus be over there," Roark said pointing to the farthest corner of the room. "And

17

put yer goggles on."

"Fine. Brilliant idea." Jones pulled his goggles over his eyes. "Okay, are you ready now?"

"Yeah."

Roark squatted, like a small child, in the corner with his arms wrapped around his legs. He still took up a large amount of space.

"Wait. Help me push the table over."

Roark rose to his feet, cleared off all the papers, grasped either side in his large spread out hands, and lifted the entire table. He placed it so the top blocked Jones and the writing tool arm rested perpendicular to the opening in the door in order to use it to push the lever. He then thundered his way back to his place of safety and squatted on the floor.

"Ya can start now."

Jones assumed a crouched position behind the table and pulled on his goggles. He carefully guided the long skinny end of the tool right up to the lever and stopped. He waited for a moment mumbling the procedure.

"Roark," Jones said.

"Ye'ah?"

"I'm having one small doubt."

"I know that ya'd be doin' it anyways."

"Yes. Your assertion is without a doubt true, however, I am at once taken with the thought of failure and the burden of success."

"Me thinks you can do this 'cause yer the most clever man I've ever known."

"Thank you for your confidence, Roark. That actually means a lot to me."

Jones pushed the lever and could hear, through the door, the whirling of gears picking up speed. The low vibration began to hum in the closet followed by an eerie silence. Jones opened the closet door and from behind him, he heard a swooshing sound, like a hard wind through a cracked open door.

"Eureka, Roark. The machine is now over there." Jones pointed and snatched out his pocket journal and writing instrument. "Quickly, what time is it?"

"Eight fourteen and forty-one seconds."

Jones glanced at his watch. "I have eight fourteen and forty-five seconds now. I will quickly toggle in the closet coordinates."

Jones waited at the far side of the room with Roark.

Both men went silent. The Atomotron spewed steam and picked up speed, faster and faster, until the machine disappeared right before their eyes. A smaller vibration whooshed and the time machine rested in the closet with the last of the steam swirling above the frame. The metal box rested as if it had never traveled anywhere.

"It takes nine seconds to exit." Jones laced his fingers behind his head, pacing back and forth. "I will not be able to sleep tonight. I am just too excited about the possibilities." Jones cautiously placed his hand on the frame of the machine. "This is excellent, Roark, feel this. It is barely warm, much less hot. I think, dear friend, it will not be necessary to wear a shield against the heat. That will make the Atomotron lighter than I originally anticipated."

Roark reached past Jones but hesitated to touch the Atomotron.

"When d'ya expect ta try wearing the machine then? I mean… and where ya gonna go? How long will ya be gone?"

"You needn't worry over those details right now. Let me answer this way. The first human trial will be in a couple of days. I have not the slightest idea of how to narrow down the infinite possible destinations. Moreover, I know this may come as a shock, but I will be able to travel both forward and backward in time, therefore, although I will still have a linear progression of my own age while in travel, the timeframe can appear as an instant should I return at the exact time of my departure. Does this make sense to you, Roark?"

"No."

Roark placed his hands on his head as if to keep it from exploding.

"Okay, well, another time then. My mind is racing. What can we do?"

"Let's go ta the gym. Ya can practice yer Hung Gar whilst I spar wif a coupla the fellas."

"Brilliant. Allow me to change my clothes and I will return shortly."

Jones donned his black gi and Chinese bamboo sandals, while Roark pulled on a pair of boxing shorts, a shirt, and grabbed his gloves and boots from his room. They walked the one and a half miles to the gym in the sea infused summer night air. Jones chattered on regarding the multitudinous possibilities of time travel. He pushed through the main door of the gym into a pungent odor of sweat and musky leather. Gas lamps hissed a dim light casting a candle-flame effect of color in the low-slung hallway. In the faint glow, Jones caught a glimpse of Ma Chun Lee, apprentice to Wong Fei-hung and professor of science at Harvard.

"Roark, I will be in here with Master Lee."

"Okay, meet ya back 'ere in an 'our," Roark said over his shoulder as he walked toward the ring.

"Master Lee, I am profoundly glad to see you are still here tonight. If I may, I would like a few moments of your time." Jones bowed from the waist. "I need your advice on matters concerning my tattoo."

"Yes?" Master Lee indicated for Jones to sit with him. Both men assumed a cross-legged position on mats facing one another.

"Master Fei-hung has given me the name Time Traveler." He pulled up his sleeve to reveal the tattoo of his Hung Gar name. "Since my days in Foshan with him, I have spent many years designing a machine that will enable me to travel both forward and backward in time. I have only recently come to realize that I have manifested my goal, but without a clear understanding of why and for what purpose, it shall serve. Master Lee, I need your assistance to clarify my purpose."

"Jones… you must not allow yourself to leave the sanctity of your Ch'i. Your life force will guide you effortlessly on your path with a sense of balance for all you may encounter. Live your life in such a way that others will want to emulate you. You must commit to a strong integrity and ethic when you travel, for you will have the ability to influence circumstances and must not use your fortitude and strength to significantly change the past or the future."

Master Lee closed his eyes in contemplation.

Jones sat up straighter and cleared his throat.

"My machine travels along a universal spatial/time path similar to the meridians running through our bodies as Fei-hung taught. It would also seem that to influence the past could have dire effects on the future, on my future."

Lee opened his eyes and smiled.

"You are confused because you rely only on your mind for answers, when answers must come from your heart as well. Once you comprehend *your intentions,* the deepest answers will come to you. It is now time to meditate."

Master Lee closed his eyes again.

Jones had one more question, but followed Lee's example. As his breathing became easy and relaxed, his mind filled with a vivid recollection of his time with Master Fei-hung.

Friday, 12 June 1883, 6:30 am

Foshan, China

At dawn's breaking, the steam ship glided through the turbid waters of the Zhujiang River. A massive gray plume billowed from the stack as the shoreline of this strange and exotic land passed in silence. Billowy white clouds settled low on the mountains below the highest peaks. Scores of unusual floating vessels tied to one another along the docks bobbed just off the bow of the steamer's wake. The smoke from makeshift chimneys rose snaking its way into the cool morning air. People in round, wide brimmed hats and loose fitting pajamas scurried here and there, tightrope walking the rails of their houseboats as they made their way to shore to begin their workday.

A low toned voluminous steam-whistle indicated a reversal of engines as the steamship began to slow in anticipation of docking in Guangzhou, China. The dark wood deck glistened from fresh water the crew used to slosh away the salt that had accumulated overnight from the stormy seas. They then arranged the redwood lounges neatly against the cabin walls.

"Good morning, son. How did you sleep last night?"

"It was adequate."

Jones propped against the ship's rail.

"May I again say I am comforted by your willingness to take the summer for rejuvenation? Your mother feels much the same as I do. We feared you might have ended up regretting your lifestyle choices in the end."

Jones's father joined him against the railing.

Jones turned around, leaned back and folded his arms across his chest. He stoically studied the older version of himself. His father had the same blue eyes, more salt-than-pepper short hair and a fit stature. His clean-shaven face contrasted Jones's scraggly beard, mustache and dark black hair.

"Can you explain further this odyssey I am about to undertake?" asked Jones.

"I can, and will, once we are in Guangzhou. The ride to Foshan will provide ample opportunity for us to discuss all matters at hand." He placed his hand on Jones's arm. "Shall we eat our breakfast aboard the ship?"

Jones stroked his longish beard as he pondered the possible consequences and benefits of the next three months. Only after being at sea did his father disclose to him, though the trip to China was indeed to teach him the skill of acquiring textiles from the Chinese, he also had arranged for Jones to meet Wong Fei-hung, master of Hung Gar and tai ch'i ch'uan, physician, acupuncturist, and revolutionary. Jones could acquiesce to his tutelage, and become a student of the master, or decline and learn to live without his father's approval. He decided that ninety days would be a small price to pay for a continued sound relationship with his parents.

He and his father made their way down the gangway to the busy docks of Guangzhou and joined the throng of colorfully clothed foreigners parading around arranging transportation to their destinations. They secured their offloaded bags from the ship's dock and flagged down a rickshaw. Jones's father spoke enough Mandarin to hire a driver to transport them to Foshan where accommodations, arranged earlier in the year, awaited the arrival of one Jones Whitman.

The streets teemed with the patrons of the bustling markets, and ornamental rickshaws crowded the already brimming streets, racing in all directions. Away from the docks, the traffic dissipated. Two drivers, brothers, who made their sole living pulling rickshaws for visitors through the countryside, divided the fifteen-mile trip. Jones admired their physical prowess, and endurance, as he and his father chatted while one of the two brothers clung to the back of the rickshaw.

They arrived safely at the Po-ch'i-lam Temple in Foshan, Guangdong, where a hearty greeting awaited from Wong Fei-hung. They collected their items for the short walk to the temple steps, warmed by the rising sun. The two men joined the Master amongst the rattle of rickshaws whizzing by on the cobblestone and the laughter of children playing in the street.

"Master Fei-hung." Jones's father returned a measured bow, placing his luggage on the ground. "I am James Whitman and this is my son whom I mentioned to you in my letter of introduction. Jones, this is Grand Master Wong Fei-hung."

"Pleased to make your acquaintance." Jones extended his hand and Fei-hung bowed. Jones awkwardly bent at the waist. "This is… truly amazing." He looked over the surroundings. "I am fascinated. The temple is so different from anything I have yet experienced. Is this where I will be staying?"

"You must be striking young man under all the hair," Wong remarked with a warm smile.

"This is to honor my Uncle Walt," Jones said. "He is a poet and philosopher."

"And you? What are you? *Who* are you?" Wong asked quietly.

"If I may interrupt, I would like to have a bit of a chat with Jones before I depart."

James placed his hand on Jones's shoulder.

"I believe that would be helpful," Wong said. "Please take your time."

He retreated through a carved wooden gate into the courtyard of the temple surrounded by ten-foot high walls made from stone.

"So as your studies advance, you will be afforded personal time to visit our merchants who will teach you on my behalf how to choose the best textiles." Jones's father reached out and pulled him into an embrace. Holding his grip firmly, he whispered, "I am happy with the choice you have made to exhibit such courage. I look forward to beholding the man that returns to me, to us, in the fall."

"I have every intention of making you proud. Time will tell."

Jones shook his father's hand.

James Whitman hailed a rickshaw for the ride to his hotel near the textile markets.

The next three months became a day-by-day routine, which began with morning stretching and meditations, rice for breakfast, warm lavender tea and the daily rigorous practice of Hung Gar and tai ch'i chuan.

On the third day, the temple barbers greeted Jones and two other young men.

"Please take a seat on the bench," Master Fei-hung said. "The journey you have embarked upon will begin by becoming invisible. We shall shave your hair and beard. You will wear the same clothing as all students. Your daily routines will be similar. However, in the end, you will become man who is distinguished from all others by your strength of character and determination, your destiny by your new Hung Gar name."

"I am excited and intrigued, Master, although I feel as though I should be frightened."

They provided Jones with several pairs of loose-fitting peach colored pajama-styled pants and loose fitting shirts that buttoned to the neck. The only means for Jones to observe his new look was a reflection pool in the middle of the courtyard where he returned often, to study the changes in his face. At first, he appeared young and boyish to himself with his shaved head and naked face, but over time, he morphed into a confident strong man. He took advantage of walks in the garden, the smell of blossoms in the air; children's laughter from the other side of the walls, needles tapped gently into meridians, realizations of an energy shift, a feeling of power that came from deep within, Master Fei-hung's quickened fists, the strict but calm sound of his voice of encouragement.

Grand Master Wong Fei-hung, in the last days, readied Jones to receive his Hung Gar name. On the third to last night in Foshan, in a room filled with lanterns, burning incense and fellow students, Jones assumed the Lotus position, quieted his mind, and extended his left arm. He waited patiently as the artist created a tattoo with ink from a sharp bamboo instrument on the inside of his left forearm: **時光旅行者**, Time Traveler.

Foshan, Guangdong, had transformed from a challenging,

possibly dangerous place, into a community filled with mystery and mysticism as his own metamorphic journey evolved. The richness of life became more evident each day under the guardianship of the Master. The infinite possibilities lay before Jones as numerous as the stars in the night sky and he intended to discover how far he could go.

Wednesday, 2 September 1891 9:05 pm

Boston, MA

Master Lee broke the silence.

"Yes, it was all planned from the beginning by your father. He became concerned with your choices and did not want you to waste your life on drinking and carousing. He believed, given a choice, you would see the error of your ways yourself and become a different man than your previous manifestation. I only wish your mother and father were still with us to see the man you are becoming."

Jones smiled without opening his eyes.

"Thank you for answering my question. I am honored to be in your presence."

"And I, in yours."

"Master Lee, if I may?"

"What is your question?"

"Ling Lee, how is she?"

"My sister is well. Last I heard. You understand that Master Wong Fei-hung took us in after our parents were killed during the Taiping Rebellion when we were left destitute. I graduated two years before she and one year before your arrival at Foshan. Ling chose to stay behind to continue where my parents left off. It is difficult to communicate with her in China, so I only hear from her once in a great while."

"I thought that to be the case as we have also lost contact. She is gentle yet fierce, and an inspiration to us all. I hope to see her again someday."

Jones opened his eyes to see Master Lee's robe floating away into the darkness.

As he disappeared, two young men from the university, one Chinese, one Caucasian, took their places on a large mat. Jones rose and bowed, as did they. They began a dui lian exercise, originating from ancient katas where two or more combatants practiced martial arts to increase balance, flexibility and focus. The three performed several sets, sparring with deliberate control so as not to do extensive damage to their opponent. Jones demonstrated the Shadowless Kick made famous by Master Fei-hung in China. He drew his clenched fists to his side and shifted his balance onto his left foot. The university student moved forward in a sashay fashion preparing to strike from his waist using his fist when he suddenly felt the hair flutter on the side of his head. He felt a slight sting to his ear but saw nothing. After a summer of training with Fei-hung, Jones had managed to increase his effectiveness dramatically, following the careful practice of the forms that included the Shadowless kick. The student bowed to Jones and smiled.

"That is faster than lightning," he said.

"Thus the name, Shadowless Kick. It is an honor to have been taught such a remarkable move."

The young Chinese man turned to Jones and bowed.

"You have represented Master Fei-hung well. Thank you for your time."

The two men gathered their belongings and walked out the side door toward the campus.

Jones made his way through a second door to the boxing ring where he saw Roark towering over his opponent. Roark lumbered deliberately, as if stalking his prey. His bulky chest and arms were pumped and intimidating, but his wiry opponent continued to throw punches and jabs to the stone jaw of Roark.

"You're losing on points," Jones shouted. "Move your feet."

Roark sneered at Jones, looked back at his opponent, threw a right hook and down went his stringy antagonist to the canvas with a flump.

"Well, now I see you had a strategy all along." Jones held open the top two ropes of the ring for Roark to step through.

"Ya didn't wait enough, did ya?" Roark leaned on the middle rope and looked up at his opponent. "Thanks, Nico. Ya 'round on the weekend?"

"I'll be around, but dis next time... I'm'a gonna bring a small stool," he said with a grin.

Nicoli gathered his towel, threw his gloves over his shoulder and walked into the shadows holding his left jaw.

Wednesday, 2 September 1891, 10:15 pm

The rectory, where Franciscan Father Carlini resided, reflected a great deal of Italian influence, housing large masculine dark furniture and two walls lined with shelves overflowing with books in perfect alphabetical order. Neatly stacked materials for his next sermon and a few writing utensils, hand carved by Australian aboriginals, lay on

Carlini's desk. Inside his desk drawer, he kept a bottle of Irish whiskey and several bottles of wine from Spain, as well as tobacco for his pipe and the hand-carved humidor for his cigar collection. The claw copper tub, trimmed with oak, highlighted his preference for acquiring the best for his living quarters. Large woven rugs imported from India covered the area between his desk and bed. A family crested Italian jewelry box held various rings and necklaces he had obtained over his years of travel as a missionary. As he prepared for his evening bath, he heard a knock.

"Yes, who is it?" he said as he leaned into the door.

"Father, we hear ya want a meetin' wit us."

The priest recognized the voice and opened the door. Two slender young men entered the rectory, their hands crossed in front of them. They waited patiently as Father Carlini turned off the water filling the tub. The olive skinned Drago, an Italian fisherman, looked as if he had come in after a day at sea. His dark bushy hair and gray clothing were in dire need of a wash to rid him of the crusty layer of sea salt and the strong odor of fish. Nicoli was similar in build with small blue eyes, which darted back and forth while Drago's dark heavy-browed pupils stared straight ahead.

"You are good men. You fight the honorable fight. Would'a either of you care for a drink?" he asked as he poured his own.

"None for me, tanks," Drago said.

"No, dun't drink, Father," Nicoli said.

"Why do I not'a believe that?" Father Carlini continued. "I need'a your assistance in a matter of great importance, but it will need'a to be kept secret for a short while and I know I can'a count on you."

Drago smiled.

"You can'a count on us, Father."

Carlini then placed his hands on his desk and bowed his head.

"I need'a for you to investigate a certain person whom'a I believe not only to be a heretic, but a danger to one of God's children right here in our own congregation."

"Yeah? Who we talkin' about?"

He looked up. "One'a of my favorite children, Emily Fuller, has'a taken to favoring Jones Whitman. In fact, they are'a to be married here in the garden chapel at the end of this month. I do not wanna to see that happen and require your and God's help."

"Whatta ya asking us ta do?" Drago asked while glancing at Nicoli who shuffled nervously.

"Oh, not to harm him, no, I plan'a to humiliate him. I wanna have him committed to an insane asylum like his uncle Jesse." He came out from behind the desk. "I wanna you to enter into his house and scour for any signs he might be a lunatic and report to me." The father stopped mid-step. "I know there is something going on'a in that turret room but I know not what'ta … yet. I'm'a sure it will reveal Jones's predilection to transcendentalism and acts of heresy toward the God Almighty.

"Emily has'a told me that she and Jones will be on a ride tomorrow. That leaves just Roark in the house. You must figure out a way to distract him long enough to search the third floor room."

"I run inta him at da gym a couple times," Nicoli said. "He's a boxer. I could challenge him to a sparring bout."

"Dat could work." Drago shook his head in agreement.

"Tomorrow, go over to the house and talk'a to him after Jones has left to spend time with Emily. Drago, you'a walk

31

part way to the gym and then return to the house. I need'a evidence I can take to people of influence. I will'a express my concerns based on whatta you bring me. Hopefully, it will'a be enough to have him picked up and committed for observation."

Drago reached out to shake the father's hand. The priest stared directly at the hand and did not offer his in return.

"You are on your own should'a you get caught," he said. "I will'a deny ever having had this conversation. Do you understand?"

"Yes, Father," Nicoli said.

"Yes. Good night, Father," Drago said.

"Now go… and wash yourselves thoroughly."

Thursday, 3 September 1891, 7:30 am

"It's Emily. She wants ta talk ta ya."

Roark handed the phone over to Jones and left the room.

"Good morning, Emily. I meant to call you earlier but I started solving a cal—"

"I just want to know if I can expect some attention from you today or not?"

"Yes, as I promised and I am a man of my word. Where shall we go? You may have my undivided adoring attention for the next four hours."

"Oh, that makes me very happy. Shall I come over to your place or would you like to meet me here?"

"There. Should I bring the Columbia?"

He braced for the disdain.

"Absolutely not. I shall never ride on the back of that

contraption. It is far too loud and fast for my liking."

"Bicycles it is then. I am looking forward to sharing the same space and time with you. I shall see you in fifteen minutes?"

"I'll be waiting."

"I am sure you will be. Goodbye." Jones placed the phone back in its cradle and turned his attention to Roark. "I will be out of the house for a few hours. How would you like to do the shopping for dinner at the Haymarket?"

"Dat's me job. What ya want for dinner this evnin'?"

"Surprise me," Jones said. "I am leaving now and will return at 1:30 and set up a new trial. It is really too bad we don't own a small pooch." He reached for his top hat. "Come now, smile. I am only jesting. Well… maybe… never mind, we can attach an apple or some other living matter."

"Ya 'ad me goin' there fer a second." Roark pointed his finger. "If ya can wait tirty seconds I kin walk part way wif ya."

"I'm going to retrieve my bicycle and I'll wait on the front porch."

Thursday 3 September 1891- 8:00 am

Nicoli and Drago walked the back streets near the harbor to Jones's house. They stationed themselves at a far corner to watch the morning's activity.

"Dere's Jones now and look who'sa walkin' wit him," Drago said.

"Dat's good 'cause I ditn't feel like boxing Roark anyway. 'e's mean and hits like a train," Nicoli said as he adjusted the brim of his hat. "Do ya see this?" He pushed out his chin. "A right hook from Roark."

"Let's go 'round back and check the door."

Large bushes and a white picket-styled fence concealed the back of the house making their clandestine activity easy. Drago climbed the back staircase with Nicoli in tow.

He reached for the doorknob and turned it. The door opened smoothly and they crept into the kitchen.

"People make it so easy," Nicoli said.

"Yeah maybe God unlocked the door afore we got here."

Drago stopped long enough at the bottom of the stairs to make a plan.

"Nicoli, go ta da parlor window and keep me posted… case we need to get out fast."

"Ya don't wanna get caught by Roark. So, if I call out, you betta fly down dose stairs. You understand doncha?"

"I ain't worried. I'll work fast. What we lookin' for 'xactly?" Drago asked.

"Anythin' that'll tell us he's crazy."

"We ditn't need ta come here for me ta be able to tell ya dat."

Drago mounted the steps. "I'll be upstairs."

He made his way to the turret and opened the door. He gasped at the spectacle of clocks, gears and cogs; the writing tool and floating lamp; the smell of machine oil, and the parchment map covering the full wall. Before him, several projects in progress lay neatly organized on small worktables next to the curved wall. He would not soon forget the sight. Drago picked up one of the Atomotron drawings and turned it sideways and then upside down. The formulas and equations written on the edges made him shake his head. He carefully replaced the drawing. He took one last look and started down the stairs.

"Drago," Nicoli called out in a loud whisper. "It's Roark. I kin see 'im coming up the street. I think we'd better get da hell outta here."

Drago jumped over the last few feet of banister and landed next to Nicoli who ran full out toward the back door. Drago caught up just as Nicoli scaled the fence.

The pair walked quickly toward the harbor for a block or so and then slowed down.

"Well, what'd ya find?" Nicoli asked, catching his breath.

"A most amazin' room, Nicoli. He ain't no madman, I tell ya, but what he *is*, I can't be sure either."

"What'd ya see? Tell me."

"There's clocks everywhere set to different times. Maybe dey're broken? Maybe Jones repairs clocks. I don't know." Drago jumped a step ahead, whirled around, and stopped. "And, there's drawin's of a machine of some sort. He must'a be working on it because it was'a at the end of da table."

"I'm sayin' that's aint much of a report, Drago. Father Carlini will be disappointed I think."

Nicoli and Drago continued their walk toward town.

"Then he kin try another way. That's all I got. He shoulda do a little arm-twisting ta Jones's fiancé. Get her to spy on him."

"You suggest it to 'im, not me. I don't trust Father Carlini. I believe he gotta an eye for that girl, but I'd never let on 'at I took notice."

Friday, 1 August 1890, 4:30 pm
Dublin, Ireland, 13 months earlier

A giant man of alabaster, chiseled proportions stood before Jones. His muscular torso glistened with sweat from his spar, drenching the top of his knickers. His bare knuckles flared as red as the curls of his hair. His calloused hands showed the years of boxing undertaken in order to repay his debt to the man who sought to take advantage of his height and reach and although, he had won many bouts, his liability never seemed to diminish. Jones had come to Ireland to buy a debt contract. He was searching for a suitable youth to employ. His father had favored the Irish for their work ethic and family loyalty. The ethic of O'Brannigan, the boxer's creditor, remained in question, as the sport, relegated to back alleys and sweatshop fights, existed those days for the sole purpose of gambling.

"Mr. O'Brannigan." Jones approached the man holding the bottom rope of the boxing ring. "Am I safe in assuming this is the young man you mentioned to me in your correspondence?"

"Top of the evenin' to ya."Ya 'at would be 'im. He's a big'un that one is. Hard ta knock'im down." He paused, staring at the fighter stalking around the ring. "I'm glad ya decided ta take 'im off me 'ands. Not dat I dunt like da boy, but he's lost 'is heart, if ya know what I main."

"The sum you mentioned as having been the original debt has grown to an exacting amount and needs explanation I should think."

Jones stepped in closer to O'Brannigan and opened an

accounting sheet under the dim light.

"Not sure wha'cha ya sayin' ta me."

"I am saying you are asking more for his contract than he originally owed and I would like to understand why given that he has won as many bouts as he has during his career."

"Dem everyday particulars he owes me for."

O'Brannigan drew on a fat cigar.

"I am willing to pay you in cash his original debt and an additional ten percent if I can arrange for his departure day after tomorrow."

Jones reached into his waistcoat and opened his wallet. He withdrew the appropriate amount of cash and offered it to O'Brannigan. O'Brannigan pulled the contract from his back pocket and handed it to Jones.

"Ya got yaself a fine fighter if 'e can ever get the heart back."

"I shall not be employing him in that manner. I hope to assist him in any way I can to achieve his own goals. He will work as my valet." Jones folded the contract and slid it in his waistcoat, along with his wallet. "Would you be so kind as to introduce us?"

"Fogerty," O'Brannigan called out. "Over har to meet ya new owner."

"Manager." Jones said .

"Manager 'e says. Sounds like ya stepped inta the right spot and come out with no shite on ya shoes, laddy." O'Brannigan turned to Jones as he placed his hand up on Fogerty's shoulder. "Jones Whitman, this here is Roark Fogerty. Roark, this here is Jones Whitman, ya new *manager*. Pack ya belongin's cause ya leavin' soona than expected."

"Not soon enough ta be honest wif ya."

Roark reached out and took Jones's hand, dwarfing it

with his own.

"Roark, your hands are enormous," Jones said. "But I suppose you know that already. My apologies. You took me by surprise."

"Not like I ain't neva 'eard 'at before."

They began to stroll out of the ring area toward the washroom.

"So I understand you were abandoned by your mother."

"Ya and I abandoned me da and me uncle, so no claims on me at all. Ya tell me where ta be and I make it happen."

"Very well. Why don't you clean up and change. Have you eaten?"

"Not taday yet." Roark ran his fingers threw his hair and smiled. "I could eat a fair amount right now though... bein' honest wif ya."

"Fine, I will meet you outside, oh and bring your belongings. I shall purchase room and board for you tonight. Tomorrow we can get to know one another on a more personal note."

Thursday, 3 September 1891, 6:00 pm

Boston, MA

"Roark, excellent dinner. Thank you."
Jones pushed away from the table.

"I gotta letter from the court about me contract. I don't suppose ya know nofin' about it."

"What did it say?" Jones asked.

"I dun't read much but I could make out a lot of it. It says paid in full, that me debt has been paid. It says I'm a free man." Roark pointed to the 'free man' in the last paragraph of the correspondence.

"This must have come as a surprise." Jones leaned back against his chair and folded his arms across his chest. "I must tell you that over the past months I have come to value our friendship more and more. I would like you to know how much I appreciate you and your talents." He paused for a moment. "I am no longer in need of a valet," he said and looked straight at Roark. "I need a companion and perchance, a bodyguard. So, having said that, I now would like to know how you would feel about working for me in the same capacity and receiving a paid wage?"

Roark sat fixed for a moment and then laid his face in his hands. He raised his head and stared at Jones. A single tear made a path down his check to his chin.

"I'll take this to mean I have made the correct decision. You owe me nothing. In fact, as of right now, you do not owe anyone anything."

"I owe ya me life. I've neva felt 'is way. I'll accept yer offer and I'll serve ya with honor and loyalty, so help me God."

"Well... I am of the opinion that you will not need God's help in these matters. You are a strong and powerful man, Roark, and I am a great judge of character. My intuition tells me I have nothing to fear when you are around."

Roark stood, wiped his face on his sleeve, and began to clear the table. Jones followed him into the kitchen with an armful of dishes.

"So, our first official outing together as a team, of sorts, is tonight. There is a transcendental gathering at the club to honor the work of one of my uncle's friends, Thomas Treadwell Stone.

"He believed it is imperative to follow one's own instincts in matters of self. What you conceive you can achieve. Thusly, I have over the last six years or so, undertaken the task of creating the Atomotron to free us to travel anywhere in time that we please." Jones sat.

"My strongest apologies, I become mesmerized by the possibility of time travel."

"Yeah, but I know 'is about ya."

Jones laughed and then asked, "Roark, did you happen to see anyone prowling around today?"

"No."

"Strange. There is an interesting energy shift in the lab. Someone seems to have left their energy. Not sure. I plan to meditate up there in the morning. Shall we leave for the meeting?"

"Ya. Let me get me guns and lockup the 'ouse. Be right back."

"You won't need a gun and since when do we lock our doors?"

"Let me do me job, Jones." Roark smiled.

The two made their way to the university auditorium where an aged Thomas Treadwell Stone and thirty others had gathered to discuss the need for the individuation of thought on all matters. Stone lectured that there is inherent goodness in both people and nature and that transcendentalists believed organized religion and political parties corrupted the innocence of the individual.

Outside, the gathering protesters waved placards heralding the end of the world due to scientific exploration. Inside, Stone taught the belief that an individual is best when self-reliant and independent of organized doctrine.

The sound of breaking glass startled the participants, and

Roark in particular, who bolted straightaway with derringers drawn. Someone picked up the brick and held it up for everyone to see.

"Well, that was exciting."

Jones once again took his seat.

Roark crossed over to the outside wall and made his way to the front window. The protesters had run away after they tossed the brick, and from the opposite direction came the Boston constables to inspect the damage.

"Folks dunt care fer ya much do they?" Roark said as Jones approached and looked out through the hole in the window.

"Yes, I suppose. Understandably so—after all, we have chosen a lifestyle out of the mainstream. That alone can bring undeserved retribution from a frothy group of religious zealots."

After paying their respects to Treadwell, they took their leave. Jones chattered on about philosophy while Roark kept an eye out for shadowy figures on the dark side streets.

Friday, 4 September 1891, 7:30 AM

Jones entered the lab and assumed the lotus posture he had learned while in China. After taking three deep breaths, he quieted his mind. He could sense someone had entered the lab with malice in their heart. He could see, in his mind's eye, a shadowy figure, male most probably, but he was unable to make out the person's identity. The intruder had left a faint odor of cigar behind, however, Jones knew many men and women who smoked cigars at the clubs to try to discern who it might have been.

41

After meditating, he opened the door of the lab to the smell of breakfast being prepared. Strangely, he could hear Roark singing what sounded like an Irish lullaby.

"Top of the morning to you, my friend. This smells wonderful and accompanied by song as well. You seem happier than usual."

Jones reached into the pan for a piece of bacon.

"Aye. I've not felt this rested in years. Ya've unburdened me from me debt and ta be sure added years ta me life."

Roark dished out pancakes, eggs and bacon. He then poured coffee for them both.

"Hopefully you will be spending those years with me in some fashion, assisting me with adventures, traveling through time."

"I ain't so sure of 'at idea. I ain't much inta aventures. And I'm sure expandin' and contractin' don't seem right."

Roark strolled over to take his seat.

"I know this about you," Jones said with a mocking smile.

Friday 4 September 1891, 9:30 AM

"Emily."
Father Carlini waved.

She paused in front of her favorite boutique with the intention of purchasing another pair of bicycle bloomers. She had admired herself in the store window and had just decided to enter the shop when she heard Father Carlini's voice.

"Emily."

He approached her, took her by the arm and pulled her in his direction.

"Ouch, Father." She brushed his hand from her upper arm. "That hurt me."

"Please forgive me, I did not mean'a to be rough. There is a matter of'a great importance."

"Yes, I suppose so, but do tell what has you in such a state. I've not seen you like this before."

"Let's walk together, shall we?" Father Carlini took her arm again as they strolled alongside the storefronts. "I need'a for you to understand what I'm to say to you. I need'a for you to trust me completely, for your own sake."

Emily halted and looked straight at the priest.

"Is this once again concerning Jones? My marriage? Father, you seem overly invested in my circumstance. I am a grown woman with a mind of my own and quite capable of making my own decisions."

He placed his hands on her shoulders.

"I seem'a to have offended you and we have not even begun to talk. My apologies to you." He pulled her in and constrained her with a hug.

Emily brought her hands to his chest and with cultured decorum forced him away.

"Father, I am somewhat confused by this. I think it is time I take my leave. Good day to you."

"But Emily, I need'a to know from you exactly what Jones is inventing. It may be dangerous and I have my concerns. If it is nothing more thana his usual tinkering then I will leave it alone. I promise you. Sincerely, you have'a my word."

"He is— why do you want to know? I don't think I care for your tone."

"I promise if it is harmless, then'a I will leave it alone."

"Well... he has said... that what he has been attempting

for the last six years is impossible, but it gives him great joy to imagine what it would be to finally achieve the goal of a working time machine."

"He is a lunatic, as I suspected. God will'a rain down on him from on high for the heresy of exposing our flock to this kinda sin against God himself. We have'a but one life confined to God's time and no one else's. It is in'a this life you are forgiven and *only now* exists."

"I really do not know much about all of that, Father. I mean I understand some, but truthfully, I am taking your word for the rest. He does not believe, I do not think, that it can be accomplished, but it is also not like Jones to give up."

"I have'a much to mull over, Emily. I wanna you to know my love and concern for you comes from the purest of places." He took her hand in his and showing temperance, kissed it.

Emily withdrew from his clutch and walked past Father Carlini. Only the moment before entering the haberdashery did she dare to look back in the direction of the priest. It seemed to her that he had turned recently to walk away leaving her with the impression he had been staring after her.

"Em'ly." The familiar voice startled her.

"Roark, what are you doing out and about?"

"Makin' a stop at Haymarket for some fresh vegetables for supper, I mean dinner, this evnin'."

"Where did *you* learn to cook?"

" 'at's a long story."

"Then tell me the short of it. Please Roark, I am truly interested."

Roark pushed his hands into his pockets, looked down and started.

"Me da was a drunk and me uncle watn't much betta, so

44

when me mudder left da tree of us, I become da keeper of all tings 'ouse."

"I see. You are a very unusual fellow. I think I would like to know more." Emily crossed her arms, took a step back and looked up. "Was your father as statuesque as yourself?"

"I dunt know about 'at. What I do know is me da was mean and 'ed beat me." Roark shifted and leaned against the wall.

"I see. That must have been a terrible life to live." Emily stared at Roark with a quizzical look. "However did you escape?"

"When I was fourteen, I learned ta box, I 'ad ta defend meself, but truth is I started ta like beatin' men up—maybe a little too much." He looked away. "I got into a pub fight, bait a man close to death and got meself into debt wif the man who bailed me out. Jones bought me contract and ya know the rest."

"I had no idea." Emily said touching his massive forearm. "Well, between Jones and me, you are in good hands now." Emily shared a smile filled with warmth—a smile befitting a mother.

"I seen ya wif Father Carlini. Ya seemed a bit a-fraid."

Roark looked up the street where the priest had been.

"Oh no, not... really." She stared in the direction where Father Carlini had been standing. "He seems strange these past few weeks."

"I work fer Jones now." Roark's chest swelled. "If ya ever needs me fer anythin', just let me know."

"Thank you, Roark," Emily said softly. "I will." She curtsied and smiled as she took her leave.

Roark pushed away from the wall and continued to lumber in the direction of the market.

Friday, 4 September, 1891, 1:45 pm

Drago knocked hard on the rectory entrance and waited anxiously. Father Carlini opened and peered through a small crack in the door to make sure it was Drago and Drago alone. He pulled him in by his arm and pushed him back against the wall.

"Drago, I need'a you to return to Whitman's lab. I wanna you to bring to me the plans for the machine he is'a working on." He stood uncomfortably close to Drago wafting the odor of whisky in his direction.

Drago tried to pull away from him. "We kin do that for ya. I'll find Nicoli."

"I will'a use these plans to put him away." The priest released his grip and took a wavering step backwards. "He is not to know until it is too late. I'm convinced… no, I have a driving conviction to see to it that Jones never marries Emily while at the same time, putting an end to his meddling in God's affairs."

"Dis may take some time to set up." Drago pried Father Carlini's other hand from his arm. "When I got da plans I'll come straight to ya."

"And notta before. Do notta return without those plans." The priest raised his hand and made the sign of the cross. "May the Lord have'a mercy on you and may the hand of God guide you. You will'a see I am right about this… lunatic… mongrel… thinks he canna just take Emily away from the Church and me. He will'a spend eternity in hell for his refusal to repent his ways."

Drago watched as an agitated Father Carlini paced the room. He opened the door to the rectory and slipped out into the garden leaving him in his drunken state.

✿✿✿✿✿

Drago searched their usual haunts for Nicoli, and at last found him in a pub near the docks.

"Nicoli, Father Carlini wants them plans from Whitman's lab," Drago said as he sidled up next to Nicoli at the bar. "Yuh in?"

Nicoli studied Drago for a couple of seconds.

"Yeah, I'm'a in, but I ain't crazy about any of dis."

"We should'a ask for money or some kinda payment, you know whatta mean?"

"Yeah sure, I kin hear it now, 'God will'a reward you, Drago.' But God don't carry cash on him, at least dat I know of," Nicoli said laughing.

"Let's take a stroll over to Jones's place."

The two stationed themselves a block away to observe the comings and goings of Jones and Roark. When the coast was clear, they used the same back access but found the door locked. Forced to pick the key chamber, it took Nicoli a few minutes to gain entrance. They eased their way through the kitchen listening carefully. Drago prowled up the stairs to the lab and opened the door with caution, worried what he might encounter. Convinced the room was empty, he rushed to the table, folded the mechanical drawings, and stuffed them into his waistcoat. He could feel his heart pounding in his chest. He closed the door, and ran downstairs alerting Nicoli to catch up as they dashed for the backdoor to escape. They made their way to the rectory to deliver the plans. Drago along with Nicoli knocked on the door once again.

"So soon?" the priest said as the door swung open allowing them passage. "God bless you, you have'a made me happy indeed. You are good men and your service will'a be

47

rewarded, I assure you. If'a you have any doubts concerning what you have been a part of, I will'a hear your confession, even today, and you can be on your way."

Drago reached into his waistcoat, withdrew the plans and handed them over to Father Carlini.

"I don't need to confess, do I, Father? I mean we did da right thing, right?" Drago asked.

"*Sì. Meglio dire…* I stand corrected." He unfolded the plans as he marched to the dining room table. He laid them out and pressed them flat with a sweep of his hands. "It is'a obvious this is the work of a lunatic, but what'a does it all mean?" he asked as he surveyed the drawings dabbled with scribbled equations and measurements along the edges.

"I haven't no idea what an Ato… mo… tron could be, but I did hear dat he's buildin' a time travel machine."

Nicoli, in the spur of the moment, jerked straight when the penetrating glare of Father Carlini forced him to back away from looking over the priest's shoulder.

"And this is exactly what I need'a to convince the powers of influence that he needs to be committed for observation. I'm'a very excited. This will'a ruin his reputation… the marriage will'a be called off, and I'll have my Emily back. Gentlemen, I thank you." Father Carlini opened his desk draw and pulled out a bottle of Spanish wine. "Please, have a glass of wine with me and a cigar, will you? Drago? I know you don't drink, Nicoli, so I shouldn't offer my wine to you. Although, you do have'a the faint distinct odor of cheap whiskey." He looked back in Nicoli's direction. "I assume'a my nose must be playing games with me," he said with a wicked grin.

"No, Father. It wouldn't be right fa me to turn down a drink of wine if'a ya gonna offer."

"Well then…" he fetched three goblets from the bookcase and poured a dark red wine for all of them, opened a carved wooden humidor and handed over a cigar to each.

"I will'a not implicate either of you in this matter should a protest arise. As my name is Giovanni Carlini, I do swear by that name." He raised his glass and, in one gulp, emptied the goblet of wine. "I must take some time to myself and pray diligently. Finish your wine and take'a your cigars away with you."

He escorted the men to the door and when they had taken their leave, he crossed over to the garden chapel to pray. The chantry, bathed in subdued warm light from the stained glass windows, vibrated with quiet reverence. Even though it was a small basement chapel, it boasted large arches and a gilded podium from where Father Carlini performed mass during the week for a number of older, in large part, Italian women. In direct view above the podium, a large wood carving of Christ on the cross, meant to give solace to everyone who entered, stared back at the Father as he knelt down to pray.

"You'a are my Shepherd, my Lord. You'a are my reason for living. I'm'a committed to your flock, and with your guidance, I shall'a find a way to bring light to the heretical teachings of transcendentalism and the diabolic followers, Lord. They are the source of many vain and self-centered acts. We are in a fierce competition for the very souls who, in their innocence, fail to see the errors of their ways, oh Lord. The mere notion that'a any human being could possibly create a time'a travel machine is the epitome of arrogance and exposes the insanity that accompanies the mere attempt. I will'a do my best, Lord. In the name of the Father, the Son and the Holy Ghost. Amen."

Friday, 4 September 1891, 8:00 pm

"**F**ather Carlini, is that you?" Jones approached the unmistakable figure, in a cassock, standing next to the tree adjacent to the fence at the Fuller's home.

"Yes. I'm'a out for my evening walk." He glanced at Jones in an unconcerned manner.

"Why are you so far from the rectory and why do you stand here at Emily's home?"

"I was walking and praying and I ended up here. I thought maybe I would'a stop in to speak to Emily."

"Whatever would you have to speak of at this time of night?" Jones came forward a step and loomed over the priest.

"What'a you after?" he asked, taking a step back.

"Father, you are standing below the window of my fiancé's bedroom. I am quite sure I have the right to inquire as to your motives, would you not agree?"

"You'a don't mean to imply—you disgusting man." He stepped around the tree and caught his cassock on the trunk. He lurched forward tearing a small portion at the bottom hem. "Now look'a what'a you made me do," he growled and adjusted his hat.

"I think you should take your leave before I get any other ideas," Jones said, stepping closer.

"No one would'a ever believe you anyway." Father Carlini held his ground. "Your word against mine?" He extended his long disjointed pointer finger in Jones's face. "I have'a no reason to worry, but I dare'a say you do. You'd better learn to watch'a your back."

Suddenly, Jones took him by the scruff with a sure grip.

He turned Father Carlini toward town and gave him a little push to assist in his departure.

The priest did not look back.

Jones made his way through the gate to the front of the Fuller home and knocked. He removed his top hat and waited.

"Ah, it's you," Mrs. Fuller said as she opened the door. "This is not a good hour to be calling. I am sure that Emily has disrobed by this time."

"Yes. I apologize for my indiscretion. This will only take but a moment. It is a matter of serious concern."

Mrs. Fuller hesitated, looking Jones up and down.

"Wait here."

Emily bounded down the stairs into the foyer throwing her arms around Jones.

"Good evening," he said with a broad grin.

"To what may I attribute this pleasure, Mr. Whitman?"

"It is a question of concern. Roark related to me this evening that he saw you walking away from Carlini this afternoon and that you seemed anxious. And I, just now, confronted him outside the fence below your bedroom. What do you make of this?"

"Roark is right, I was upset. When Father Carlini approached me, he took my arm so forcefully that I made comment that he had hurt me. He was apologetic but somehow it left me feeling a bit frightened. Perhaps he was coming by to make sure my anger with him had subsided."

"How was his manner at the symphony?" Jones asked.

"Oh Jones, don't be silly, I didn't really go to the symphony with Father Carlini. I was hoping you would become jealous enough to accompany me."

Emily tightened the sash of her pink satin robe.

"I see," Jones said. "I should have known. In regards to keeping your dealings with the priest to yourself, I have changed my opinion on this matter. Please keep me informed, if you will."

"You do not believe for a moment that he would be spying on me? He's a priest after all."

"And you are a beautiful amazing young woman. I could see myself spying on you if you were forbidden fruit to me."

Jones pulled her in close.

"Emily," her mother said with that particular tone in her voice.

"Yes, Mother, right away."

"Well, Miss Emily Fuller, I shall see you tomorrow?"

"Yes," she said. "Tomorrow." She took a step back. "That is unless you plan to spy on me tonight." Emily looked at the floor with a smile on her face, laughed and then bounded up the stairs.

Jones kept a watchful eye on her as she disappeared.

"Good night, Mrs. Fuller," he called out. "Thank you very much for allowing me this time with Emily. Take care."

Mrs. Fuller stepped from behind the library door and ushered him to the front porch. As Jones replaced his top hat, he heard the door shut from behind. Strolling out to the street to make his way home, he glanced back to see Emily's silhouette in her bedroom window.

"Father, you are making a big mistake," Jones whispered aloud.

Friday, 4 September 1891, 8:50 pm

Father Carlini pushed his key into the door of the rectory. It opened before he could turn the handle.

"Who'sa in here?" He eased the door open. "Jones Whitman is that *you*? Roark? Show'a yourself." He felt his heart pounding in his chest. "Drago? Who is there?" he demanded as he moved with caution farther into the rectory. He kept glancing back to see if anyone would assail him from behind or worse yet, if someone would slam the door and trap him inside. He eased open the bathroom door, turned on the light and surveyed the scene. It was just as he had left it for his evening walk. "Sweet Mother of Jesus, please be with me now."

He stood rigid, cocking his ear to listen for any sound other than the pulse in his throat. When he decided no danger lurked, he sighed in relief, closed the front door and threw the bolt. He turned on the lights in the rest of the rectory and made his way to the wine cabinet, opening a bottle of imported vino. He retrieved his humidor and chose a cigar. He walked into the bathroom and turned on the tub faucet. Setting the glass, the bottle of wine and his cigar next to the copper tub, he then poured a small vial of lavender oil into the hot bath.

"Please'a, Lord, forgive me for not relying on you. I should'a have known that I live completely safe inna your grace." He looked toward the ceiling, removed his cassock and stood naked. He opened the closet to toss his dirty clothes into the hamper. "Ahhhh, dear God," he yelped. "Wait, Roark, you are a God fearing man. Please don'a kill me, I beg of you." He stood, holding his folded hands out in front of him. A few seconds passed without Roark strangling him giving the priest the courage to assert, "How did'a you get in here?" Then seeing the expression change to a scowl on Roark's face, he changed his tone and uttered, "Please don'a hurt me."

He glanced into Roark's eyes and saw a calm that made him shudder.

"Ya talk a lot," Roark said, then ducked under the doorframe and stepped into the bathroom. "Not 'ere ta kill ya and not goin' ta hurt ya... 'his time anyway. A simple warnin' ta ya. If ya ever lay a 'and on Em'ly again, I'll come back and ya won't like what I do. And that goes fer ya meddlin' in the affairs of Jones too. Do we have an understandin'?"

"It was an accident, I assure you. I will'a make sure to keep'a my hands to myself." Father Carlini cowered before the towering man. "You have'a my word."

Roark pulled the drawings from his coat pocket.

"And I ain't gonna ask ya how ya put yer grubby hands on Jones's drawin's, but I'll be takin' 'em wif me now. Ya have a good evnin'."

Father Carlini stood naked and watched Roark cross the rectory and tromp out the front door, not bothering to close it behind him. He grabbed the bottle of wine and took several swigs to relieve his anxiety. He scurried to close the front door and latch the bolt. He collapsed against the door and wiped a single tear from his cheek.

Saturday, 5 September 1891, 3:30 pm

A s Jones exited his meditation room, he encountered

Roark standing with a square box secured by a brass lock. Roark held the key out to Jones and steadied the box for him to open.

"What could this be?" Jones took the key. "I do love surprises."

He inserted it and turned, lifted the lid, and beheld twin derringers with stocks made from walnut and four inch barrels crafted from a copper-nickel alloy. The hardware, commonly referred to as German silver, glinted in the light from the window.

"These are remarkable. But have you forgotten my Shadowless Kick?"

"I'm thinkin' yer legs ain't 'at long." Roark smiled. "This'll give ya a longer reach if yer surprised by a man who keeps 'is distance."

"I have no real experience with guns and why, pray tell, would I be in need of them?"

"I got 'ese from Father Carlini."

Roark showed him the drawings of the time machine.

"It is highly unusual for me to not notice a change in the lab. Shall I inquire as to how he came by them or your reasons for being there?"

"All's part of me new job protecting ya and ya loved ones… and I'll teach *you* somethin' fer a change."

"Ah, I see, well then, I guess I should remain quiet as you enlighten me to the intricacies of shooting a man."

"Good fer you," Roark said without missing a beat. "Now, theys." He pointed to the guns, "can be the woundin', or worse, the death of ya if ya don't do exactly what I tell ya. Let's sit at the table."

Jones, amused by Roark's newfound confidence, obediently followed him to the kitchen table and took his seat as the student. Roark took the case from Jones and handed him one of the derringers. Jones thumbed the small firearm, tracing the outline before raising and aiming it across the room.

"First," Roark said. "Don't do 'at. Never point a gun unless ya mean to kill somebody, because ya only get one more chance. That's why derringers come in twos. Remember, 'is is a single shot forty-caliber cartridge. It'll hurt a man but ya gotta hit 'im first."

"This is an interesting side of you." Jones laid the pistol on the table. "You seem confident in knowing precisely of what you speak. Does this mean you have killed a man?" Jones's curiosity peaked.

"No. It's a lot harda than ya think," Roark said. "These be best at close range." Roark retrieved the tools used for loading the derringer from the case and placed them on the table in front of Jones. "Now, break away yer barrel ta da side. That makes it ready fer loadin' or reloadin'. 'ere's a small bag of black powder. Pour just this much inta the barrel and use 'is ta pack it." Roark performed the procedure with the second gun.

"This could take up a lot of time. I assume that is why the need to be precise the first shot or second as the case may be. I know… I will keep a log of my time and make every effort to surpass my previous attempts. I cannot get mine to pivot to the side, however."

Roark held his pistol close to Jones and showed him how to move the hammer to a half-cocked position allowing the barrel to open.

"Yes. I see. Okay, this is not as difficult as I thought it might be. I am getting excited now."

"Ya need ta slow down until ya get the 'ang of it. Ya

need practice so ya dun't shoot yerself instead of tha thug."

"What thug?"

"Ya got a reputation and me thinks there's people who want ta do ya no good."

"Father Carlini? I do not believe we have to worry. What would he attempt to do other than influence some of his associates to have me committed for observation?" Jones paused and stared into the distance. "Hmm. Now that I have said as much, it sounds worse than I was thinking. Well, I have you to thank for setting me straight on this matter."

"Let's look at one more 'ing. Ya shove a patched lead ball, like 'is one, down the barrel next ta the powder. Ya have ta do this right or the gun will explode and I don't think ya would look good with just one hand. Last, this half-cock notch 'ere keeps the hammer from falling if the trigger gets bumped while carryin' 'em in yer waistcoat pocket. Ta fire it, fully cock the hammer like 'is, point the gun and squeeze the trigger. Me advice is take'em bof out at once. If ya wing 'em, yer gonna need ta shoot agin. Ya should fire the pistol every day and reload. 'at's me advice."

"You've done remarkably well, Roark," Jones said as he held both pistols. "I have a lot of practicing to do, I'm sure, but I am a quick study."

"Yeah. I know 'is about ya. I'll help ya in any way I can. Just, please, Jones, don't shoot yerself because 'at would make me feel bad."

For the next week, every evening, Jones would load the pistols, fire them and reload. He would then make note of his starting time for each trial and log his entry into his journal. He recorded notes as a means of increasing his speed.

Sunday, 6 September 1891, 8:00 am

"**R**oark, please make haste. I am excited to perform this trial."

Jones bounded the stairs two at a time toward the third floor turret. He entered the room, seized the machine and placed it on the worktable center. He stood in front of the parchment map and calculated the coordinates, logging them into his journal.

"Roark, where are you, kind sir?"

Jones called out and then smiled when Roark stumbled through the door with an arm full of vegetables and fruits.

"I watn't sure which would be best so I brung a whole bunch."

"Yes. I can see that." Jones laughed. "We will need but one. I will allow you the honor of choosing the innocent victim."

Jones stepped aside to observe.

"Me thinks that maybe da apple should be the one. Yeah the apple… or the head of lettuce cause it's bigger. Nah, the apple."

"Excellent choice. The apple is symbolic of good and evil in many ways. It would seem appropriate that the apple makes the first ever organic time travel excursion even if only from here to there and back." Jones attached the apple to the Atomotron using a belt and connected the steam valve to pressurize the machine. "We are on the precipice of making history, that, or I shall be recalculating my mathematical calculations for another seven years."

"Maybe a baked apple."

"Ha. You utter the most unexpected proclamations on

occasion. Perhaps, should this perform as expected, we could use a live chicken in the next trial."

"I bought a chicken fa dinner."

"That would not do as it is already dead. I thought briefly to perform the experiment with a live chicken, however, it would seem problematic to get the chicken to wear goggles and a dustcoat." Jones waited for Roark's response.

"Me thinks ya makin' a joke on me," Roark said, displaying a broad smile. "I kin see the chicken in my head and he looks funny."

"He does indeed." Jones prepared to flip the lever. "Are we ready? I think we are. The purpose of this trial is to evaluate the effect time travel has on an organic molecular structure." He scribbled his words into his journal and slid it back into his waistcoat pocket. He donned his goggles and crouched over the Atomotron. "Three, two, one." He pushed the lever.

Steam spewed from the side, filling the area around the time machine and clouding their view.

" 'at dunt seem right," Roark called out.

"I must agree. When it settles, we shall determine what failed."

Jones stood with his fingers laced behind his head.

The steaming time machine reflected in Jones's goggle lenses. Finally, the Atomotron slowed to a quiet.

"This is a worrisome state of affairs." Jones leaned in to get a better look at the problem. "Ah ha, as I believed. The valve has a minor crack. I can replace this in a matter of moments and we can attempt another trial."

After his repair, he pressurized the machine once again. He attached the apple and flipped the lever. This time the steam escaped in a controlled manner. The hum began and nine seconds later, the machine disappeared, and as hoped for, reappeared on the table assigned as the destination.

"Me sees the apple, Jones," Roark called out.

"Yes indeed. I do as well. It appears to have made the first leg intact."

Jones toggled the return coordinates and flipped the lever. The machine began to whirl once again and at precisely the nine-second mark, it vanished as the molecules began to fall away. The Atomotron and apple then gathered once again at their point of origin.

"Eureka!" Jones shouted. "Shall we?" He picked up the apple. "Roark, observe that the apple is exactly as it appeared when we attached it to the machine. However, we still, as yet, do not know if it will taste the same… or what its effects will be on the digestion." He took a bold juicy bite from the side and smiled. "So far so good." He chewed slowly savoring the sweetness and swallowed. "I am convinced."

"Ya should let me eat first cause I'm bigger. It would have a harder time killin' me."

"Nonsense. I would never put you in such an unfavorable position. That is not to my liking at all."

They waited as Jones paced the room, making short notes in his journal. After five minutes, he stopped in his tracks.

"I am fine. What would you think of acquiring a chicken next?"

"I kin get ya one from the market."

"Let me think." Jones paced the room in a circle. "Well, as a matter of choice I think we can foreswear the chicken. I will wait twenty-four hours to ascertain any ill effects from the apple and make a qualified decision at that time."

Jones turned to see Roark holding the apple up high in the air.

"Take a bite, Sir. It is delicious, I assure you."

He pulled it down to his mouth, nibbled a small bite, and smiled. He then bit off half of the apple in one chomp.

"Me thinks it tastes better," he said grinning and finished it off, putting the core in his pocket.

Monday, 7 September 1891, 9:30 am

"It is not quite twenty-four hours, but I can wait no longer," Jones said. "I am fine, I assure you. Not to mention, that I am excited and optimistic that we are about to make history."

He lingered over his drawings, surveying the plans, one last time, before assembling his gear to execute the first ever attempt to time travel—parlor and back.

He paced over to his map and checked his calculations for proper aligns. According to his math, he could leave from his meditation room, travel to the parlor and return within three minutes time. Jones took a deep cleansing breath, donned his dustcoat and goggles and pocketed his journal in his waistcoat. Roark had picked up the machine to haul it to the meditation room. Jones followed closely with a piece of scratch paper, containing the exact coordinates to toggle into the machine. Roark placed the Atomotron on a table set up with incense and effigies.

"So 'is is where ya toggle in the date? 'ese are fer location?" He toggled through coordinates, dates and times.

"Yes. I will put in this location and we shall be on our way," Jones said. "As close as I can figure the approximate field of transfer is eighteen inches deep created by my personal gravitational field in relationship to the time machine. The maximum vibration generated by the Atomotron will induce the dematerializing and assemblage at arrival based on the internal clock connected to the gyroscopes. Once the coordinates are satisfied, the machine will countermand and in this reduction, materialization will manifest. Okay… now I am talking to myself. Roark, can you help me place the straps? If you can hold the machine up for moment, I will try it on for fit."

"All right 'en, hold yer arms out behind ya and I'll slide it onta ya."

Roark slipped the straps up Jones's arms, coming to rest on his shoulders. Jones adjusted the balance.

"It feels a little low." Jones pulled to tighten the straps and then reached behind to adjust the position on his waist and accidently tripped the lever.

"Take it off," yelled Roark. He started to reach for Jones but held back as his friend and benefactor began to dematerialize right in front him. A sound like an approaching tornado engulfed the room followed by a deafening silence. Roark stood dumbfounded and desperate. He, without question, skulked to the parlor, pulled on his Donegal, and tramped out the front door.

He walked in the direction of the Haymarket station with increasing speed as his mind roared with angst.

"Roark," a woman's voice called out.

Roark glanced in the direction of the summons and saw Emily strolling toward him. He went to make his escape but heard her call out once again.

"Roark, whatever has gotten into you?" she said as she sashayed up next to him and took his arm. "Why on earth are you shaking like this? Are you ill?"

"No. I… eh… yeah… me thinks I have a cold. I need a

good walk."

Emily disengaged their arms and stopped, allowing Roark to walk a few steps ahead.

"I would feel better speaking from here, that being the case. Does Jones know you are not feeling well?"

"Can't say that fer sure."

"Well, when you see him next, tell him I will be stopping by this afternoon."

Sunday, 17 June 2012, 6:30 am

Snohomish, WA

Jones all at once became aware of his senses again. He had made it. It had worked beyond imagination with no ill effects as far as he could tell. He opened his eyes and realized he stood right on the edge of a steep bank. As he turned to assess the predicament in which he found himself, he lost his balance, crashing sideways to the ground with one tumble. He lay there for a moment, steeling his mind, while he took in the expansive blue skies and mountains off in the distance surrounding a lazy river glistening in the morning sun.

"Where am I?"

He could see what appeared to be automobiles moving rapidly over a black roadway. The green train trestle over the river appeared much the same as he had beheld in the rural areas of Boston. He climbed the slope to assess his immediate surroundings to discover a small house reflecting the same architecture as the Victorian houses he had inadvertently left behind, only dwarfed in size.

"Excuse me?" a voice called out from the first floor

window. "What in hell are you doing in my backyard? Are you an exterminator? Are you lost?"

"I am a bit shaken to be honest," he called back, brushing off the debris. "And may I say you ask a lot of questions at once making it difficult to answer."

Jones unloaded the time machine from his back. He placed the metal box on the picnic table in front of him and investigated the nature of the damage. Two bent cage gears.

"This is unfortunate—I cannot believe this has happened," he groaned. "This creates a very serious situation." He looked up and yelled in the direction of the window, "Where am I?" Jones closed his eyes as he connected with his Ch'i and took a deep breath to center himself. After a couple of moments, he called out again, "I am asking your forbearance and will attempt to explain my predicament."

Darcy bounced out the backdoor, down the porch steps, and within seconds stood in her own backyard before a person dressed in a dustcoat and goggles. "Do you always dress in steampunk gear?" She cautiously approached him near the berm's edge, keeping a safe distance. She considered her intuition to be rock solid but still felt undecided regarding the odd man in front of her.

"Steampunk?"

"Your clothes and the metal backpack?" She pointed to the time machine.

"This is an awkward situation to be sure and I have a lot I need to explain. I do not understand of what you speak when referencing 'steampunk', however—"

"You have a weird way of talking," she said as she wrapped her arms around herself.

"I might say the same about you."

64

"Awww, sweet, our first argument."

Jones blushed upon realizing the short length of Darcy's skirt. He had never seen a woman dressed in that manner. He brought his attention back to her freckled face and brown eyes, at once feeling rather mesmerized and confused. Ever the gentleman, he struggled not to stare at her bare legs.

"You're not hard on the eyes at all. If you clean up your act—"

"I beg your pardon? What does that mean?"

"Take off those goggles, you look kinda weird with 'em on."

"This seems incredibly contentious for a first time meeting," Jones said, removing his goggles.

"That's the kind of girl I am. What's your name?" She took a tentative step forward and found the silvery blue of his eyes captivating.

"Jones Whitman. And yours?"

"I'm Darcy Champagne." She squinted in the sunlight and dropped her arms to the sides. "Are you from England?"

"No I am not. Please, may I have a few moments to explain the situation in which I find myself?"

"Sure, but this better be good, 'cause I'm running outta steam for this get together."

"Yes, as I have as well with the Atomotron." Jones pointed to the machine. "Well, how shall I begin?" He laid his goggles and dustcoat on the picnic table and took a deep breath contemplating a way to move events forward. "What do you know of time travel?"

"H.G.? I've read a few books. I'm in a steampunk sort of mood these days. I even have a corset to wear for this year's Steamcon."

"What?" Jones asked. "So, wait, where am I? And what

65

date would it be today?"

"Okaaaay. Now that's a really odd question."

Darcy began to back up, crossing her arms in front of her once again.

"It will not seem strange in a few moments, I assure you."

"You're in Snohomish, Washington and it's Sunday, June 2012, and I don't off hand remember the exact date."

"This is incredible. I am stunned." Jones glanced at the toggles on the time machine. "I left Boston, Massachusetts on Monday, 7 September 1891, at precisely 9:30 am."

"Yeah, right," she said with a nervous grin. "I'm starting to think you need some help."

She pulled out her cell phone and looked at it.

"I know how this must sound but please bear with me. I am Jones Whitman, nephew of Walt Whitman—"

"Oh right. Sure *you're* the nephew of Walt Whitman and *I'm* the niece of… of Joan of Arc."

"You are making light of me, I can tell. So how can I prove to you that I am who I say I am?"

"Wikipedia. If you're somebody famous, that invented a time machine—well that's ridiculous because if you had, we'd all be using one right now! Who are you?" Darcy's eyes widened, the angst apparent in her voice. "I think I'll call Taylor and have him take you to a shelter."

Jones wiped his forehead on his sleeve and sat down on the picnic table.

"There must be a way I can explain. I assure you these circumstances came to be by accident. I tripped—"

"Okay. Let's say you're telling the truth, then why can't you just travel back to where you came from?"

"Because I have bent two gears that are crucial to

generating the low vibration used to expand my atomic gravitational field to allow for a lateral time and space displacement."

"What the...? What did you just say?"

Jones sighed.

"May I intrude upon you for a glass of water?"

"That is *not* what you just said."

Darcy flopped down next to Jones.

"Yes, I know. However, my immediate need is to quench my thirst." Jones glanced in the direction of the house. "Would this be your domicile?"

"Yeah. Came by it from the death of my father."

"And your mother?"

"She's in a facility. She never got over my Dad's death. And what business is it of yours anyway?" Darcy looked Jones up and down.

"I realize it is none of my business. I am a curious kind of fellow." Jones waited.

Darcy stared at Jones for a moment. "Come on. I'll take you inside."

"You can feel completely assured that I mean you no harm," he said as he rose from the table.

"Not necessary, I'm highly intuitive. I wouldn't be asking you in if I had even one red flag." She traipsed over the yard toward the house and bounced up the steps with Jones in tow.

"Red flag?" he asked as he fell in behind her.

Jones stopped and went back to retrieve the Atomotron from the table. Once again, he caught up with Darcy at the back door of the small yellow house with white trim. He followed her through the rear entry leading to a quaint kitchen.

"May I?" Jones draped his dustcoat over the back of the

chair and took a seat at the square oak table set for two. "I am still feeling somewhat disoriented," he said. "I have a plethora of emotions and thoughts running through my mind. Please forgive me if I start to babble on about all that has happened. I never considered time travel would be so exhausting or maybe I am feeling the effects of displacement in an unknown location. *Maybe* if I can explain myself, we will both feel better."

"Sure, babble on. Would you like a cup of java? I make a mean cup of coffee. I've been a barista for around two years." Darcy pulled out a French press and her favorite grind.

"Yes. That might help."

She proceeded to make two cups of coffee.

"Do you take half and half or milk or black?"

"What would half and half be?"

"Half milk, half cream?" Darcy said. "Okay, I guess you might not know about that little discovery."

She raised her eyebrows wondering if he was an excellent actor or crazy?

"A barista sounds like a fugitive from the Mexican war."

"Italian. It's Italian for bartender. Clueless when it comes to history. History isn't my finest subject. I'm more into computers and languages. Writing software. That sort of stuff. But I do love working as a barista, making coffee for my customers. Enough about me because I could go on all day, but I want to hear your story."

She placed a glass of water in front of him.

"Computers? Software? Perhaps you can show me these manifestations later. Should I start?"

"Sure. Knock yourself out."

"Really?" Jones asked in surprise.

"Geeze, an expression, Mr. Jones."

Darcy pressed the plunger on the French press and wondered about the man behind her. From his reflection in the kitchen window, he *looked* as though he came from another time-period but so did many people she ran into all the time. She would not allow her undeniable attraction to him to cloud her vision.

Jones took a couple of deep breaths.

"Well then, I will share my story. I am Jones Whitman, son of my father, James Whitman, who was brother to Walt Whitman. I have an unbounded admiration for my uncle as both poet and philosopher. I grew up in Boston society and graduated cum laude from the Lawrence Scientific School at Harvard. I was not always as I am now. Growing up in a progressive family, I was given ample opportunities to make my own decisions, which in the beginning were fairly well informed, but as soon as I left the refuge of my home for college, a different fellow began to emerge."

"That's what I hear about college."

She retrieved the half-and-half from the refrigerator and placed on the table. Darcy brought over the French press and cups. She took a seat across from Jones and poured his coffee.

"Well, I developed strong friendships with three other students that led to drinking nightly, secretly cavorting with women of ill repute , and engineering devices that when wound produced various levels of vibrations for up to three minutes at a time. We issued them to the women in lieu of payment. The devices seemed to add a great deal of pleasure to the lives of libertines of the night. Thank you." He took a sip of coffee after stirring in the cream.

"That alone should have you in the wiki. Those little devices became a major industry, dude."

"Really? I suppose that would make sense. Shall I continue?"

"Sure. I'm all ears." She sat back in her chair in a comfortable manner to listen carefully to his story.

"My father soon caught wind of my exploits and sought the advice of his close friends. The summer of my freshman year, I found myself on a steam liner headed for Foshan, China with my father, who explained he had business there and wanted me more involved with our import textile company."

"You must be from a wealthy Boston family then. That's cool. Sorry. So go on."

"Yes, by most standards."

Darcy rose from the table.

"Well, upon arrival, I found his ulterior motives had much to do with my introduction to a recommended instructor of sorts. Wong Fei-hung, acupuncturist and tai ch'i master, became my teacher and mentor. My Father informed me I would be residing with Fei-hung for the next ninety days where I would be his pupil and his patient. I had no hope of escape. We were in China after all. We reported to Wong's establishment, the first morning of our arrival, and to my amazement, the dwelling turned out to be a temple."

"A temple? This is gettin' good, Mr. Whitman."

"It was fascinating to say the least. Lit mostly by lanterns, the rich colors of gold, orange, and brilliant red silks danced in the evening breezes. It dazzled my mind. Fei-Hung brought a special tea the first night to help me sleep."

"Whoa, cool. We should be able to look up the Wong on the Wiki."

Darcy laughed.

"What is this Wiki, of which you speak?""

"I'll be right back." Darcy sprinted down the hall. She reentered the kitchen and pulled her chair around next to him. "Check this out. This is a laptop computer. These are awesome machines. If you stick around or come back—which I'm not saying that I'm a believer just yet—I'll teach you all things internet. It's crazy amazing. It's booting up." Darcy logged on, typed in www.wikipedia.org, and waited. "Okay so how do you spell this guy's name?"

"W-o-n-g F-e-i-h-u-n-g."

"Here we go." Darcy clicked on the search engine. "Get out of town, dude! He really existed."

"Exists."

"Okay that's creepy in a weird funky sort of way," she said, glancing into his eyes.

Jones pointed at the screen.

"Am I listed?"

Darcy typed in Jones Whitman. No information came up.

"Sorry. I wonder what this all means? Wong is there but you aren't. Let me think. Okay, let's attack this another way. We can do a public record search in Boston for your name and see what shows up."

She flipped through screen after screen as Jones watched in amazement.

"Where is all of this stored?"

"In the clouds."

"Truly? You are jesting with me again? I must admit, my head is reeling. Have you, we, somehow learned to store information in the atoms of a cloud? That is fantastic! A marvel, to be sure."

"Well not exactly, but, sort of... no, not even... nope that's not it at all. It's a reference to the ethers? The net is an interconnected system connecting computers around the world using TCP/IP protocol. The Internet enables the World Wide Web to exist. When I searched, do you remember me typing in www?"

"Yes. I see it right there," Jones said, touching the screen.

"Okay, well that connects us the World Wide Web and we can get to places almost as fast as light."

"Seriously?"

"No, not really, but very fast."

She smiled.

"What kinds of information does it hold?"

"Everything, I don't know, ask me a question about anything."

"Is there anything smaller than an atom? I have pondered this question often."

"I'm typing in the question. Okay, the easy answer is— the smallest particle that has mass is a neutrino. However, there are three million three hundred and eighty thousand results to your question."

"I am intrigued by the possible ramifications of having access to such extraordinary knowledge." Jones sat still, contemplating for a moment. "A time traveler could easily be enticed by the promise of fortune and power, utilizing such information when traveling back in time."

"How is it different than you coming to the future and returning to Boston?"

"I surmise it is not, and maybe, that is why I am not found in the Wiki. Time travel, in the wrong hands, with such vast knowledge available could provoke one to choose an unintentional dark path. Time travel must be concealed. Thusly, it must be safe to assume, I have kept it secreted. I did commit to a high standard of secrecy prior to my departure, but I am seeing now that may be a problem when one shows up in the middle of someone's backyard adorned in strange gear."

"Oh dude, I think you may be on to something. Listen, does that mean, since I now know about time travel, I too can—do I need to take an oath?"

"An oath? Um, yes, do you, Darcy Champagne, swear not to speak of time travel to another living soul?"

"You mean other than yourself?"

"Of course."

"I do. So does this mean we could go back in time and I could meet your parents and you meet mine?"

"You move rather quickly for a woman I have only just met."

"I meant in theory," Darcy said, glancing away to hide the heat in her cheeks.

"My father and mother were killed in a train derailment on the way to New York. I was close to them both. However, I feel it would be unethical and dangerous to cross paths with myself. Perhaps someday when I have much more experience as a time traveler."

"Ouch, that's got to hurt. What if you could go back and make them late for the train?"

"I cannot permit myself that luxury at this time. A debilitating experience, to be sure, which makes the proposition attractive. The idea of seeing both my mother and father again has kept me motivated to achieve my goal, however, I now understand I have no idea how that might alter the future. I feel obligated to honor my commitment to Wong not to modify the past, present or future without weighing the possible outcomes. And in keeping with Tao, allow the natural progression of things to come to fruition."

"I don't think I could resist going back and altering the

future to save someone I truly love."

Jones looked impressed.

"I cannot begin to tell you how fortunate I feel to have landed in your backyard. Your hospitality and fearless approach to this situation is remarkable."

"Fearless could be my middle name," Darcy said with a broad smile. "The truth is I'm fascinated by oddities and in your case… the jury is definitely in."

"You use the most peculiar terms. It sounds like English but—"

"What kinda stuff did you do in China?"

"Well, we would rise each morning at five o'clock—"

"Okay, right there, that would *not* work for me."

Darcy chuckled.

In the midst of all the confusion, Jones had not yet taken full notice of Darcy Champagne. He had not studied her until the moment when he felt a surge of energy pass through his body like an opened meridian. He drank in her features for the first time, as she moved around the kitchen, lingering particularly on her tawny full lips and dark brown eyes.

"Not contentious, but assured, and judging from your surroundings you have lived a full life with courage and strength."

"Let's keep going 'cause I have to leave for work in an hour, so I'll need to shower and get dressed, comprende?" Darcy tilted her head back and smiled.

"And there is the small matter that I have no place to go."

"It's okay, I'm known for picking up strays and helping them find their way back home or to a new home as the case may be. Mostly animals, you understand–the four-legged kind, but you can stay here until I get back. You can watch some TV."

"What is TV?" Jones asked.

"Oh… maybe we should wait on that for a bit. I'll find you a something to read and when I get back we'll continue." Darcy strolled over to the bookcase and pulled out a book. "Hey, before I leave to get ready, do you mind explaining how you ended up in my yard?"

"It is rather embarrassing to admit," Jones sighed. "However, as I adjusted the fit of the Atomotron, I inadvertently tripped the lever and you became the recipient of an errant time traveler."

"I think I understand, except how?" She approached.

"Ah. Well, Roark's curiosities lead him to play with the time and location toggles. This destiny was random."

"That my friend is an oxymoron."

Jones stroked his chin. "I will have to agree. I would have better served my purposes by asserting this *destination* was a random event."

"And who knows yet? Maybe this *is* a destiny of sorts. Anyway, you're more than welcome to stay."

"I can pay you for any inconvenience. I have money." Jones reached into his pocket and brought out three half eagle and two double eagle coins. He held them out to Darcy.

"Dude, are these for real? They look like real gold."

Darcy's eyes gleamed.

"As opposed to what kind of gold?" Jones asked.

"No, I just mean these are probably worth a whole lot more now than back in Boston. We should take this over to one of the antique stores and ask for some kind of valuation. You're going to need spending money while you're here. I mean, I can help out, but if my brother finds out, he'll hit the roof."

"Sounds like Roark and he quite literally doesn't live far

from the roof."

Jones chortled.

"Who's Roark? Oops, maybe later. We can talk about Roark later." She glanced at the clock on the wall. "Right now I need to shower, so here… this is right up your alley." Darcy handed Jones a book. "Gott wrote this book on time travel. It's good. Part of my steampunk anthology. Maybe you can read it and explain some of the concepts to me. Stay in the house." She pointed a finger in his direction. "Showering," she said as she left the room.

Jones glanced through the book for a moment and then stopped to look around. His body tingled with excitement at the realization that everything he believed could and actually had happened. He was living proof time travel was indeed possible. He sat in the kitchen of Darcy Champagne's home, in Snohomish, Washington, in the year 2012. He had traveled one hundred and twenty-one years into the future and yet he resided here and now. *All time is local*, he thought. *I am still aging as I would, and will, wherever I am. I am alive here but dead somewhere else on the continuum.*

"This experience is simply excellent," Jones said aloud. "I cannot wait to see the look on Roark's face."

He grinned like a little boy discovering how delightful it is to play in the mud for the first time.

A sharp knock on the front door surprised him.

"Darcy!" the voice called out as he stepped inside. "Darcy, I'm dropping off a list of things I need help with. Helloooo?"

Jones tightened his body in expectation of the new person entering the kitchen. He tried to shrink himself to become inconspicuous, but alas, nowhere to hide, he sat still, holding his breath.

"Whoa," the young man called out in surprise. "You scared me. Who're you?"

"Jones, Jones Whitman."

Jones faltered as he stood and extended his hand to the man standing in low-slung jeans and a baggy T-shirt who was examining him from head to toe. His eyes gazed across Jones's odd attire of a gabardine vest with a golden chain running from his vest buttonhole to the watch pocket. "Darcy has a reputation for bringing home strays but you're even a bit much for her," he said and scrunched his nose. "What are you supposed to be? Is this that steampunk look she keeps going on about?"

"I'm sorry if my—"

"Where's my sister?" he said as he ambled farther into the house.

"It's a pleasure to make your acquaintance," Jones mumbled as he withdrew his empty hand. "Darcy is taking a shower," he called out and made his way past the bookcase as he followed the same path as the stranger toward the back rooms.

"So you don't know her that well," he said, turning back to face Jones.

"No. I am not exactly sure what that is supposed to mean. We've only recently met, but I assure you I am—"

"Homeless?" he asked.

"Well, yes, you *could* say that… and it would be a true statement at this point in time," Jones answered. "However, I do have—"

"Figures. She can't seem to help herself'," he said. You would think she'd been abandoned as a pup."

He chuckled and shook his head at the thought.

"She seems mentally and physically strong and adequate

enough to fully take care of herself," Jones said. "It is an admirable quality."

"She's combative."

"Yes, she is that as well."

Jones broke into a full smile.

"By the way, I'm Taylor, Darcy's older brother."

He finally extended his hand for a handshake.

"I see the resemblance in your brown eyes and hair and the way you both project your energy."

"Uh oh… energy? You're not one of—"

Suddenly, Darcy raced in with a towel wrapped around her. "Taylor, I see you've met Jones. Be nice and don't be telling him stories about me."

Jones froze at the sight of Darcy clad only in a towel.

"Should I take my leave?" His voice was two octaves above normal.

"Too late," Taylor said to Darcy with a teasing laugh. "But I didn't get to the story where …"

"I should definitely take my leave," Jones muttered to himself and started toward the back door.

"Stop it, Taylor. And Jones, you can stay."

Darcy pointed in Jones's direction.

"But you don't even know—" Taylor said with a raised voice.

"Okay. That is fine then. I will just stand over here."

Jones turned his back on the two siblings and began to peruse the bookshelf.

"Taylor, you're walking on thin ice here, this is my home. No more kiddin' around."

"Okay, fine. I'm joking," Taylor said. "I need you to run some errands." He handed her a list. "I have to get to work now and Mom needs a couple of things. Can you drop them by the care place?"

"Sure. But it will have to be later today because I'm headed into work myself."

"Maybe Jones could drop them by?"

"No. Definitely not, Taylor. I'll take care of it and let you know the next time I need *your* advice." Darcy placed her hand on Taylor's back and ushered him to the front door. "Have a nice day."

She closed the door behind him and returned to the kitchen.

"You were somewhat combative," Jones said with a grin. "I have no siblings so I cannot empathize with your plight. And may I say your attire is very appealing."

"No, you may not." Darcy strode to the back of a short hallway to her bedroom. She partially closed the door, obstructing Jones's view as she dressed and said, "My brother feels the need to be in on every decision I make. Since my father died, Taylor thinks he has to take my Dad's place. Sometimes he's more of a pain in my ass than helpful," Darcy called out. "But I understand what motivates him so I tolerate more than I should. Once in a while, I wish I were a boy so I could just knock him out."

Darcy returned wearing a tight pair of jeans and a white button down shirt sporting a red bowtie.

"Where is Taylor employed that he would be working on a Sunday as well?" Jones looked Darcy up and down. "This is what women are wearing now?"

"He's a motorcycle mechanic and artist. He paints designs on the tanks. What's wrong with what I'm wearing?"

"Absolutely nothing at all." Jones held back his sheepish grin but the sparkle in his eyes was plain to see. "I find the style most appealing. I think I'm going to like it here."

"So you're staying?"

"No. Well, perhaps coming back at some point in time." He closely watched Darcy move about the kitchen. "What are his ambitions?"

"Taylor? He wants to open his own shop to design and build custom motorcycles." Darcy finished her coffee and gathered her necessities for work. "And I'm glad you approve of what I'm wearing... *not*."

Jones's eyes widened upon hearing the word motorcycle. He chose to ignore her last statement.

"Do you think I might see the shop at some point? I have a steam bike back in Boston that I thoroughly enjoy riding through the streets down by the harbor."

"Steam bike?" she asked. "That's a hoot. Maybe later I can take you out on my '78 Triumph Bonneville T140. That'll blow your mind."

"I must admit I am completely baffled by some of your expressions."

"Yeah? Well, stick around and I'll teach you all you need to know," Darcy said with a wink.

"Is the Triumph a motorcycle? I would be pleased to accompany you. And I suppose while I am here anyway, perhaps we might go for a ride in an automobile?"

"I'll see what I can do. I need to head out, so stay here. I won't be gone long, okay? You gonna be alright?"

"I will use this time to examine the damage to the Atomotron. Perhaps you could assist me in finding a source for some small cage gears."

"I think I know just the place. Make sure to help yourself to anything in the frig or icebox or whatever you call it."

"Thank you, Darcy, for bringing me into your home. I will do my best to repay your kindness."

She had a couple of ideas how he might pay his debt, but chided herself. *You don't even know this guy. He's a stranger, you fruit.*

Sunday, 17 June 2012, 8:00 am

"Hey, how's it goin'?"

"Great. Sarah, I'm entertaining a visitor this afternoon, so I'm anxious to get back home."

"Relative?"

"No. Let's just say he's a guy from the past." Darcy smiled. "Would you be upset if I asked you to close?"

"Nope, not at all. Old flames can be a lot of fun," Sarah said as she scooped coffee beans into the grinder, preparing for the morning rush. "Be careful though. Sometimes they come back with the same ole baggage."

"Yep… or none at all."

Darcy pushed through the double doors into the counter area where she faced twelve tables adorned with mini flower vases. The tables sat empty for the moment, but soon enough the café would be filled with happy voices.

The popular Crêpe Escape coffee bar drew both Snohomish locals and vacationers. The summer Sunday morning rush of customers often formed a line winding around the side of the building. Darcy had a reputation for having lots of energy and a knack for 'getting it right the first time'. She prided herself as a coffee buff with extensive knowledge of all matters java. The two years as a barista had given her a different perspective on life. She had explored many countries via coffee beans and plantation posters, often daydreaming of traveling to the faraway tropical estates and

81

meeting, in person, the coffee growers to buy beans for the coffee house she hoped to own one day.

"Good morning, everyone." Darcy opened the front door and pushed a doorstop in place allowing in the fresh air. The mountain breeze cooled the café while patrons sipped coffee and dined on pastries and crepes. "You know the drill." She addressed the long line of customers. "Place your order at the counter and we'll bring it out for you. That's it, soooo… *bon appétit*!"

The breakfast and lunch shift felt endless to Darcy. She longed to return home to Jones and his magical tales of travel through time. She had left him alone to tinker with the damaged Atomotron and secretly hoped it would take some time to repair.

Jones mulled over several critical issues, notwithstanding the importance of locating gears to replace those bent during his fall on the embankment upon his arrival. After much contemplation, he decided to center himself by meditating on a solution to his dilemma. Jones made his way to the living room where he removed his shoes and striped bare to his waist. He assumed the Lotus position and breathed deep and slow, calming his mind and relaxing his body, which allowed his life force to flow in a more balanced way. He reminded himself of the words of Chun Lee, 'Stay within the sanctity of your Ch'i'. Jones felt his life force organizing itself around the challenge before him and a great calm came over his body and spirit. When he achieved his centered mental state, he could meditate for great lengths of time. While he hung in suspended animation, his mind returned to his days at Foshan.

Master Fei-hung took a seat next to Jones by the

reflection pool. The temple was calm but bustling with activity as the monks began preparing the morning meal.

"Master, what is my destiny?"

"To become yourself."

"How will I know when I have achieved the goal of being myself?"

"When extraneous events have no impact on your personal happiness." Fei-hung paused. "You must follow your bliss."

"How do I ignore the outside influences?"

"It is not a matter of ignoring but embracing that which is different from yourself. You will stand strong with the understanding that differences do not threaten your centered self or personal happiness."

"So am I to pursue only my happiness?"

"That would not be fair in universal terms. You are to commit to the utmost integrity and seek happiness for all that you encounter along the way." Master Fei-hung slid his hands into the sleeves of his gi. "On this path, you will find happiness for yourself as well." He bowed. "It is time to start a new day."

"I am grateful for the opportunity to be under your tutelage," Jones said, returning the bow. "I will be forever in your debt."

"I too am grateful, for this is my bliss and I am immersed in happiness."

A faint smile crossed his lips.

Jones heard a distant voice bringing him back to the present moment.

Sunday, 17 June 2012, 2:30 pm

"**H**i honey, I'm home. Took care of my mom, so we can..." Darcy called out as she entered her house from the front door. She rounded the corner to the living room and found a cross-legged young Jones meditating. "Wow, what do we have here?" she whispered.

Jones maintained his posture both physically and spiritually. His palms rested face up on his knees, pointer finger and thumb joined to form a circle with his spine straight. His controlled breathing highlighted his taunt abs. Out of both respect and awe, Darcy slowed her pace as she entered the room. She had no idea that under the waistcoat and white shirt lived a man of such striking appearance. A tattoo of Chinese characters ran the length of his left forearm. A charge of heat flushed her face.

Jones stirred and squinted one eye.

"I do hope your work was productive," he said. "I am very happy to have you return. My mind has been racing with thoughts and questions so I did what I always do to calm myself. I must apologize for my state of undress. Time is not apparent when I meditate."

"It's no problem... at all... I think you... well you look really... it's no problem."

"That was clear." Jones chuckled.

He rose from his seated position and pulled his shirt on. His body moved with fluidity, physical strength and prowess. He buttoned his shirt and straightened his collar. He took a seat on the couch and smoothed his dark hair with his hands.

"What's with the tat? What does it mean?" she asked, pointing to his forearm.

"Tat? What does *that* mean?"

"Tattoo. Sorry. I keep forgetting."

She sat down on the couch next to him.

"Ah, Fei-hung assigned it to me. It is my Hung Gar name: Time Traveler." Jones rolled up his sleeve and held out his forearm.

"That is seriously cool." She ran her fingers over the Kanji characters, touching his smooth, soft skin. Her body responded, causing her to abruptly stand and withdraw her hand from his forearm. "Let's get one thing clear, though. From now on, should you feel the need to meditate… you can do it in the guest room. Cool?"

"I'm sorry? You are using 'cool' in a manner with which I am unaccustomed."

"Meaning 'do you understand'? Nothing to do with temperature. Except… when it's chilly."

"Really? Cool now means 'do you understand'?"

Jones raised an eyebrow.

"Oh, among many other things. Just… just follow along, will ya?"

"Where are we going?"

He stood up and moved closer to her.

"No. I mean… OMG never mind." Darcy raised her hand, palm out, in Jones's direction.

"OMG?"

"Geeze, sit down and be quiet for a moment. I want you to listen and I'll try my best to speak in the Queen's English."

"I'm not English—"

"Not another word from you until I say so. Do you understand?" Darcy waited. "Well?"

"So I may speak at this moment?"

"You are a piece of work, dude… and don't say

85

anything... please." Darcy held up one finger in Jones's direction. "No, not even a whisper."

Darcy plopped back down on the couch and took a few moments to assimilate into her brain the human being sitting next to her. She found him baffling, irritating and intriguing all at the same time.

Jones waited with a slight grin on his face.

"You can speak now," Darcy said.

"May I ask one question of you?"

Jones waited for her permission.

"Dude, ask your question," she said with a scowl on her face.

"Am I inadvertently causing you to experience frustration with me?"

"My apologies, but you can certainly try the patience of a woman without meaning to."

"So I have heard... back in Boston. Emily is rather fond of reminding me that I try her forbearance."

"Emily?" Disappointment filled her gut.

"Yes, she is to be my wife by the end of the month. Therefore, you can see why I must get back to Boston as soon as possible, which brings me to my plight at present. This is all so very complicated. Would you be willing to allow me the liberty of answering your questions as we move toward my return to Boston?"

"Yeah, not a problem, and you just answered one of my biggest questions." Darcy sighed.

"And what answer would that be."

Jones squinted.

"Where you'll be sleeping tonight," Darcy said. "The guest bedroom is exceedingly comfortable."

Jones captured her heart by rocking his head back and

forth like a discombobulated and fascinated puppy. He adjusted to face Darcy. Without thinking, he stretched out his hand onto the back of the couch only to find Darcy's hand occupying the space.

"Excuse me… my apologies." He quickly withdrew his hand. "I didn't mean to… touch you."

"Really? That's too bad. I kind of liked it for a split second. Your hands are soft… and warm."

"Well truth is I rather enjoyed the experience myself," Jones said, his eyes bright with excitement.

"Are you always going to talk like that?"

"Like what?"

"Say 'man that was excellent'."

"There are so many reasons why I cannot speak to you in that manner."

Jones looked at her in a way that left Darcy feeling warm and tingly inside. He again placed his hand on hers and smiled.

"That feels nice," she said, locking her brown-eyed gaze onto Jones's blue eyes. She shook her head, breaking off the connection. "Back to the future or past or… whatever. So my first question is this: How does the Atomotron work?"

"Do you want the get-to-the-point answer? Or shall I recall the last seven years in some type of chronological order cross referencing progress?"

"Well… when you put it like that, what's a girl to do?" she said. "I think a shorter version, for the sake of time, will be fine for now."

"Democritus."

Darcy stood and went about the country-styled kitchen, gathering what she needed to make her afternoon Blue Mountain drip.

"When he and another Greek by the name of Leucippus joined mental forces, they concluded that all things are made of atoms and atoms are the building blocks of everything. Can you hear me okay?"

"Yes," Darcy said from the kitchen. "So Demo and Leu were from where?"

"Ancient Greece. They were from an era of deep thinkers. They lived surrounded by many philosophers that our current ideas are based upon. Current being a relative term."

"I see. Haven't really heard of those guys before."

"Well, suffice it to say they have made a huge impact on my life and my decision to pursue the Atomotron as a means of time travel. The key idea for my purposes is that between atoms therein lies an enormous amount of space relative to the atom itself. Therefore, I concluded that if one could generate a low frequency vibration to match the frequency of the Universe, logically, one could become one with the universe, expand and therefore be enabled to travel freely back and forth in time and space."

"We may have to go over that again." Darcy placed her cup on the end table and took a seat next to Jones. "Sometimes when you speak, I become mesmerized and I'm listening but not necessarily understanding. So why, if you become one with the universe, are you able to time travel?"

"Because there are timelines, like the meridians in the body, where the energy of the universe travels, and if you attach yourself, you can then travel along that timeline."

"Well obviously it works or you wouldn't be here right now."

"So you do believe that I am presently here in this location, having traveled from Boston 1891 to Snohomish and your backyard?"

"Well honestly, I was stuck between you being insane or a proficient actor, but yes you've made me a believer. I mean the way I feel when I'm close to you… well… it's hard to deny the ease and comfort."

And titillation, she thought, hoping her attraction hadn't muddled her brain.

"I am relieved to hear this. I shall attempt to make my explanation palatable. When I explain procedures to Roark and ask if he understands, usually he simply says 'No'. Shall I resume my attempt?"

Darcy nodded.

"The Atomotron is based on the idea that we are mostly liquid that can be heated and cooled allowing for the appearance of dematerialization but the truth is when we expand it makes traveling far easier. And it is theorized that there is more space between atoms than we could ever imagine. Leu, as you call him, theorized atoms are flexible because liquids can become gases and change shape without losing their original foundation, glass for instance. Glass is a liquid in solid form. Every element has its own location and attraction to itself."

"So you look like you're disappearing but you don't really?"

Darcy moved closer, her eyes wide with fascination.

"No, you do not. I believe you experience suspension in universal time/space. Our local time remains intact while universal time is transitional. The machine captures local time and gravity and moves through the universal space/time by means of meridians or timelines."

"Right… like with acupuncture."

"Yes, exactly. Those are the pathways in the human body where energy travels at enormously high speeds.

Acupuncturists utilize needles in the meridians to release debris in the paths, restoring the free flow of Ch'i. Your life force is the most powerful instrument for understanding the universe where you reside. Become one with the universe and you are free to travel."

"What does it feel like?"

"Perhaps the clearest analogy I can use to describe the experience is to equate it with falling asleep, as you might after a long, exhausting day. Akin to passing out."

"That's gotta be a little scary!"

"Trust me when I say I was a bit terrified when I mistakenly flipped the lever on the machine, but only for a brief moment. A rushing noise accompanied my arrival behind your house, and a ringing in my ears that diminished thoroughly. This being my first foray, I felt understandably disoriented when I materialized in your backyard. However, once aware... I experienced a rush of exhilaration, as you can well imagine."

"Wow, that's *so* cool. So it doesn't hurt at all? So what do ya think about me taking a little ride once it's up and running?" Darcy waited but Jones simply stared at her. "Okay, so what exactly does the Atomotron do? We'll get back to the ride later."

"Hmm. Well it uses a steady low vibration that resonates at the same frequency as the universe creating synchronization with the time/space meridians. Once accordant, you are free to move throughout the time/space continuum. Our entire human history could fit on the head of a needle, which underscores how infinitesimal our history is in relation to all of time. Therefore, the idea of time travel did not seem difficult to comprehend. At least not to me."

"Dude, we gotta get this thing working again."

"I have examined the entire system and I am in need of only two gears to restore it to good measure. I could use my pocket watch I suppose, but it was a gift from my Father and I do not imagine they would be an exact fit anyway. Might there be a watch or clock manufacturer around?"

"There is!" Darcy yelped. "Right around the corner from here is Legends in Time. They have a whole bunch of wicked devices. They're really cool." Darcy caught sight of Jones tilting his head again. "Oh wow, okay so let me interpret for you." Darcy explained in a stilted voice, "Legends in Time happens to be a shop and they procure and sell devices from the 1800s. They're antiques and I really like the way they look. Better?"

"Yes, thank you," Jones said. "So when can we go?"

"Right after we eat linner? That's a cross between lunch and dinner."

"Fascinating. Sustenance, a wonderful idea that has only just this moment overwhelmed me with hunger pangs. I often find I am unaware of what I need until someone distracts me from the path I am on."

"Maybe I can distract you later." Darcy jumped up from the couch wishing she had more control over her impulse to blurt out her thoughts. "Come on, big guy, let's get something to eat."

Sunday, 17 June 2012, 4:00 pm

"You need to take off that waistcoat and shirt. I might have a T-shirt you can wear." Darcy reached into a basket of washed clothes. "Yeah, here, let's take this off."

She assisted Jones out of his white button down dress

shirt and tossed him a T with Steamcon 2011 across the front. "So whatta ya think?"

"This is amazing. I recognized the Jules Verne illustration. The gears meshing throughout in the fade is fantastic to the eye. I can truly say I have never encountered this type of art or interesting innovation."

Jones pulled the T-shirt over his head, which accentuated his biceps and round shoulders.

"Yep. Amazing... and the shirt looks good too," Darcy said with a wink.

Jones stood back for a moment, pondering Darcy's flirtatious behavior. Although Emily would often bat her eyes and make suggestive comments, coming from Darcy, he could not help noticing the excited shift of his energy.

"We should make a run to Goodwill in Monroe and get you a couple of pairs of jeans and T-shirts. We can take the Triumph. It's not too far from here, but for now, let's walk over to Legends and check out what they have. We also need to find a buyer for those coins of yours."

"Sounds fine then. I am in full agreement with anything you say..." Jones marveled over the trust he felt with Darcy in the short period of time they had been acquainted. He looked at his reflection in the window. "I am enjoying this change. The shirt is unusual and expressive, except I do not get to see it often, do I? Maybe you should wear it and I can enjoy my observations of you while you are wearing it?"

"You'd be staring at me..." Darcy said and blushed. "And well... that could leave a girl feeling a bit uncomfortable."

"I think I understand. I suppose it would feel strange to have a man ogle you constantly."

"Yep, at least some men," she said. "Not so sure about

you just yet."

Their eyes locked as they stood there, lost in the moment.

Darcy shook her head, breaking the magic.

"Let's get out of here."

"I'm pretty sure you're going to like this place," Darcy said as they stepped onto the sidewalk. "They've got some great stuff from the 1800's. He should have some spare gears you can take a look at."

Darcy had a stride that left no doubt she had plans. Although tiny, she held herself straight and assured giving the impression of more height. Jones listened with eager attention as they walked around the corner from the house to the shop called Legends in Time.

The quaint storefront lay between an antique shop on the left and the Oxford Bar and Grill on the right. The Oxford had survived since 1898, mostly intact, including the ghost of a man walking his dog.

Legends left its patrons feeling as if they had embarked on a stroll back through history, where they got to see and purchase remarkable pieces of primitive engineering. Encased in glass and speckless, lay various precision cut instruments. The antiques filled every corner and shelf in the shop. Jones wandered through the maze fingering each case with a knowing touch.

"This is remarkable. And... these are your antiques while they are working instruments of my day in the 1800s. They have been well kept and with this one, I have much familiarity." Jones pointed and stepped aside in the tight space to let Darcy see. "It is called a chronograph and its use is to set longitude. Longitude and latitude are important aspects of time travel. This is unless one has a poorly designed lever mechanism that can be tripped by any imbecile adjusting the fit of the machine."

Jones laughed and Darcy could not help joining with a heartfelt laugh of her own.

The shopkeeper doddered in from the back and joined them, standing among an array of clocks and instruments that predated Jones's departure from Boston in 1891.

"Hi. Mr. Evans this is Jones Whitman. He's a friend visiting from Boston."

"Hi and welcome. What can I help you with?"

Mr. Evans tugged on the peak of his Mariners baseball cap and adjusted his glasses. His bulging blue eyes stood out as a unique feature among other oddities. He wore a plaid shirt with striped shorts and sneakers.

Jones stood still, for a moment, observing Mr. Evans and then blurted out, "I want a pair of those." He pointed at Mr. Evan's shorts and smiled. "And those shoes, what are their purpose? Fashion or—"

"They're running shoes." He furrowed his brow. "Where're you from that you've never—"

"I think what he meant to say was that he has never seen them in fluorescent green color," Darcy said, staring hard at Jones to get him to shut up.

"Undoubtedly. I must endeavor to get a pair for Roark."

"Right. We can get *you* new shorts and *shoes* for Roark later, k?" Darcy leaned into Jones and whispered, "Be cool, dude. You sound a bit mental."

"This must be one of those variations on the syntactical use of the word 'cool'."

Darcy rolled her eyes as her gaze left Jones and returned to her conversation with Mr. Evans. "My friend here is working on a little project and needs some small cage gears. I thought you might be able to help."

"What size?"

Jones pulled up the image in his mind of the Atomotron and scanned the damaged area.

"I need two at 14 millimeters and two at 10 millimeters."

"Hmm... let me look in the back. These for a pocket watch?"

"No. They are—"

"Yes." Darcy glared at Jones.

Jones chuckled and said, "May I just say they are for a time piece."

Darcy took the opportunity to hit Jones on the right shoulder and share a glower of disapproval.

"Knock it off."

Jones looked around his immediate space.

"Knock what off?"

"Jones, I want you to breathe the way you breathe to get in touch... no... never mind... I don't want you to do anything. Just stand there and be quiet. I'll take care of this. I do have a question however; I thought you only needed two gears."

"I calculated getting two of each would assure an accurate fit."

"Cool. Smart thinking. I mean they can't be that expensive."

Mr. Evans reentered the store from the back, displaying several gears on a cloth that he laid out on the counter.

"Some are gold, some are brass. Depends on what you need."

"Brass would—"

"Speaking of gold, Mr. Evans. Could you take a look at a couple of pieces he has— show him Jones—and tell us what they would be worth these days? I mean on the market."

"Sure. What do you have there?"

"I have five dollar half eagles and four double eagles worth twenty dollars each."

Jones pulled the pieces from his pocket and extended them to Evans who broke into a huge grin.

"Where did you come by these?"

Evans fingered the coins using the corner of the cloth.

"By legitimate means I assure you. Would that influence their market value?"

"Well, every good piece from the past should have a good story to go with it. It makes it more fun and interesting to buyers. The condition is extremely important. You have been carrying these around in your pocket?"

Jones laughed and held up a five dollar half eagle in one hand and a twenty-dollar eagle piece in the other.

"These coins have magically traveled a great distance over a long period of time to get here today."

Jones turned to Darcy smiling. She raised one eyebrow.

Mr. Evans opened his laptop and signed on. He typed in London Gold Fixing.

"Nice. Now the twenty dollar piece has .9675 troy ounces of gold and the half eagle has .242 troy ounces." Mr. Evans pivoted the screen of the computer around so they could read the website information. He turned the screen of the computer back while Jones eased around the counter staring at the machine with complete fascination. "It's Sunday, but I can tell you the value for Friday of last week. Let's see the troy ounce price for gold on Friday was $1509.92 melt value and now we need to add the numismatic value which won't be as much because you've been handling them and carrying them in your pocket." Mr. Evans shook his head and chuckled.

"Now, I can put on their numismatic value at… say… two hundred dollars? I can offer you the melt value plus a hundred for each twenty dollar eagle in order for me to make a profit."

"I think you and I have made a transaction, Sir. How many will you take?"

"How many are you looking to sell?"

Jones turned to Darcy.

"What do you think? Should I sell but one or two and take the rest back to Boston?"

"Yeah, that's a good idea," she whispered into Jones's ear. "You don't want to bring too much attention to us right off the bat. This is a small town and I mean small."

"Yes much smaller than Boston," he whispered back.

"Yes, Mr. Evans, I would like to sell one double eagle twenty dollar coin."

"Okay. Let me get my checkbook and I'll write you a check and bring a contract to sign for your legal protection, although, I assure you this check will be good."

"No problem, Mr. Evans. Could you make it out to me, since Jones is from out of town? Thanks a million for helping out," Darcy said. She turned to Jones and moved in close. "I'll deposit it in my bank account and I'll give you the money. Trust me?"

"Remarkably and without hesitation or explanation, I do."

Jones lingered a bit longer than fashionable on her features, as she focused on the transaction. He became fascinated with the light wispy eyelashes that framed her brown eyes.

Mr. Evans handed the check over to Darcy who folded it and slipped it into the front pocket of her jeans.

"Now back to the gears," Darcy said as she took Jones's face in her hands and guided him to look at the cloth holding the gears.

"Yes. How much for the four gears in brass?" Jones asked and then glanced back at Darcy.

"Ten dollars and twenty-four cents."

Mr. Evans punched the number keys on an eighteen hundreds National Cash register that produced the first paper receipts.

"I am sorry but I…" Jones muttered.

"Here ya go, Mr. Evans." Darcy handed him eleven dollars. "My treat. You can buy dinner."

"Yes. That is a wonderful idea. Thank you very much." Jones redirected his attention to the shopkeeper. "It was nice making your acquaintance, Mr. Evans."

Jones extended his hand and bowed slightly.

Mr. Evans dropped the gears into a small clear plastic bag and handed them to Jones.

Jones held the bag up to the light. "Fascinating." He slid the bag into his pocket and then pulled it out again. "This material—"

"Let's go." Darcy grabbed him by the arm. "Put that away and I'll tell you everything on the way home."

✿✿✿✿✿

The mottled shapes cast by the warm afternoon sun elongated the shadows, highlighting buildings and streets. The quiet of Snohomish counterpointed the hustle and bustle of Boston.

Jones and Darcy strode back to the house. She pushed through the front door and made her way, with Jones in tow, straight to the Atomotron.

"So what do you need to repair this, I mean in the way of

tools?"

"I'll need a pair of needle nose pliers and do you have a magnifying glass?"

"I have a tool box for repairing computers. So let me get it from my room and we can ask Taylor for anything else we might need." Darcy ran her hands along the edge of the Atomotron as if to heal it in some way. "Be right back."

She reappeared at the kitchen table with her toolbox filled with instruments used to work on the mainframe of a computer's hardware.

"This is extraordinary. I must strap a kit like this to me when I return to Boston."

"Not a good idea. Was any of this around in your time?"

"Do not make me sound so ancient." Jones examined the tools. "These are perfect."

He squeezed a pair of rounded tweezers to loosen the cotter pin, which allowed the gear to slide off.

"Nicely done, sir."

Darcy moved closer so the two of them were shoulder to shoulder working as a team to repair the time machine. She felt an energetic pull to her left and found herself inches away, staring at Jones's face as he focused on the Atomotron. His slight but knowing grin made her quiver; she had no choice but to linger in his smile, mixing her own delight with his.

"Thank you," Jones said. He then proceeded to release the second gear in hopes of beginning his travel back to Boston that same night. "These are not exactly the same as the originals. I fashioned these two gears myself. This could well present a problem that I cannot solve. Thus, no Wiki for me." Jones pointed to the two gears and tried to match them. "You see, the landings are slightly different and therefore will not match the meshing gears. Does that make sense?"

"Oh no, we're gonna fix this sucker." Darcy tapped her chin with her pointer finger. "Okay, here's what we're gonna do. I have a friend with a monster brain. He's waaaaay cool. I'll call him and see if he can stop by and help us out. I'll tell him it's for Steamcon and he'll be so jazzed he'll faint when he sees this thing."

"What can he do to facilitate the correct sizing of the gears?"

Darcy smiled.

"Well you know how I keep talking about computers? This is why they are so cool. He can measure and produce your gears on a schematic. Then we can take it to the foundry and have them made using a computer program."

"Really? Fascinating. How then would that be accomplished?"

"Too much too soon. You'd have to be Einstein to take it all in at once."

"Is he also a friend of yours?"

"Yeah, close friend." Darcy laughed. "Nah, I'll turn you on to Einstein tomorrow. I'm gonna call Caruthers and see if he can come by tomorrow morning."

"Or maybe tonight? I am feeling anxious to solve this issue… although once repaired, I will be able to return to the point of origin at a time of my choice. With that revelation, I am not feeling as pressured as before. Tomorrow will be fine."

"Thank you. I'll assume that I *now* have your permission to call Caruthers."

"Sorry, I was mostly thinking aloud."

"Sure. No problem. I was busting your chops. Oh wait before you go crazy asking a million questions it's just an expression to say that I'm… let me see… jesting with you."

"I see. So you have made a joke at my expense?"

"Correct," she said, smiling.

Darcy reached into her jean pocket and retrieved her cellphone and Mr. Evans's check. She punched the keyboard and held it to her ear. Jones watched with great interest. She then laid the check on the table.

"May I speak to Cars please?" Darcy paused. "Thank you."

She looked at Jones whose face now sat right next to hers, peering at the small instrument in her hand.

"I am simply awed. Is that… could that possibly be… a telephone? OMG," he said with delight and took it out of her hand to examine it more closely.

"What are you doing? Give me that." She wrenched the phone from his hand. "Hey Cars, yeah it's me, Darcy." She pushed Jones away. "I need a favor and you're going to be so freaked out. A friend of mine from Boston is here and has a sort of time machine kinda thingy for the next Steamcon that actually rotates and everything, but he bent a couple of gears and we need your help. And dude, I promise you, it'll be worth it just to see this machine."

Cars said something Jones's could not hear and Darcy giggled into the phone.

"Yeah, rock on Steampunk." She thumbed the phone to disconnect. "He's on his way. He didn't even say goodbye."

"You seem well acquainted with Cars." Jones held out his hand. "May I?"

"Yes and yes. But nothing between… I mean no way." Darcy moved next to Jones. "Yeah, it's a phone and other devices in one. It's called a smart phone but it's only as smart as the person using it."

Jones sat down and held the cell phone as if he were inspecting an ancient fossil, turning it repeatedly and holding it up to the light. "I must say this is a fascinating period in time." When he accidentally hit the trigger for the screen and it lit up with a photo of Darcy, he beamed.

"Absolutely wonderful."

He then turned the screen to her.

"Yeah, not bad for a girl from Snoho. Thanks." She retrieved the phone and pushed it into her jean pocket. She withdrew it again and held it up toward Jones. "Okay smile. This will be proof that you still exist when you return to Boston."

"How so?"

"Well, if you dematerialize into space the photo will disappear right?"

"Let me think. Yes, I believe you are correct. You constantly impress me with your ability to deduce in the same manner as a scientist. May I see?" Jones grinned from ear to ear. "Not bad for a boy from Boston."

"Yeah, not bad at all," she said as she ran her pointer finger over his photo.

There was a knock at the front door drew their attention away.

"That must be Cars. Coming," she called out as she ran to the front door. "Hey, what's up?"

"You called me, remember?" Cars said with a quizzical look on his face.

"Oh no, not two literal junkies," she mumbled. "Yeah, I did. Come on in. I want you to meet a friend of mine." Darcy hopped next to Jones. "This is Jones Whitman, Steampunk aficionado and time traveler extraordinaire."

"I'm Cars," he said, craning his neck to see around both

of them. He clapped his hands together twice expending his excited energy. "So let's see this time machine."

"Right over here... and this to can be yours..." Darcy held out her hands as if presenting a product on a game show.

"No. I mean... not this one... or any duplication," Jones said. He regained control and slowed his pace. "That is to say... I have worked many long hours on this time machine and do not want it duplicated until I have—"

"A patent," Darcy jumped in. "He wants to get a patent so he can sell it at Steamcon. Right?"

"Yes. Exactly. So you can understand, correct?" Jones asked.

"What? Sure." Cars marveled at the steampunk time machine, his eyes wild with expectation. "This is sweet, man."

Jones looked back to Darcy and shrugged his shoulders. She mouthed the word "later". He raised his eyebrows and turned back to face Cars.

"Tell me it really does run on steam," Cars said. He took a seat next to the Atomotron and began his inspection. "So are you using dry ice to create the steam effect?"

Jones hurriedly took a seat next to Cars.

"Actually, this valve is an inlet for pressurized steam which generates the turning of gears in order to produce—"

"The effect of what a real time machine might look like," Darcy said. "But we'll never know if we don't create these two gears to the exact specifications of the original."

"So why are these different?" Cars asked.

"Well, because I made them. But that task took many hours of labor and Darcy assures me your monster brain will facilitate a much easier solution. So, is that a possibility?"

Cars wheeled around to look directly at Darcy.

103

"You called me a monster brain?"

"Sort of." Darcy dropped her head in embarrassment.

"Sweet. Didn't think you ever noticed," Cars said, catching Darcy's eyes. "I'm gonna run out and get my laptop. I'll be right back."

He leapt to his feet and skip-walked out the front door to his car.

"Do you date Caruthers?"

"Cars? It's not like that between us."

"Might you be missing the obvious?"

"Might you?"

She turned to face Jones and wondered if the engaged-to-be-married man could be jealous. She smiled inwardly. The surge of emotion threatened to spill out, when she was saved by Cars who jumped at the chance to sit on the couch next to Darcy. He opened his laptop and booted up. He carefully laid out the damaged gears on a black square of cloth he had brought with him. He then photographed them to send to a program that would measure and replicate the original two gears producing a schematic ready for delivery to a foundry for the replication of the original gears.

"I see what's going on here," Cars said.

"What?" Jones and Darcy said in unison.

"Eh, these gears are thicker than the normal gears."

"Correct. They have to be to be able to—"

"Mesh with the fat ones below them to make all the gears move inside the frame. Makes it look really authentic."

"Thank you, Darcy, for a wonderful explanation."

Jones reached out and touched her arm.

She felt the zap of his energy and stepped away to look over Cars' shoulder.

"Okay got it," Cars said. "Let me scan the measurements

and plot the points. Check this out, Jones. These will be easy to make. Okay, so I'll send these to the printer and we can call it a night. But … you've *got* to promise that I can be here when you crank this awesome machine up. Promise?"

"Unequivocally. How long will it take to get this back from the printer?"

From down the hallway, behind Jones, emanated the snapping, swishing, grinding sounds of Darcy's printer that was spitting out the finished plans.

"Dude, the schematics are here. What are you talking about? Oh, did you think I would have to take them to a commercial printer? Nah. I sent them over to Darcy's printer."

Jones looked at Darcy with surprise.

"You have your own printer?"

"Yes, I do. And I'll show you later and we can discuss it then, comprehende?"

"Certainly. I can detect by your tone that we are in an area in which I am to enjoy an evolutionary leap in understanding."

"You're a little freaky, dude," Cars said and then pointed to himself and said, "Pot … kettle." He continued to chatter as he hoofed toward the front door. "I like you though and I really like what you've done with that sweet time machine. Thanks, Dar. Gotta run. Ciao."

"Wow, what a day," Darcy said. "You can to shower and eat and tell me more about Boston and Emily. So what would you want to do first?"

"I would like to ring Roark and tell him I am okay. I am convinced he is worried sick. I can feel his angst over the time/space meridians."

"Now that's what I'm talkin' about. That's true love."

"Not to dissuade you from your liberal thoughts, but I am, in fact, not *in love* with Roark. We're friends and although dedicated to one another, in a special kind of way, we limit our affections to… how did you say… jesting with one another."

"No, I get it. I'm just thinking. What if true love got separated by the time/space continuum thingy and the only way it could ever be restored is through time travel. How romantic would that be? And what about Emily? Shouldn't you be equally concerned for her?"

"Yes, I should be. A lack of expressing my genuine concern for Emily as well does give me pause. Separated love is a cause for Shakespeare and my uncle. However, just now… in this moment, may I say, I *can* understand the notion of being in love with someone only to discover this love might not be true love?"

"True love? And there is a difference?"

Darcy moved in a little closer.

"Well, as you know, I'm going to marry Emily and we are in love. But as you mentioned, my concern surrounds Roark and not Emily. Emily and I have great affection for one another, but sometimes I feel as if I am going through the motions and I am not experiencing—"

"The heat," she said with a knowing smile. "Okay what I mean… is the rush… eh… excitement. That feeling when you want to say WOW and 'you're so cool'… cute, handsome."

"I actually cannot imagine speaking in that manner but yes. I actually thought I had experienced that *rush*, if you will, in the past, but truth be told, my first time seems to have taken place in your kitchen."

"What?" The warmth of his disclosure played across her

skin. "With little ole me? Nice," she said far more casually than she felt. "So what are we gonna do about that?" Darcy could feel her heart pounding and her face flush. "If you hear a loud thumping sound, pay no attention to it."

"Darcy," he said slowly. "I have a commitment to marry Emily Fuller in Boston at the end of September 1891. I fear it is set in stone by now and it shall take place. Moreover, I cannot stay here any longer than necessary in order to fulfill my obligations."

"Yeah. I thought you might say something along those lines. 'Cause that's the kinda guy you are. And truth be told, I like that about you."

Monday, 7 September 1891, 6:00 pm

Boston, MA

Roark made his way back to the house and spent the day shaken by his encounter with Emily. He made dinner as usual, waited for an hour and then cleared the table and washed up. He took a bath and dressed for bed, all the while listening intently for any sound that would indicate Jones might have returned. His heart felt heavy with grief and his spirit became angry, the kind of anger he used to feel for his father. It was not an anger directed toward Jones but those feelings of helplessness he had experienced so long ago. He finally wept while sitting on the edge of his bed. He simply fell back and cried himself to sleep.

Sunday, 17 June 2012, 8:30 pm

"Thanks for helping me clean up." Darcy flopped the dishtowel over the cabinet door. "You're quite the catch, young fella." She joined Jones on the couch. "Let's see… time traveler, inventor, yoga dude, reasonably handsome…kidding, you're very handsome, a bit stilted, but cool in many other ways. Oh and oops, a fiancé. Let's not leave out that little tidbit of info," Darcy said sardonically with an ever so slight frown.

"I will assume you have complimented me and I will leave it at that." Jones leaned back against the couch and threaded his fingers on top of his head. "I am anxious to see the foundry tomorrow. I keep referring to linear time rather than universal time, so I panic to think I have been gone for almost a whole day. Everything will work out fine as long as I keep my wits about me and return at the proper moment. I can assume that most will not have missed me but the persons who have missed me will deduce they have experienced a collective dream."

"You're gonna have a whole lot of questions to answer."

"Darcy, I want to thank you for taking me into your home. I also want to thank you for not calling the local authorities and having me arrested. There would have been much calamity and perhaps an assurance of a page in the Wiki. I cannot imagine what you must have thought when I stated my business here. You are a brave and self-possessed woman. I admire this a great deal."

"I'm possessed alright." Darcy stood up. "I made up your bed in the guest room. Well…I pulled down the covers. No AC in the house but it will cool off as the night passes. I'll show you the shower and then you're on your own for the rest of the night."

"What is AC?"

"Oh sorry, air conditioning. It's similar to central heating but kind of the opposite—oh, well maybe you don't know about that either. Let's see, so instead of using a fireplace or furnace to heat your home, you push a button and set a thermostat to the desired temperature and your house will either cool or heat. We don't have much need to cool our homes out here so most people have heat of some sort but no air conditioning to cool their homes or a lot of businesses."

"I want to assure you, I plan to pay for all services."

"Hey what kinda girl do you think I am?"

Darcy flipped her hair.

"Oh no. No way did I mean—"

"Chill, Jones. I know what you meant. Let's go. The shower is a bit quirky sometimes, so don't say I didn't warn ya."

As they made their way toward the bathroom through the bedroom, Jones stopped, tested the firmness of the bed with his hand, sat down on the side of the mattress and began to pull off his shirt.

"Hey, what are you doing? You can't just get undressed in front of me."

"Ah, maybe I should explain. Besides being a transcendentalist, I am a nudist as well. Since I am not encumbered by religious guilt or shame of the human body, I find the state of dress or undress should be strictly driven by the circumstances in which I find myself. This time of the year I sleep in the nude as a method of overcoming the heat and humidity of Boston's summer nights by the sea."

Darcy laughed and blurted out, "Alrighty then. I'll show

you quickly how to turn on the shower and let you get a good night's rest. I'll be just down the hall if you need me."

She bent over the tub and turned both the hot and cold to mix.

"So what temp do you like?"

"Warm, but when did you light the furnace?"

"No, we have hot water on demand. You turn this faucet and hot water will eventually come out and continue until you shut it off again. Flip this lever should you want to take a bath. And you already know how to trip a lever I hear."

"Extraordinary. In that case may I take a bath?"

Darcy spun around and came face to face with Jones once again.

"Yes," she said quietly. "Yes, take a bath if you want to."

This time her face heated and she felt the magnetic pull of her body toward his. She quickly looked to the floor for escape.

"Are you unwell?"

Jones lay the back of his hand gently across her forehead.

The unexpected concern and genteel touch made her feel lightheaded.

"Oh sure. Probably dinner. Wow, this bathroom is smaller than I remember."

"Well... if you should need *me* tonight. I will be right here."

"Okay then... yeah... so... excuse me." She moved around him. "Man, is it hot in here?" she said as she exited the bathroom.

"I'm finding it quite nice," he called out after her.

Jones peeled off his new T-shirt, shoes, trousers and lastly his boxers. After the bath filled, he immersed himself slowly, taking the time to breathe in relaxation and focus on his Ch'i.

Monday, 18 June 2012, 4:30 am

He awoke energized and ready to make their trip to the foundry. Dawn had started to break and he could hear the songs of the morning birds and cars whining down the highway off in the distance. From his window, he could see the Snohomish River weaving its way underneath a train trestle heading west to the Puget Sound. Pushing against the wall, he stretched his calves and thighs. He then lay chest up and drew his knees up tightly to stretch his lower back. After popping forward into a cross-legged meditation pose, he placed his hands on his knees, straightened his back, and took a deep breath to quiet his thoughts. He focused his breathing and experienced the bliss of timelessness, no past, no future, no time.

Sunday, 14 June 1883, 2:00 pm

Po-ch'i-lam Temple, China

"Who are you? What is your name?" her soft melodic voice cooed.

"I am Jones Whitman and who may you be?" He turned to discover a petite beautiful woman dressed in like peach pajama pants and shirt.

"I am Ling Lee."

"It is a pleasure to make your acquaintance."

He smiled broadly and bowed slightly from the waist.

"You are not from here. England, perhaps?"

"No. I reside in America with my father and mother."

"I see. And how long will you stay?" She bowed her head slightly.

"That depends."

Jones found himself mesmerized by her demeanor and delicate features.

"Depends on what exactly?" she said as she raised her head and peered into his eyes.

"I am at a loss for an explanation of what I am to say." He wiped his forehead with his sleeve and muttered, "That was clear."

"I want to get to know you better. I have watched you perform your katas and I find your agility most promising. Shall we walk together?"

"That, I imagine, is a wonderful idea. May I invite you to the reflection pool?"

"You may and I accept."

As they walked, Jones had the urge to reach out and take her hand, but realized the reason for being in Foshan did not include engaging in physical relationships.

"You have a powerful sexual energy," she asserted boldly, as if she read his mind. "You cannot hide it from women."

"You have me at a disadvantage. I am unable to surmise your feelings other than a friendly conversation."

"And that is all it is... for now. Relationships blossom over conversation and familiarity, brought by time and experiences together. We have only just begun."

She stopped, looked up and smiled at Jones. He melted.

The next morning Master Fei-hung greeted Jones as he rose from his bed.

"Good morning. Today we begin sparring with our assigned partner. After consideration, you have been assigned Ling Lee. I have chosen her to allow you the opportunity to rein in your sexual distraction in order to hone your focus."

"I must confess I am not looking forward to this challenge, Master. She seems so fragile."

Master Fei-hung laughed out loud, placing his hands on his stomach—rather surprising Jones. Wong strolled to the door of Jones's room, turned around and softly spoke, "A purring cub will someday turn into a powerful tiger."

Jones donned his orange gi and made his way through the quiet corridors of the monastery on his way to breakfast. After eating, he strolled to the garden where he sat quietly by the reflection pool. The trickle of water calmed his spirit. He stretched on the ground and meditated, conjuring his Ch'i. Once finished, he rose and ambled across the garden to the crowded arena. Sitting cross-legged, he waited for his summons to the sparring mat. He looked around the circle for Ling, scanning the many faces but he did not find her. The first match culminated in a knockout of one opponent and the second match ended in a draw.

Ling entered the arena in a purple gi with an orange headband. Her face no longer resembled the face of a young Chinese woman but that of a fierce warrior. Jones heard his name through the fog of viewing Ling's presence.

The officiating master used hand gestures to bring them to the center.

"You are not my enemy," she whispered as they bowed to one another. "But I cannot lose a match—because I am a woman and Master Fei-hung has expectations."

"I understand... at least I assume I understand." he whispered back as he rose.

Ling drew back into a horse stance, fists cocked at her sides and waited. The moment Jones shifted his weight she attacked with a fury unexpected. He blocked most of her onslaught, but took a punch to his right cheek. He then made a forward move, expecting to throw a right fist followed by a swiping kick to bring her down, but instead felt a sting to the left side of his face and then everything faded away as he lost consciousness.

✿ ✿ ✿ ✿ ✿

"You will be fine," Master Fei-hung said quietly. "You have met the tiger and lost. You must be clear that your sexual nature can trick you. It is most powerful and distracting. Keep vigilant when in the presence of a woman to whom you find yourself attracted. She may not always be the woman of your first impression." The master dabbed a bit of cold water on Jones's forehead. "You will know her fully only after walking together a great distance and it is likely that in your walk, you will learn a great deal regarding yourself." He stood and placed his hands inside his sleeves. "Although two streams have different points of origin, they, nevertheless, can join forces to become a river that nourishes much of life living alongside. Ling is not a stream you will join. That stream is in your future."

Monday, 18 June 2012, 6:30 am

Snohomish, WA

"Good morning." Darcy stopped in the doorway of the guest room. "Whoa, dude, you need to put some clothes on." She covered her eyes with her forearm and backed out. "How about a cup of coffee to wake us up and then off to the foundry?" she called back to Jones. *Damn, that boy needs to travel on out of here!* She quickly headed toward the kitchen.

Once dressed, Jones entered and took a seat at the table.

"What time did you get up?" asked Darcy.

"Four-thirty, when dawn broke."

"What's up with that?"

"I assume it has something to do with the time differences. I am living three hours ahead of you, right now, were I in Boston, which I am not. Therefore, you are three hours younger than I at any given moment in time plus our age difference."

"Too early, Jones."

She bounced her head lightly against the refrigerator door with her eyes closed.

"Yes. I can see that. Do you have an extra toothbrush by chance? I'm in need of a good brushing, I assure you."

"Yep. Right under the sink on the left in the bathroom, I should have mentioned it last night. Brand new, just for guests. If you see a purple one—my favorite color—that would be for me."

"Very well. I shall make note."

Jones disappeared into the bathroom.

"How'd you sleep?" Darcy yelled down the hall. "Any good dreams?"

"I do not recall any specific dream. However, I did return to the temple this morning while meditating."

"*You* traveled?" Darcy quickly trotted toward the bathroom door.

"No, not in the same manner as my travel here. I did travel, however, to the past and recalled a lesson taught to me by Wong Fei-hung and one Ling Lee. I must say, it was a vivid recollection. And I assume there is a reason I am hearing and seeing this lesson in particular."

"That sounds ominous."

She put her cheek to the doorjamb.

"It is not meant to. However, the lesson emphasized not allowing my sexual nature to cloud my judgment."

"Where have I heard *that* before? Oh yeah, it was me. The small voice saying 'keep it under control there buddy'. So what's this all about, Alfie?"

"Jones. This relates directly to my attraction to you and the obligations I must clear prior to our continued walk."

"Alrighty then. Let's get outta here and pick up those gears, shall we?" She stood upright to leave. "The sooner we get you home to clear up a few things, the sooner we can rock on."

"That would be walk… walk on."

"Okay, dude, have it your way."

✿✿✿✿✿

The building had stood for many years at the same location. A pedestrian could not help but see from Main Street the large sign "Snohomish Foundry" hanging over the entrance. Darcy and Jones strolled past the Oxford Bar & Grill and the American Legion Hall, to the four-way stop where Jones paused to marvel at the different styles of vehicles, each stopping in turn as if to be judged, and then proceeding on to their destinations.

"I could never have imagined the many different designs that would come from such a simple machine. Do you have one of these automobiles?"

"Well sort of. I walk most places here in town but if I do need to go somewhere, I use the Bonneville. I told you about her. She's my pride and joy." Darcy squinted against the morning sun. She swung around and started walking backwards to talk with Jones. "Don't let me hit anything."

"Here, let me hold your hand in case you trip."

Jones reached out and she placed her hand in his.

Darcy immediately noticed the warmth, the strength, and then, the tingle. She broke his grip. "I should turn around. I'd feel horrible if I lost it right here on Main Street in front of everyone in town."

"I agree whole heartedly. Walking backwards and falling on your bum in front of others leaves one subject to ridicule." Jones grinned.

"Ah, here we are. We can hand these over and find out exactly how long it'll take. Maybe we can put a rush on the order."

Darcy pushed through the front door and into a small reception room with a narrow worn countertop and various business cards under glass next to the register.

"Good morning," Darcy called out toward a closed door.

An older woman entered the room and shut the door quickly trapping the noise behind her. "Good morning. How can I help you?"

"How soon can we get these back?" Darcy opened the schematics on the counter.

"I'll have to show these to the fellows in the back and get you an estimate." She left the room, back through the door where a rush of noise and light filled the storefront momentarily, followed by stillness once again.

"Déjà vu. That reminded me of a situation I recently experienced," Jones said. He raised his eyebrows and tilted his head slightly.

"How's that?"

"Hopefully you'll see in the next few days," he said. "There it is again."

The noise from the back flared and then the door slowly shut, restoring the quiet.

"It will take around a week," the woman said.

"A week?" Jones cringed at the thought but shook it off. "No matter, I am not used to having control of time and space. I need to relax."

The clerk scrunched her forehead. "Excuse me?"

"We'll take it," Darcy said to the woman. "What do you need from us?"

"Nothing but a name. You can pay when you pick them up." She eyed Jones with interest. "Oh let me get your phone number, just in case the boys have any questions."

"No problem. Darcy Champagne." She recited her cell phone number. "I love small towns."

"So Miss Darcy Champagne, how shall we spend the next week?"

Jones pushed through the door onto the street and held it open for her.

"Let's walk back to the house and—wait, how about some breakfast? We can walk up to the Snoho Bakery and get some coffee and Danish."

"Sounds fine then and I will pay next time."

"After breakfast we can run over to Monroe, make a deposit, get some cash and pick you up a couple pairs of jeans and see if they have striped shorts. We can take the Triumph. You're gonna love her."

On that clear day in June, the tops of the surrounding mountains reflected snowcapped ridges against brilliant blue skies. The air smelled clean and crisp in the morning sun as Darcy escorted Jones to the Snohomish Bakery for breakfast.

"This place is great. It has a long history. It was probably here when you were there… Boston, I mean."

Darcy reached for the door only to watch Jones's long arm take hold of the handle and open it for her.

"Thank you, but not necessary. I can open my own doors, ya know."

"Yes, of this, I have no doubt." He leaned in close to her. "Possibly we could trade niceties in the future. Being polite is part of my culture, so I must apologize ahead of time for any future acts of kindness that might trigger your disfavor. I learn quickly," he said. He withdrew to a safer distance.

"You're offended. I'm sorry. Let me make amends by pulling your chair out for you."

"I see. It is going to be like that is it?" He pursed his lips.

"To what do you refer?" she said in a most sophisticated manner. "Did you like that? Did you see what I did there? I did a Jones!"

Darcy laughed as she pulled out the chair for him.

"Thank you very much."

"Hold on. We need to go up to the counter to order. Got too wrapped up in the banter."

"Hi Darcy, what can I get for you?" said the cashier as they approached.

"Hi Kiki. This is a friend of mine from Boston, visiting for a few days."

"Good morning," she said as she reached across the counter.

"The pleasure is mine, I assure you," Jones said in a cheery voice.

"Excuse me, I'm standing right here," Darcy said and laughed. "Americano, twelve ounce with room." She looked back to Jones. "Rich coffee with room to put in cream."

119

"Yes. Well then, I shall have the same."

"Anything to eat?" Kiki asked. "Pastry, pie, quiche or—"

"Nothing for me, thank you," he said. "May I say you have an arresting smile and beautiful eyes?"

"Right. They go well with the sheen of perspiration from working in the kitchen."

"I had not taken notice of that fact. The compliment still stands."

"Come on lover-boy; let's get back to our table."

Darcy took Jones by the arm.

"How old is this establishment?"

"Old. I really don't know, but I bet Kiki probably does."

"Darcy, coffee's up."

"Okay, cool. Kiki, how old is this place?"

"Hang on and I'll come over in a minute."

"Jones, it's time to fix your coffee."

She waved him over to the counter.

"Fix? Fix my coffee?" he mumbled. He approached the coffee bar and asked Darcy, "Why do you use the term 'fix' when referencing preparation."

"Because everyone else here knows exactly what I mean. Use the cream and sugar, or whatever else you deem necessary to prepare *your* perfect cup of coffee," she said in the most proper voice she could muster

"I see and please forgive my ignorance."

Kiki joined them at their table and brought along a photographic paperback of early Snohomish.

"This is a great little book if you like history."

"I do. It is most interesting to have a perspective of the past as if it were the present," Jones said.

"I guess so." She thumbed through the book. "This place has been here from the beginning of Snohomish but a lot of different store fronts occupied the space. Antique shops, hardware stores, bakery... many changes over the years. This particular bakery has been here for seven years now. There's a basement where previous owners just left their stuff, but nobody wants to go down there."

"This area exists, I mean existed at the—"

"This historic district hasn't changed much since the 1800s. That should make you feel right at home. Big steampunk fan like yourself."

Darcy pointed at Jones.

"Ah, that explains the funky pants," Kiki said.

"We're headed over to Monroe for a couple of pair of jeans from Goodwill."

"You don't own any jeans?" she asked.

"Well, he didn't bring any because... well you know how guys are. They don't always pack everything they need."

"Yes, you see, it was a split second decision to visit. And I must admit I was a little unprepared for this particular journey. Now, concerning the basement. Why do people avoid going down there?"

"Rumors about ghosts and such. And it's creepy and dirty I'm sure. Still piles and piles of stuff from the first occupants."

"Really?" Jones rubbed his chin. "What is the probability I may see it?"

"I can ask. Maybe this would be a good time to go down there. What the hell. Let me see if I can get someone to cover me for a few. Be right back."

"I hope she is successful in convincing the proprietors," Jones said.

"I guess. But if she does, you go first." Darcy looked at him over the top of her cup. "Nooo ... I don't believe in ghosts but I most definitely believe in spiders!"

"Yes. I myself have no particular reason to support the hypothesis of ghosts, however, I did not support time travel in the beginning either."

"Alright, it's okay," Kiki said. "We can go down. Don't be surprised if a couple of others join us. We've been threatening to do this for years."

Kiki grabbed a lantern from underneath the counter and pulled the floor door open. The greeting of stale air and musty odors caused the three to step back. She flipped on the lamp and held it high to illuminate the stairwell.

"Maybe I should get you flash lights as well."

"Yeah that's a good idea," Darcy said. "It looks a little creepy. What's down there?"

"Not sure. Stuff." She laughed. "Old newspapers, books, machines... crap mostly that should be thrown away."

The three descended the steps into the darkness.

The large room felt dangerous and caused goose bumps to climb up Darcy's spine.

"What's that?" she whispered, gesturing to the other side of the basement.

"It's a giant mixing bowl of some sort," Kiki whispered back.

"Excuse me," Jones said in his full voice. "Is it possible that the need to whisper under the present circumstances is not necessary?"

"Holy crap, Jones, you scared me to death."

"May I assume then, you are now a ghost?"

"Look at this," Kiki said. "I should tell my friend Linda about these magazines. She owns the antique shop next door. Looks like 1895, Strand."

She held the light high to get a full view of the magazine

cover.

"Really?" Jones moved in close to her side to peer at the cover. "That would make them four years old at the time." Jones lifted a heavy container onto a stack of wooden boxes and opened it. The box contained rusted nails from the hardware store that once occupied the storefront upstairs.

Darcy shined her flashlight into a corner and found it filled with hand plows used to turn the rocky soil for crops that still filled many of the surrounding lowlands. A thick fog of daddy longlegs spider webs covered the area so she quickly headed in the opposite direction.

"This is fascinating."

Jones spanned the room with his light.

"This is nasty," Darcy said. "I thought my place was dusty."

The three milled about carefully checking the labels on the boxes, magazine covers and newspapers.

"Eureka," Jones whispered. "This is the ultimate serendipity." He flashed his light in Darcy's direction. "Darcy, you must avail yourself to marvel at this item I have found, but keep yourself from overly expressing your feelings when you see what I have in my hand."

Darcy sidled up next to Jones and took a quick look.

"Oh cool. It's a Boston Globe newspaper." Darcy slapped Jones lightly on the back. "I guess we had some Bostonians move here around eighteen ninety-one."

She dragged out the last few words, as she comprehended the year.

"And this particular article is of great interest."

Jones laid the paper across a box and pointed his flashlight at the article's title: *Jones Whitman's Home Burns to Ground.* The article continued: *Young Jones Whitman, missing in the tragic loss of the Whitman home, was the nephew of Walt Whitman, poet and philosopher...*

"Jones," Darcy said and put her hand firmly on his arm. "What the hell does that mean?"

"I am truly baffled. And may I say a bit disturbed at the thought that I never made it back." He called out across the dark room, "Kiki, would you mind terribly if I took this newspaper with me?"

"Nah. That's fine. One less thing to clean up."

"Oh yeah, that'll make a big dent in this mess," Darcy said. "Did you check the rest of the box for more articles?"

"Yes, and this is the only one I found. The rest of the boxes are marked otherwise and have different time periods."

"Let's get out of here."

Darcy moved past Kiki on her path to the stairs. She led the way back into the light of the present day, followed closely by Kiki and Jones.

"Thank you so very much." Jones shook her hand.

They returned to their table with the newspaper shoved underneath Jones's arm.

"Drink up, buddy. This is very freaky stuff. My curiosity is burning me up inside. We can talk about this on the way home. By the way, I've got another serious surprise for you back at the house."

They finished their coffee and placed their mugs in the bin provided.

Darcy pushed open the door and held it for Jones.

"This is gonna be a long day, I can tell."

"It was very nice meeting you, Kiki. Thank you for everything. I do hope to see you again before I leave."

"Stop by anytime. I won't always be here but you never know."

"Bye," Darcy waved.

They strolled the three blocks back to the house, discussing the possibilities of what might have happened when Jones attempted his return to Boston.

"Do you think it went badly?" Darcy asked.

"I'm not sure because there are, after all, many paradoxes in time travel, so I will read the article in an attempt to prepare myself for the consequences of my return. I am thinking this would be more than an appropriate time to meditate, gather my Ch'i and open myself up to answers unexpected."

Darcy halted and looked at Jones. "Damn that was deep."

"I shall continue reading if you are comfortable?"

"Please, I gotta know what happened."

> *Jones Whitman, missing in the tragic loss of the Whitman home, was the nephew of Walt Whitman, poet and philosopher and a mainstay in the transcendental philosophical movement in the latter part of the eighteen hundreds. Jones Whitman graduated from Harvard with an engineering degree and was well known for his inventive pursuits. He was an outcast of the Brahmin Society due to his antipathetic attitude towards organizations in general.*

"This article lacks certain valuable details concerning my life. They say nothing of Roark or Emily. I believed that I had greater favor with the Globe than it would appear. A rather short article," Jones muttered.

"Jones, this is no time for a sulking ego."

"Yes. You are quite right. I need to surmise if this incident occurred when I accidently tripped the lever or upon my return. The date of the paper is Tuesday, September 8, 1891. This would indicate the incident arose at or soon after my departure."

"Or your return because if you go back just before leaving then none of this has taken place? Am I right about that?"

"Yes, very well said, and therefore, there is a high probability the occurrence took place upon my return. But whatever must have manifested in the lab is not a part of my memory and that gives me serious pause."

"Maybe you left again before the fire, but where would you go?"

"I must repair the Atomotron expeditiously. It would seem there is a mystery to be solved." Jones paused, smiled to himself and turned to Darcy. "Once again, I find your company to be rather stimulating. I will have to venture back to see you on occasion."

"I can live with that... eh, only don't drag Emily along and I'll be quite happy. Oh man, sometimes my mouth just runs away without me." They approached the garage. "Let's go over to Monroe, whatta ya think? Meditate later?"

"If this is the right time, then I concur. Yes, I can do that."

"Okay, close your eyes." She opened the garage door. "You can open them when I say 'now'. I can't wait to see the look on your face."

Darcy pulled the cover off the Triumph to display the powerful conglomeration of chrome, leather and horsepower. Taylor had customized the bike to fit Darcy's personal tastes. The seat had been recovered with purple leather and the frame had been somewhat modified to accommodate Darcy's smaller size.

"Open your eyes," she said excitedly. "What do you think?"

"I have nothing to say."

"Oh my god, I broke you," she said putting her hand to her lips. "You always have a ton to say."

Jones stumbled, wide-eyed, over to the motorcycle and began to stroke the machine ever so lightly.

"This is so beautiful." He stood and stared, as if in a trance.

"Thanks. Wait 'til I crank this beauty up. That'll take your breath away," she said with a big grin on her face. "Are you ready to go for a little ride?"

"Yes, I think so. I am exhilarated beyond words."

Darcy pulled on her leather jacket and straddled the purple leather seat. She balanced its weight to the center, turned the ignition key and pushed the small black button that ignited a thunderous exhibition of power. She revved the perfectly tuned engine a couple of times and smiled at Jones.

"Get on. You've ridden before so you know you have to flow with me as we ride, right?" she called out over the rumble of the bike. "You're gonna want to put this on."

She handed him a rider's helmet.

He placed the newspaper down on a toolbox.

"It's all about the physics. Climb on and wrap your arms around me."

Jones squeezed her tight against his torso. He pressed against Darcy's back and spoke directly into her ear. "Indeed. What is your top velocity?"

"I really don't know. Taylor said he's had her up to ninety easily, but there's no place you can do that around here with the winding roads and hills and surprises on the other side. I try my best to ride as responsibly as I can." She turned her head back to him. "Physics, ya know, but I love speed as much as the next guy."

She clicked the bike into gear and slowly released the clutch, increasing the speed. They smoothly rode out of the garage into the sunlight.

"This is brilliant. My excitement is coursing through me with such force—I may have to call out loudly."

"When we get to the highway," she shouted to him. "Feel free to 'whahoo' when I accelerate." She cruised over to 88th street and made a right. She followed the curve to the freeway entrance to pick up highway 2 to Monroe. "Hang on," she said as she approached the merge.

The sudden surge of power and the thunderous roar of the Triumph sent chills up Jones's spine. The motorcycle lurched forward, filling him with adrenaline. Darcy's driving had his nerve endings heaving with an unadulterated, urgent need for release.

"Whahoooooooo!" Jones screamed out. "This is… beyond phenomenal." He patted her on the shoulders like a happy little boy. "Thank you."

Jones reveled in the speed of their travels until he noticed what appeared to be a large bird gliding in the sky with something falling from its side. As the objects fell, they suddenly exploded into colorful rectangles and glided in a spinning motion toward the earth.

Jones tapped Darcy and pointed.

"What, may I ask, are those objects that have come from the giant bird, and should we be frightened?" he shouted.

"Hang on a sec," she said as she slowed the bike, pulled over and stopped. "That was not a bird, that was a plane and those objects are people called skydivers. You don't know about planes?"

"Would seem apparent."

Jones sat quietly gazing at the swirling rainbow of colors as the parachutes collapsed one after another in the open field.

"Are you okay?" Darcy asked as she laughed.

"I do believe that I may be suffering from stimulus overload." He watched the skydivers float to earth one after the other. "Thus, the glazed appearance you may be witnessing at this moment."

"You'll be fine. You've got a lot to learn and it'll take more than a week to teach you everything. Maybe you can come back to see me in the future."

"We shall see. I would take you back to Boston as my cousin, but I could never forgive myself if the Atomotron failed and something horrific befell you."

"Yeah. That would sort of piss me off too. You ready to continue on? You're gonna be fine."

"I assumed you would be bothered by a possible unfortunate outcome and I do have some reservations regarding your maintaining such a positive expression relating to my psychological state."

Darcy laughed, fired off the motorcycle once again, and rejoined the traffic to Monroe. Once there, they rode to the other end of town to the Goodwill store.

"What size is your waist? I'm guessing thirty, thirty-two maybe. Here try these on. The dressing rooms are right over there."

Darcy asked a stock person for a key and tossed it over to Jones.

"How's it going in there?" Darcy said, speaking through the slats in the door.

"Fine, I am guessing. Are these supposed to be this well

fitted? And I'm not sure about this sophisticated advance on the original zipper. Did you know the zipper was patented by Whitcomb Judson, 1891."

"Geeze, Jones, did everything happen in 1891?"

"Everything of significance, I suppose."

"How can you say that after all you've seen in the last couple of days?" she said through the slats.

"I assume these are simple evolutionary advances on the same products and inventions from the 1800s."

Darcy could see Jones's feet moving under the door.

"What's the problem?"

Jones stepped out and pulled his shirt to his chest exposing his washboard abs.

"Holy smokes," Darcy said. *Behave.* "There is a metal tab at the bottom of the opening, can you feel it?"

"Yes."

"Pull up on it."

"This is my first experience with such a garment *on* my person."

"I can look for jeans with buttons, if you prefer."

He glanced up at Darcy, finally looking away from the zipper. "No thank you, but I'm not sure of the fit."

"Turn around and let me see the back." she said as she twirled her finger.

"This is interesting."

Jones chuckled and held up his shirt so Darcy could see his backside.

"It sure is," she said, not bothering to hide her silly grin as he had his back to her. "Those look great on your butt and they'll loosen slightly as you wear them. Let's see if there is another pair like those."

Jones pivoted around. "They are a bit tight in this general

area." He made a circular motion around the zippered section.

"Yeah, well, they're supposed to be. It's all part of the dance, my friend, all part of the dance."

"Can we look for those striped shorts Mr. Evans was wearing?"

"Sure. Man, are you gonna get spoiled."

"Darcy, we are completely charmed. Look at these gigantic green shoes."

"Sneakers."

"Yes. Sneakers for Roark. I shall return with these in hand as a gift from this century. He could wear these to spar, perhaps."

✿✿✿✿✿

After purchasing two pairs of jeans, striped shorts, a few T-shirts, boxers, ridiculously large fluorescent sneakers and a bag of strawberry licorice Twizlers, the two mounted the Triumph for the short ride back to Snohomish. Darcy swung into her bank to the outdoor ATM. She pulled out her bank card and deposited Mr. Evan's check and withdrew cash for Jones to have on his person, should a need arise.

"Remarkably different experience." He shook his head. "Do humans still engage customers?"

"Oh yeah. If we went in you would see lots of folks banking, but this is an easier method. Whatta ya think?"

He rubbed his chin. "Far too many questions I assure you."

"Next time then. Maybe we can open you an account and that way you would have your very own bank card and I'll teach you how to use it."

"I believe that would be an excellent experience."

"Here, put this in your pocket. It's walking around money."

Jones pocketed the cash after examining the bills.

"Interesting. Since when has American currency proclaimed 'In God We Trust'?"

"Since the 1950s, if I remember correctly."

"That is a rather provocative move on the part of the government, unless, of course, it includes all gods. That must place a bit of a strain on the atheists."

"Money spends, so why worry?"

"There are, in my opinion, some issues that should not be ignored. However, this is neither the time nor the place, shall I say?" Jones took Darcy by the arm as they walked back to her motorcycle. "When we arrive, I would like to request that you meditate with me."

"Okay. But *I'm* keeping my shirt on."

She throttled up the bike and they rode the rest of the way home in silence.

✿✿✿✿✿

"Thank you so much for the enormously stimulating experience," Jones said as he dismounted the motorcycle. "Perhaps we could take another ride before I return to Boston. Maybe we could ride over to Taylor's place of employment. I would most enjoy being in the presence of so much machinery."

"Sure." Darcy removed her helmet, allowing her hair to fall free. "Taylor loves to talk about his grand plans for having his own place; I know he'd love a visit."

She removed her leather jacket and laid it across the Triumph. She turned to face Jones.

"You are a stunning woman… in so many ways. I am honored to have made your acquaintance and I am convinced we shall see each other again at some point on the time continuum."

"Wow. No ambiguity there. Do you want my number too?" Darcy waited, staring at Jones's puzzled look. She waved her hand dismissively. "Never mind, it's a girl thing."

"I am sure I am lost in this conversation. Nevertheless, I feel compelled to express my newfound affections for you. In this short period, you have managed to make a grand impression on me, leading me to desire a… a… hug."

"You are so damn cute." Darcy careened straight into Jones's body and wrapped her arms around him in a heartfelt embrace. "I thought you would never ask and I didn't want to make the first move."

"Am I to understand that you may also have feelings of affection toward me?"

Jones gazed into her eyes.

"I thought I had made that obvious." Darcy broke the embrace and strolled to the backdoor. "Is it just me or have men stagnated in the evolutionary process?"

"I cannot be sure, at this point in time, but when the Atomotron is working again, I will project forward and return to let you know."

Jones opened the door and hesitated—Darcy sashayed through.

"Well, based on you being here from 100 years ago and the fact that my experience is the same with you as it is with many men, I'd say at least in the short term of a century, you guys have completely stagnated."

"One hundred *and* twenty-one years ago." Jones sat down on the couch.

"Right. You get sidetracked easily, don't you?" Darcy laughed and left for the kitchen. "Can I get you anything?"

"No, thank you. I am feeling the need to meditate and you promised to join me with your shirt on, I believe?"

"Right. So what are you contemplating this time?"

"I am pondering the possibility of ethereal communication with Roark. I am convinced we have the kind of connection where I could transmit my thoughts to him and bring some relief to his anxious state of mind. I will attempt to send comforting thoughts to him this very evening. I believe that having you by my side will strengthen my resolve."

"I really like this about you." Darcy opened the refrigerator. "You talk about your concern for Roark and you want to reach out to him… that's just way cool. Not many guys would do that so openly. I would love to help in any way I can."

"Roark is like family now and I very much enjoy his company although we are truly different in so many ways."

"In what ways?"

"Well, for instance, he is six feet eight inches tall."

"No way," Darcy called out from the kitchen. The slamming of the cabinet doors reminded Jones of Emily's comings and goings at the house on 4 Garden Court Street.

"I assure you, meeting Roark in a dark alley would make the hair on the back of your neck bristle. He is not a monster by any means; however, his formidable size can cause one's heart to quicken upon unexpectedly encountering him." Jones paused. "I like Roark a great deal."

"Sounds like a really good bodyguard to have around."

"There is no greater truth. I hope everything is okay with him."

A knock on the door took the two by surprise.

"Yeah who is it?" Darcy yelled. She put her snack to one side and listened.

"Cars."

"Come on in," Darcy shouted. She flounced toward the front door to greet him. "So, what's up?"

"Check this out," Cars said. "I've made this so that it'll fit into the steam chamber. The whole thing will run on batteries. How cool is that?'

"How are you gonna do that?" Darcy asked.

"Well, we can uncap the tank here and slide this into where the same shaft connects to the first turbine that essentially runs the whole gamut of gears and gyros."

"But they need to run at a certain number of revolutions per minute." Jones excitedly pondered the possibilities. "I suppose the knob with the resister provides the actual flow of energy creating... this is excellent... it could work."

"Of course it'll work. I'll disconnect the lever, and you'll use the knob from now on. Let's attach this sucker and crank it up."

Cars gathered his tools and Jones brought the Atomotron to the kitchen table. For the next four hours, the three worked as a team, to modify the machine. They surgically removed parts and reattached the new modern electric motor to power the geared system.

"Okay, I think that's it," Cars said. "You should have the honors of turning it on."

"Not yet, I'm afraid. We must reinstall the cage gears for the machine to actually work."

"But it doesn't matter really. We can at least see if the motor works. What's a couple of gears in a demo?"

"He's right," Darcy said. "We can at least see if this new contraption is going to turn."

"Alright then," Jones said after a moment's reflection. "That makes perfect sense to me."

Darcy and Cars watched as Jones hesitantly approached

the switch with trembling fingers.

"May I say, this is exciting indeed?"

"Go on, Jones. I'm freakin' here," Darcy said in a high-pitched voice. Her eyes were wide with anticipation.

Jones turned the switch and marveled as the gears began to mesh. He looked back at Darcy with a wide grin.

"Give me a high five," Cars said.

"What?" Jones said. "Do you have a question?"

"You are a funny guy." Cars laughed.

Darcy immediately shared a high five with him and patted Jones on the back.

"We did it," she yelped. "We need to celebrate. How about a glass of wine?"

"None for me," Cars said. "This is good enough. I probably won't sleep as it is."

"Cars, thank you very much. You are brilliant." Jones put his arm over his shoulders. "You do have a monster brain and I am truly impressed with what it is capable of accomplishing."

"Hey, give me a hug," Darcy said. She took Cars by the hand and pulled him into an embrace. Cars stood motionless with his arms by his side, eyes rounded, his head stiff, looking straight at Jones, who broke into laughter.

"Take this moment to return the embrace." Jones approached Cars' face. "After all, I don't expect Darcy would care as she has initiated."

Cars then threw his arms around Darcy, drawing her into a bear hug.

Darcy attempted to laugh but could hardly catch her breath. She managed to sputter, "Hey, easy, buddy. Ya breakin' my ribs here."

"Oh, sorry." He winced. "I think I'm going to go now."

"No, you don't have to," Darcy said.

"Yes I do."

"Yes he does," said Jones. "Thanks once again, Cars. You have been an excellent help. I will endeavor to find a way to give you credit for your accomplishments in the modification of the Atomotron."

"Seriously?" Cars said excitedly. "Wow that would be so sweet."

"Good night Cars." Darcy kissed him on the cheek. "Thanks for all your help." She patted him gently on his head and said, "Take care of this monster will ya?"

"Sure thing. See ya in the hood. Ciao."

✿✿✿✿✿

"Can you eat? Not sure if I can, I'm so excited." She opened and closed the refrigerator several times in a row and then began to open and close the kitchen cabinets. She moved in a flurry of gestures that showed the enthusiasm she barely held under control.

"I am inclined to converse about the possibilities of traveling back to Boston."

"Yeah? I'm thinking I'm sorta avoiding the possibility." She joined Jones at the table and ran her hand down the side of the Atomotron. "I like having you around, Jones. I know already that I will miss you terribly. This is hard for me to talk about and that's very unusual for me."

Jones reached out for her hand only to have her withdraw. He waited patiently as she stared back at him and then slid her hand across the table touching her fingertips with his.

"Sorry. Knee-jerk reaction. I'm scared to let my guard down and feel close to you. Do you understand?"

"Yes, of course I do. I am somewhat baffled by my

137

feelings and at the same time I am wistfully engaged in a fantasy relating to future endeavors with you."

Jones moved his hand on top of hers and gently squeezed.

Darcy felt a surge of energy pass through her heart and the rhythm jump to a faster beat. She laid her head down on the table. "What are we doing? This is dangerous territory, Jones. I'm feeling very vulnerable right now."

She did not raise her head for fear of looking into his eyes where she was sure all of her resolve to do the *right* thing would melt in his gaze.

Jones reached over and gingerly stroked her hair.

"I am committed to a marriage in Boston that does not hold nearly the power nor the real energy I experience with you. Having said that, I want you to understand it means a great deal to me that I behave in a manner consistent with how you would have me behave under these circumstances."

Darcy raised her head and chuckled. "Yeah well, the manner in which I would like for you to behave is probably inconsistent with what you would have me desire. Wow, did I just say that out loud?"

Jones laughed heartily.

"This is why I find you intriguing and wonderful to engage, this is the precise reason." He grinned broadly. "Should we risk a warm embrace?"

Darcy stood, pushing the chair away and stepped around the side of the table. Jones took her by the hand and stood in front of her. She swayed a bit as he pulled her into him. She laid her head against his chest and sighed.

"What was that?" Jones asked.

"Coming home," Darcy said. She closed her eyes, breathed him in and opened her heart to the infinite possibilities.

Tuesday, 19 June 2012, 5:00 am

Jones arose from sleep and prepared to meditate. He brushed his teeth, drank a full glass of water and assumed the Lotus position on a throw rug beside the bed before beginning his stretching exercises. He faced the morning sun as he had when in Foshan with Fei-hung. He lingered in his stretching, feeling his muscles elongate and relax. He recalled his initial shock of learning that he would be staying for ninety days in China. However, as the weeks wore on, he found within an ability to focus his energies as never before, which resulted in a dexterity that manifested from his constant and skillful practice of the rigorous katas of Tai Ch'i.

A new sense of calm and centeredness enveloped him. Jones admired this new self. He opened his eyes slightly to gaze at the tattoo on the inside of his left forearm 時光旅行者, Time Traveler. He closed his eyes again and felt the rise of Ch'i in his body and mind. He stood and began his morning Tai Ch'i Chuan katas. As he moved through the tenth form, he heard a tinkling sound and knew he could expect Darcy to stop by his door in a short time. He quickly donned his boxer shorts and T at the same time she approached. He stood frozen for a moment and then continued his tenth kata.

"Good morning," Darcy said. "How can you move so slowly?"

Jones desperately tried not to laugh.

"I'll be using coffee to wake up. I promise to drink it *slowly*."

Darcy yawned down the hallway toward the kitchen.

Jones wiped his forehead with a towel and soon joined her in the kitchen with a sheepish grin on his face.

"And good morning to you. Sorry I did not answer out loud, I assure you, I did try to send you a mental note."

"Yeah, I bet you did. And what's that little grin about?" She chuckled.

"An ever so close call one might say," he said with a soft, slightly suppressed laugh. "I find myself grateful for my acute hearing and my ability to navigate my clothing at lightning speed."

"You weren't... you were, weren't you?" Darcy shook her head as she poured their coffee.

"Yes, but I meant no harm," he said. "It seems perfectly natural to me. I am sorry. I will endeavor to make sure that does not happen again. I shall either close the door or perform in my clothing."

"Okay then. Let's try to keep it under control." She strolled over to the table, pulled out the chair and sat down. "So what's on the agenda for today? By the way, on a different topic... thanks for last night. I believe I could swim in your hugs for a very long time."

Darcy looked up at Jones feeling the flush in her face as well as an urge to pull his lips to hers for a kiss.

"I am certain I could do the same. And as for my agenda, I thought perhaps I might be fortunate enough to observe Taylor at his place of employment?"

"I'll call him to make plans but I'm pretty darn sure he will be up for it."

"Excellent."

✿✿✿✿✿

"Helloooo? Your chariot awaits. Jones, you ready?" Taylor called out as he entered Darcy's house.

"Yes and may I say, I am excited to be visiting your shop." He footed up the hallway, wearing his new jeans, a T and his last century boots.

Taylor placed his hand on Jones shoulder and laughed.

"Man, those boots must be pretty cool in Boston, but we gotta go get you some high tops. Red maybe? Yeah, red would look gooood."

"That would suit me well, I should think."

"Why so formal with the talk? Are you weird in some way I should know about?" He withdrew his hand.

"Not really. However, may I assert that Bostonians are known for their accent and well, I am from Boston. Have you had the pleasure of visiting my fair city?"

"Nope. Can't say that I have."

"So am I to assume I may be the first Bostonian you have met?"

"Right again."

"Well then, the manner in which I speak is very much in line with my peer group."

"Okay, cool. No problem. Ya just sound a bit propa... if ya know whatta mean."

"Shall we take our leave?"

"Yes. We shall. Carry on, cheerio and all that." Taylor led the way out the front door to his car parked in the cul-de-sac. "It's not far to the shop," he said as he took his place at the wheel and pulled on his seat belt. Jones stood outside the passenger side, staring at the door. "Pull the handle," Taylor said as he lowered the window. Jones took a step back and leaned down to make eye contact.

"Yes, I see now. Electricity? The windows?"

"Eh, yeah. I gotta tell ya, you're kinda creepin' me out a bit."

"I very much apologize."

Jones opened the door and sank into lush leather seats surrounded by the future. The shiny faux leather dashboard, knobs and digital displays mesmerized him.

"Put on your seatbelt," Taylor said.

"Excellent advancement. Physics is highly underrated."

"Yup. Gotta handja that."

As Taylor started the car and made the drive to his workplace, Jones sat quietly making sure his eyes and mind devoured every detail. Then Taylor reached over and pushed the button control for the radio. They drove another city block with the music blaring.

"This is amazing!" Jones blurted out. "What I mean to say is the music is incredibly strong."

"Thanks. I custom fitted the whole system." He pulled into a parking space. "Well, here we are. Prepare yourself. This place will be my main competition one day. I do most of the work but don't own any part of the shop... and... I really do want to work for myself."

"I can certainly understand your interest in a business of your own making."

"A little money would help. I've been saving up for four years now. Gettin' close."

"How much money would secure your position?"

"A couple thousand, maybe three."

"Do you not have a precise figure? What are the startup costs?"

"I've got enough to float me through the first two years if business is slow."

"Excellent planning on your part." Jones stepped from the car and peered through a smoked colored window. "This is magical. They seem like something from a fairy tale. Who may I ask paints the fire?"

"Let's go inside." He tugged on Jones's arm. "That's just the showroom. Wait'll you see the shop."

The two stepped through the door to a small front room filled with custom designed bikes. Jones stroked the chrome Ape bars while admiring the artwork on the gas tanks. His mouth dropped when he saw the different colored saddles and gas tanks painted with images of ocean scenes in blue moonlight and dramatic red flames. He gaped until Taylor led him through the double swinging doors into the garage.

"Buster, this is Jones."

"Jones, glad to meet you."

"He's a friend of Darcy's from Boston. Thought I'd bring 'im around to see what we do here."

"Make yerself at home," Buster said. "Be careful though, 'cause it's easy to fall in love. If ya know what I mean."

Buster returned to torquing the bolts on a head gasket.

"Yes, in fact I do," Jones said with a nod.

"This bunch of bikes over on this side of the room, are my bikes," Taylor said. "Well not *my* bikes, but bikes I've worked on."

"Truly remarkable," Jones said. "You have a keen eye for balance... and color, I might add. I find myself impressed with what you have designed for Darcy. Riding with her is an experience I will take with me throughout my travels." Jones sauntered back over to Buster and looked over his shoulder. "The tool you are utilizing, it appears to have a gauge of sorts. May I inquire as to its use?"

"Yeah, that's a torque wrench. You can set it so you don't over-tighten a bolt and damage your machine."

"Ah, very useful indeed. I shall have to remember should I ever need to torque my machine."

143

"You've got a bike?" Taylor said. "Why didn't you say?"

"Well, because I thought you would consider my vehicle an antique."

"Like the Bonneville, ya mean?"

"Not exactly. My bike motors by steam."

"Seriously?" Taylor stood squarely in front of Jones, squinting with his head slightly cocked to one side. "Huh… steam. Man, I would love to see that thing. Back in Boston is it?"

"Yes, as a matter of fact, the Columbia is sitting in my parlor."

"Are you rich?"

"Wealthy? Somewhat. Inheritance," Jones said as Taylor walked around him.

"Potential investor?" Taylor wheeled around to face Jones.

"Possibly. I will need to ponder on any proposition you should make and I would need to see the finite details of your business plan."

"So the plan… it's mostly in my head. You know? But I can start writing it out."

"It is obvious to me that you have talent. I believe with a bit of guidance with your bookkeeping, you will be fine."

"It would be incredible to have you as a partner."

Taylor extended his hand.

"As an investor and nothing more," he said, taking his hand in a strong grip. "I plan to be traveling a great deal in the fu—well let us leave it at traveling a great deal."

"Whatever works for you. Great, just great," he said excitedly.

"So if you will indulge me, I would like to take a day or two to ponder our discussion and I will let you know."

"In the meantime, I'll start writin' down some figures for you to take a look at. So, take your time."

Jones smiled.

"Tell ya what... I've got a test drive in a few. Why don't I run you over to Crêpes? Darcy will feed you and you can meet a couple of her friends. Whatta ya say?"

"I would feel fortunate on all accounts. Yes. You will be able to provide a helmet?"

"Pretty sure I got one with your name on it."

"Really?"

Taylor laughed out loud.

"You're strange, but I kinda like that about you. Here put this on."

"That is a vaguely familiar phrase."

Jones dropped his head for a moment and pulled on his helmet.

Taylor cranked the motorcycle and revved up the engine. Jones felt his pulse quicken and his breath catch. The tone of the engine sounded deeper, almost angry. What a male lion might sound like in the wild. Jones waited for Taylor's signal and climbed on.

"Grab the sides of my coat," he said.

Jones complied and felt the restrained power of the motorcycle as they drove out of the bay into the parking area.

"Hang on," Taylor called out and gunned the engine.

The roar was so loud it echoed off the storefront windows as they jaunted past and then merged into traffic. Jones refrained from yelping, but the urge overwhelmed his senses, causing his eyes to tear slightly.

✿✿✿✿✿

Taylor swung into a space right next to the red brick wall of Crêpe Escape and Jones quickly dismounted the bike.

145

Taylor flipped down the kickstand, revved the engine a couple of times and hit the kill button. Suddenly the air emptied of the voluminous roar and the quiet of Snohomish regained its footing.

"So whatta ya think about this puppy." Taylor asked as he removed his helmet.

"I assume you are referencing the motorcycle, so I must say this bike seems to have a great deal more power than Darcy's bike. The feel is exhilarating, to be sure." Jones handed back the helmet. "Thank you."

"Heavier and bigger, but not nearly as fast on the takeoff or the flat out run, but it'll do in a pinch." He dismounted, patted the tank like a horse and stuck his helmet on the handlebar. "I'm not staying but I'll walk you in."

"I must admit I have some concerns showing up unannounced. Darcy may feel obligated in some fashion and I would not feel comfortable forcing a situation. Perhaps I should take my leave and walk around the corner to the house?"

"Don't be silly. She'll be fine. Trust me on this one. She'll be happy to see you."

The two men walked through the open door into the breakfast coffee shop and up to the counter. Darcy emerged from the back carrying a bowl of crepe mix. She stopped short and wiped flour from her face and pushed her hair back.

"So what do we have here? What're you guys up to?"

"I'm droppin' off Jones and going back to work. He's seen the good stuff, so the rest would be boring to stand around and watch. Feed 'im and then turn him out. He can walk around town for a bit."

"No that's fine. I plan to leave a bit early today anyway. So tell me what you want for lunch, grab a seat and I'll be over with your food in a bit."

"Nothing for me," Taylor said.

"Surprise me," Jones said.

Jones and Taylor took seats at a table near the entrance.

"Thank you again, Taylor, for your company and especially for the easy trek to Darcy's place of work," Jones said, still feeling the rush from the speed and power of the motorcycle. "I hope to one day skydive. That possible endeavor causes my pulse to quicken at the mere thought, so I cannot fathom what the actual experience might be like to undertake a jump from a plane."

"Yeah? I'm stickin' to bikes. That's wild enough for me."

Darcy brought over hot coffee for Jones.

"Hey sis, I'm gonna take off. Have fun this afternoon. Just don't do—"

"Taaaylor," Darcy interrupted. "Shoo, go away. Now."

She pointed toward the door and made a grand sweeping gesture with her other arm.

After Taylor left, Jones said, "Your brother has a real skill and an artful eye."

"I think so, too. He can be a bit of a scatterbrain sometimes, just male in my opinion, but he means well and is definitely a hard worker. He's pretty conscientious himself."

"Alas, he has no business plan for me to peruse so I have to rely on my own devices to sense his commitment to a long-term project; not that I expect a return of my money should I choose to assist. I must consider over the next couple of days whether to invest in his character. As it stands at this moment... my intuition leaves me with exactly the same feelings I experienced with Roark. That is a hopeful inclination."

"Don't do it if you have any red flags. Pay attention to

the bleeps on your radar screen. They can make all the difference in how your life turns out."

"What is a radar screen?"

"Wow, too complicated for me to explain. Let me think for a moment. Okay, it's like a block in the meridian in your body. The energy runs along until it hits at some random point where it causes a flash point, right there, that flash is trying to tell you something. Take care of it and you can be all better. Comprende? It's used to track everything from storms to planes in the sky."

"I believe I understand. When assessing the present situation, should I have pause or flash, I should take the extra time to reassess my given position?"

"Exactly. Red flags. Drink your coffee and I'll fix, no— I'll *prepare* something extra special for you."

"Above and beyond yourself? I expect this will be one remarkable dish to consume." Jones winked.

He admired her intently as she strolled away until she, at the last moment, looked back over her shoulder smiling. He locked with her shiny dancing eyes. To Jones, she seemed shy, almost childlike, in that moment as she disappeared into the kitchen.

✿✿✿✿✿

"That crêpe provided me with quite an array of pleasures." Jones wiped the edge of his mouth and returned his napkin to his lap. "The flavors and aroma tugged at my senses. This experience of culinary delight will not soon be forgotten. Thank you very much."

"It's nice to be appreciated. Thanks." Darcy slid into the chair opposite Jones and continued quietly, "However, don't get used to it. That's exactly why it's *special* 'cause you don't get it often."

She glanced up and Jones read the glee in her expression.

"I sincerely hope that does not include your affections, for the sake of your lover, should you ever acquire one."

Jones stared at her with amusement.

"Yeah well, we'll see how that goes. Right now, my life is pretty full, Mr. Whitman. I've got a lot going on."

Her soft eyes drove Jones's meridians to race. He cleared his throat. "What shall we do this afternoon?" He took a deep breath and centered himself. "I am inclined to leave the historic district for an adventure. And I do promise to remain as quiet as possible when encountering spectacularly entertaining novelties."

"That would be helpful because I thought we should drive into Seattle and take in the art exhibition at the museum. You'd get to see the needle and downtown, but only if you think you can handle it 'cause you're too heavy for me to carry if you keel over from being exposed to too much too fast."

"I do appreciate your concern but I am here as a result of time travel," he whispered. "I don't imagine any further stimulation would have any grave effects upon my wellbeing. And if I may, what is your reference to the needle."

"I don't want to spoil it. Just wait and see? Okay then." Darcy rubbed the top of her thighs and stood. "I'll grab my stuff, sign out and give Taylor a call. It'll be better to head off to the big city in his car."

✿✿✿✿✿

Once away from the small town streets and onto the highway, Jones made note of all the different types of vehicles in many different shapes that crowded the roadways. His calm had yet to be challenged until Darcy pulled onto the ramp for south I-405. Jones white knuckled the dashboard and looked over at Darcy. "From whence do they all come?" he asked wide-eyed. "There are so many!"

"Easy big fella… we're fine. We're gonna take state road 520 across the lake and then we'll look for the Union Street exit. You keep an eye out for it. That'll give you something to do. It's another thirty minutes from here." Darcy reached over and took Jones by the arm to comfort him. "The population has grown a bit since 1891." She glanced to her left, flipped on her signal and changed lanes. "Dude, this isn't even rush hour which is certainly the most outrageous example of an oxymoron since the beginning of time."

"I know not of what you speak—it's difficult for me to believe at this speed people do not sense the imminent danger in making one misjudgment. It's a matter of physics." He spun around to gander at the multitude of cars following them. "Do certain cars drive themselves?"

"Excuse me? What're you asking?"

Darcy again glanced to her left and changed to the HOV lane.

"The gentleman next to us does not have his hands on the steering wheel but rather is thumbing a small object in his hands."

"Oh my god, what a jerk! That's a good example of a butthead at work; he's texting while driving."

"I will take your word." Jones closed his eyes and took a deep breath. When he opened them again, the stress of his second automobile ride had drained away. "There now, that is much better."

"Getting' a little Ch'i goin'?"

"Yes, precisely. I have calmed myself." His attention quickly fell to his right. "We are very close to this vehicle on my right and it is gigantic," Jones's voice rose with obvious angst.

"Look at me," Darcy said. "Do not be afraid. I do this all the time and I've never had an accident. We don't have much farther until we exit. Here listen to the radio."

"The radio, yes. This device was in its infancy when I left Boston."

Darcy switched on the music, much to the surprise of Jones, whose eyes danced with excitement as he gazed directly at the buttons on the dashboard.

"It works even better than I expected," he said slowly. "Not nearly as great in volume or intensity as when I rode with Taylor."

Darcy laughed. "He does like it loud."

"Yeah, Taylor's pretty proud of his sound system. Dude, it's an entire industry. This is how music is delivered, twenty-four/seven."

"Strange and ominous sounds, but I find myself enjoying… whatever this is."

"Well, that's cool, but listen to this." She scrolled through the various stations.

"I have nothing to say." He shifted in his seat to get closer to the radio. "May I?"

"Sure, punch away." Darcy then merged from the HOV lane to cross each of four lanes to exit.

"Whoooa."

"Again, I *have never ever* had an accident."

"That is most reassuring. My dilemma has nothing to do with your ability to maneuver amongst the other vehicles but more to do with the others that seem somewhat vapid in their appearance. They are eliciting from me a true concern that they are not concentrating on driving, but rather other business."

He pointed to a car in which a woman was applying makeup to her face while passing two cars, glancing first in a small visor mirror and then at the road ahead.

"That's a talent. She's running late for work... blah blah blah. Okay here we go, here's our exit." After crossing four lanes of traffic to the outside lane, the Union Street exit appeared. Jones could feel his body relax as they approached a red light, coming to a full stop.

"That was both terrifying and exhilarating at the same time." He laughed heartily. "I shall be much better prepared for the return, I assure you."

"Okay, look right over there. That's the space needle. It's the hallmark of Seattle. You can take an elevator to the top and eat dinner while the disk up there, do you see it? That puppy turns three hundred sixty degrees throughout your meal."

"That would be a magical experience. Shall I invite you to dinner then?"

"Thanks, but we need to make reservations, so not today."

Darcy drove deeper into the city and pulled into the parking garage under the museum.

"This is exciting," Darcy said as she exited the car. "I've been waiting for this exhibition for six months."

"You must be feeling quite satisfied to be here. I must see the esthetic from the outside."

As they exited the parking garage onto the First Avenue, Jones looked upward, into the sky, at structures he could not have imagined while in Boston 1891.

"This architecture is truly inspired. These buildings are made from materials I do not recognize." He glanced at Darcy and as his eyes once again climbed the side of the building. He remarked quietly, "We have evolved significantly in these past one hundred twenty-one years. The learning curve must be overwhelming."

"Nah, not really... well maybe. It's kinda like Ben Franklin saying that it was obvious to him, when visiting Paris, that all the French children were intelligent because they all spoke French fluently." Darcy chuckled. "When you grow up with it, it's not as difficult."

"I would adore being totally immersed in this time and space," Jones said, his eyes alight with the possibilities. "The adventures must be exquisite."

"I'm hopin' this will be. I love this guy, Gauguin. I don't suppose you know Gauguin?"

"No, should I?"

"Well, he's from your era. In fact, I think he left his wife and children in the 1890's, I believe that's right. He was a bit of a scoundrel, in my opinion, but an awesome painter."

"May I say you are easily influenced? You truly cannot always believe what you read or hear about people."

Jones took her by the hand and crossed the street.

"I'm not a child you know. I don't need a hand to cross the street."

"Surely you must know I am fully aware of your capabilities and that is *not* the reason I took you by the hand." He squeezed. "I am finding it strange that our cities are remarkably alike in some ways. The bay and the feel of the water... it's always there isn't it?"

"Not in Snoho."

"Yes, you are right, of course. This simply arouses memories of a different time and place. I am, right at this moment, experiencing a longing for my home and Roark and Emily. I can confess I feel saddened while at once I feel

153

elated to be in your presence."

Darcy stopped in her tracks and pulled Jones back to her. She wrapped her arms around his neck and moved in close to touch nose to nose. She could feel his loss hanging in the air.

"Listen, you're welcome here anytime. I can understand you missing your home and friends. So, I've been thinking, it's like you're going back to Boston, except I can't be in touch with you. But I hope it's just a matter of time before you return. No pun intended."

"Do you have any change?"

A rather large bearded man in a green fatigue jacket stood against the wall.

"No, I am afraid I do not."

Jones looked over Darcy's shoulder.

"Sure ya do, you asshole. You're too damn stingy to give it to me."

"Excuse me?" Jones could feel his body tighten.

"Wait a sec. I have some spare change in my purse."

Darcy opened her clutch to extract the change when she heard:

"Why don't you just give me the purse?"

The vagrant moved in closer. He held out his hand, waiting.

Jones straightened his body and stepped in between Darcy and the man. He carefully watched the man's feet for any sign of movement. The split second he shifted his weight, Jones dropped him with one swift Shadowless kick to the shoulder. It was as if an invisible force knocked him off his feet and in slow motion, he flumped to the ground.

"Who the fuck hit me and where did he go?" he bellowed looking frantically in all directions.

"It's a ghost that follows me everywhere and I apologize

for his rude behavior," Jones replied. "However, I must assure you, should you choose to threaten us again, he will return. What is rather uncomfortable for me to say is that I have no idea what he may do next."

The raggedly dressed man got up on his feet, using his forearm to shield himself from any further onslaught. He ran down First Avenue, looking back several times, and then ran around the corner.

"I assume that was not a stray of your liking?" Jones asked.

"The indigents aren't all bad but sometimes the guys get so weird. I feel bad for them but there is only so much one person can do, right? And anyway, you're my current project," she said with a twinkle in her eye.

"Let's go inside shall we?"

They strolled hand in hand into the Seattle Art Museum.

Darcy stopped and held her gaze on *I raro te Oviri* – Gauguin, 1891, on loan from the Dallas Museum of Art.

"Jones, he painted this the same year you lived in Boston. This is awesome, don't you think? And you've never heard of him?"

"I have not, but his work is captivating." He stood standing shoulder to shoulder with Darcy.

"And this one is from 1892, *Te aa no areois*. She's beautiful. Let's go to Hiva Oa Island and see him in person. I would so love to do that. Oh look it's *Le Christ jaune*. Did you know Gauguin hung out with Van Gogh? That's another artist I wouldn't mind seeing, at least from across the room."

"I suppose nothing would be out of the question. That is assuming I have truly discovered time travel that can be replicated time and time again. No pun intended."

"None taken. I'm just saying you better have gotten this

155

thing right, comprende, because I want you to come back here ASAP."

"ASAP?"

"As soon as possible."

"Yes, I agree. Shall we walk to a diner and share a lunch?"

"That would be nice. Let's walk down to the water's edge and find a… oh, I know where we can go, to Pike's Market and eat there."

"Ah, so this will be comparable to the Haymarket Station? That's our open market in Boston. You can purchase a myriad of fresh items."

"Same here *and* you will get to see fish tossing, maybe even play catch with the guys behind the counter."

"That should prove to be interesting."

"How does it feel… I mean being in the city like this?"

"Not terribly different in many ways. Fashion is dissimilar and of course, transportation, but truthfully people seem very much the same. This is reminiscent of the market place where Roark would shop for our provisions for the week."

When they reached Pike Street and made a left, Jones could finally see the throngs of visitors milling to and fro taking photos of one another riding a large pig cast in metal. Right behind them, a young man called out and the rest of the crew joined in a warning shout—a salmon flew into the crowd. A young woman valiantly caught the fish only a little shorter than her own height. The crowd roared with approval and finished with a round of applause.

"So what do you think?" Darcy threw her arms out toward the spectacle in front of them.

"Very entertaining. This is rather exciting," Jones said as

he scanned the area. "Shall we dine?"

"Yes. So what are you into? I mean what would you like to eat?"

"Hmm… perhaps we should follow our noses to a *coup de théâtre*."

"What does that mean?"

"It means a dramatic surprise."

"So you speak French? I love learning new things about you."

They threaded their way through the crowd.

"That is the extent of my French language skills. That and *oui*."

"Oh dude, something smells awesome. Let's go in there," she said as she grabbed his hand and opened the door to the restaurant. "We can sit upstairs on the patio, overlooking the Puget Sound. Watch the ferries and chill out."

"Whatever you so choose. Your choice based on aromatic *élan* is remarkable. The aromas floating in the air are exquisite."

"I think we have found our place."

"I sincerely hope this is not foretelling of what might occur after lunch, but our friend is looking up at us from the street below. Perhaps I should have a word with him."

Jones rose to his feet, but Darcy's tight grip on his wrist held him in place.

"I think we should leave well enough alone. Come on, sit down and let's order lunch."

When Jones looked back to the street, the vagabond ran down the alley frantically waving his arms and pointing back at Jones.

"I apparently made quite the impression."

"You certainly have on me. I am really enjoying getting

to know you."

"And I, you." He took her hand in his. "This serendipitous meeting in time seems to have tremendous potential for—"

"Don't say it. Don't say anything about anything that has to do with you returning to Boston. Not today, not now. Let's spend this day together having fun."

"I agree. May I kiss you?" Jones leaned in to give her a warm kiss on her cheek.

She wanted so much more, but knew in her heart the risk of being so vulnerable to Jones could be devastating in the future.

Wednesday, 20 June 2012 10:00 am

"I'm off to work," Darcy said. "Have a fun morning. Watch some TV or read a book and I'll be back before you know it."

"I promise not to be meditating when you return." He winked. "Besides I have a task of my own in mind."

"Really, well, stay out of trouble."

Darcy pinned her nametag to her blouse and headed out the front door.

Jones viewed her from the front window until she crossed over Main Street. He then put his plan for the morning into action. Teeming with ideas and designs, he strode around to Legends and pushed through the storefront door.

"Mr. Evans, how are you this morning?"

"Fine. What was your name again?"

"Jones, Jones Whitman." He extended his hand.

"Ah yes. Young Jones Whitman. Sounds like a book.

What can I do for you?"

"I am designing a gift for Darcy and I am wondering if I may impose upon your knowledge of gears to assist me in purchasing precisely what I need?"

"Well, I'll do my best. Whatta ya have in mind?"

"I have designed a flower in need of copper petals and a geared motion, such that, the petals will open and close by turning the stem at the bottom of the shaft."

"You're going to need a soldering gun and copper tubing. You'll also need a sheet of copper foil. Doesn't seem much of a challenge, except for the copper foil. I have some but maybe not enough. I can order it from Whemzie's."

"May I see the amount you currently do have?"

"Sure," he said as he left for the back workshop. "Hey, you wanna come in here and take a look?"

"Excellent, thank you." Jones rounded the counter and went through the half-opened door. "This seems familiar to me. Well organized, inventions everywhere, and your tools are exquisite."

"Here ya go," Mr. Evans said and handed him a three by six inch sheet of copper foil.

"This is grand. This is more than enough for what I have in mind."

"Do you have a cutting tool?"

"No. I do not."

"Why don't you have a seat and you can use my shop to make that contraption. No charge. I want to see it as soon as you're finished."

"I would be most grateful. And if there is a particular machine that is engineered for navigation, you may have interest in; I would gladly bring it back from Boston the next time I am in Snohomish."

"That's not necessary. Have at it, kid. All the gears are marked and here is the soldering gun. I'll just plug it in."

"A soldering gun?"

"Sure. Do you know how to use a soldering gun? It's quite simple really. It heats up and you place the solder against the metal and weld it to the next piece. Got it?"

"Mr. Evans, you are a gentleman and I count you as more than an acquaintance. I will bring out my design in an hour or so."

Jones organized everything he would need to build the flower for Darcy. He cut the tubing into the length of the flower stem and ran eight gage copper wire up the center. He fixed the petals to the stem and soldered the appropriate gears to them. He coordinated the turn screw so the petals opened in synchronization, revealing the eventual purple corolla. Purple after all, was Darcy's favorite color.

"Mr. Evans, where would one purchase purple paint for copper?"

"McDaniel's on second. I would buy a can of Rustoleum and spray the paint on."

"You can do... I mean... that is an excellent idea. So how do I get to McDaniel's?"

"You could walk it in no time. Nothing's very far. Is it finished?"

"Yes."

Jones held out the copper configuration. He had soldered wire and small pieces of excess foil to the stem to make three small limbs with leaves that closed, for ease of transport. He turned the gear at the bottom where he attached the wire and watched Mr. Evans as he opened the flower.

"That is brilliant! She's going to love it."

"Thank you once again, Mr. Evans. I will see you another

160

time, I am sure."

Jones remembered seeing McDaniel's on the way to Monroe and strolled there with ease. He searched amongst the spray paints and found a remarkable purple he thought Darcy would enjoy. He paid and excitedly high stepped it back to Darcy's house. After several failed attempts at deducing exactly how to open the can, he accidentally knocked the cap off.

He practiced on paper first and then laid out a cloth to protect the furniture. He sprayed each petal a blue-based rich purple and allowed it to dry. He imagined what he would say to Darcy as he revealed his gift. He cleaned up and placed the delicate flower in the top drawer in the guest room. He smiled at the thought of her reaction.

Wednesday, 20 June 2012, 9:00 pm

"Okay, I've been saving this one because it will blow your mind. No, not literally." She held up her hand to Jones. "But I do think you'll be even more amazed than ever before."

"Even beyond meeting you? Not possible." He shook his head.

"We're going to watch a program together called *Through the Wormhole*. These shows are right up your alley."

"I assure you, I have no idea to what you reference and you have no idea where my home is situated."

"No. I mean the subject matter is something I think you will find... fascinating. How's that?" She led him to the couch and picked up the remote control. "Hold onto your seat. Wait, I take it back. Just sit there with an open mind and breathe."

"Should I be frightened?"

"*No.*" She pointed the control at the TV. "This is a television and it does exactly as it sounds. It receives signals and converts them to pixels creating an image... well, let me show you."

And with that, she clicked on the television.

"Do these images also come from the clouds?"

"Noooo. They come from TV stations, just watch."

They sat together on the couch watching the episode *Is Reality Real?* Jones sat quietly. Darcy glanced over to find his face beaming with energy.

"Di... are we... is this... Does this have other stations as well?"

"Over five hundred channels."

She pointed the remote once again and rapidly clicked through a dozen or so.

"If I may ask, why so many channels?"

"There is something for everyone to watch and I do mean everyone. You would not believe some of the programs on cable."

"And this is reality?"

"Not in the least. It's stories acted out by actors."

"Are most of the citizens employed as actors?"

Darcy laughed.

"No. There are a lot of repeated shows. It looks like a hoard of people."

"I see. Well, actually, I do not see. However this invention must have changed the world considerably."

"Oh you betcha. And not always in a good way."

The phone rang.

"Hello?"

"Hey Darcy. I was futzing with the same switch that I put into Jones's time machine and they are faulty."

"So what does that mean?"

"If it's cool, I wanna come by and change it out, otherwise he could be ready to display the machine and it wouldn't work. That could be embarrassing."

"Or lethal, depending on the situation. Yeah, come on by. Okay see you in a few."

She hung up.

"Cars, I assume."

"Yeah, the switch is faulty that he put in the Atomotron. He wants to come by and change it."

"That could have been devastating, not knowing what I may have encountered on my return to Boston. I shudder to think my demise would come about as a result of the modernization of my time machine."

"It's cool. At least Cars found it and can fix it." She moved closer to Jones and laid her head on his chest. "I'm gonna miss you terribly."

Thursday, 21 June 2012, 7:30 am

Snohomish, WA

Darcy could hear the TV when she awoke. She strolled down the hallway with a scowl on her face.

"Hey whatta you doing? It's seven thirty."

"This is amazing. The Boston Red Sox are playing the New York Yankees."

He leaned toward the TV.

"You've gotta be kidding me."

163

"No. It is true. Come see for yourself." He glanced in her direction.

"That is *not* what I meant. You're gonna fit right into this time and space, dude. I'm making coffee. Do you want a cup?" She walked into the kitchen, pulled out the coffee and the French press.

"That would be kind of you. The Sox are winning so I would like to watch this last inning," he called out.

"What would you like to do today? I don't have to go into work until later."

"I want to spend it with you. I have no preference how we spend the time, only that we are together."

"So it's my choice? How lucky can a girl get?"

Jones walked into the kitchen.

"Within reason."

He tilted his head in the way Darcy loved.

"Sometimes I don't like that you have to be so reasonable. Sometimes I have other thoughts about how we should spend our time."

"I am confident you will make the right decision."

"I say we get a pedicure."

"That would be excellent."

"Are you kidding me? You actually like the idea of a pedicure."

"Emily would, every so often, insist I have a pedicure because of my toenails. Her insistent method of cleaning me up. She despised when I would—"

"I don't think I want to hear the end of that sentence. You have a knack for bringing me back to reality. Thanks."

"Your sarcasm is well noted and I do apologize."

"Yeah well, let's chalk it up to bad *timing*. Do you get it?" she said, trying to lighten the mood. "I'll still treat you to a pedicure. I'll call and make the appointment."

Friday, 22 June 2012, 9:00 am

Darcy's phone rang. She reached into her jeans pocket and accepted the call.

"Hello. Oh that's great," she said with an air of uncertainty.

Jones appeared concerned and raised his hands. He moved closer so he could hear the conversation.

"That's fine then… we'll pick them up in few minutes." She clicked out of the call and looked at Jones. "The gears are ready. They had a cancelation so we were moved up and now they're ready. Damn."

"Yes. Damn, indeed." Jones paused and reclined against the kitchen counter. "I am flooded with a myriad of emotions right now. Not the least of which is fear on many different fronts." Jones rubbed his chin while staring at the floor.

"That's not helping. I can't imagine you being afraid of anything."

"Nor I, until I met you," he said, lacing his fingers on top of his head. "You've bewitched me in some fantastic manner."

"Hey, you're from New England and those three words don't work well together, comprende'?"

"Yes, a poor choice surely." He chuckled lightly. "I find myself concerned that I might lose you, for a lack of better terms."

"Okay, well, think of it as you are flying back to Boston and we'll get together again soon."

"Except for the conspicuous absence from the Wiki and the article regarding my house burning down, coming back is definitely on my agenda." Jones paced the length of the living room with a slight scowl on his face. "What in the world am I to encounter upon rematerializing back in Boston?" He stood quietly for a minute staring into space and then spoke as if he had weighed all of his choices. "I assume there is only one way to find out. Let us pick up the gears, shall we?"

✿✿✿✿✿

Jones quickly pushed through the door of the ironworks foundry in his haste to secure the gears. Behind the counter stood the same woman who had waited on them the first day. She suspiciously eyed the pair.

"Good morning to you," Jones said confidently, struggling to contain his enthusiasm. "You called to say that the gears we ordered are completed?"

"Yes. I have'em right here." She reached into to a series of boxes and pulled out a small plastic bag holding the gears. "That'll be one hundred seventy-five dollars, plus tax for a total of $191.75."

"Why so much?" Darcy asked.

"Custom work. Had to make a special mold. I should've said something but didn't realize these would be custom and you didn't say. I should have—"

"I assure you, it is not an issue. Thank you very much for your services and your *timely* response." He handed over the correct amount in cash from the money he had received from Darcy, pocketed his change in his jeans and strolled out steeped in ambiguity.

"I wish they had taken a few extra weeks to finish them." Sadness overwhelmed her on the way back. She reached for Jones's hand. "I mean, I know how important this is to you, but I am going to be beside myself. I can't text you, call you, email you, Facebook you, not even a tweet. That seriously sucks. How will I know you're okay?"

They strolled, hand in hand and held on tight.

"Listen to *your* Ch'i. I will do my best to extend mine to you so that you may know I am safe. Simply quiet your mind and listen to your inner voice. Expand yourself into the universe and the universe will communicate to you. You have to trust me in this matter."

"Yeah, well I hope that works, cause I'm pretty sure I'm gonna be a little bit crazy after a couple of days of not hearing from you. I'm putting your picture on my phone as my background and you better not disappear on me."

"Remember that I can come back earlier than I leave and take away all those feelings."

"Really?" Her eyes were wide.

"To be truly honest, I have absolutely no idea. I am hoping to solve that mystery when I return to Boston."

"When will you leave?" Darcy asked quietly.

Jones halted and pulled her into his arms. He held her close for a full minute without saying anything. He could feel her heartbeat against his chest. Darcy closed her eyes. He kissed her gently on the lips, ever so lightly. They resumed the walk back to Darcy's house without saying another word.

Darcy bounded the steps and stopped at the door. She turned around. "When will you leave?" She looked down, crossed her arms and waited for the answer.

"Tomorrow will be soon enough," he sighed. "But that, my lovely person, is also based on whether or not these gears actually perform up to standard. If they do not, then I could become scattered atoms that would eventually simply decay. We do not care for this as an outcome, do we?"

"Most definitely not! I kinda like you just the way you are." Darcy whirled around and glided through the doorway. "Is it wrong of me to hope that you'll be delayed?" She looked back at Jones.

"I think not. In fact I find it rather endearing." He took his usual spot at the table, pulled the Atomotron over close, and carefully laid it on its back. He removed two of the four gears from the small bag and teased them into place, synchronizing with the mesh of the larger gears below. He turned the switch and watched as the entire machine came alive. The gyroscopes began to turn and a low audible vibration began to hum. Jones quickly slowed the speed to next to nothing and heard a clicking sound emanating from one of the new gears. "That is not acceptable," he said. He turned off the machine.

"Can you tell which gear it is?"

Darcy pulled her chair next to Jones.

"I believe it is this one. I shall switch these and try it again." He removed the gear and replaced it with the extra one he had made just in case. "Okay let's try this once again." He turned the machine back on and kept it at a slow speed. "That sounds much, much better." He then glanced at Darcy. "You are sad. This is a rather inharmonious occasion and I apologize for what I have brought to you under these circumstances."

"I am sad, it's true. I wish there was a way to make this work between us." She laid her head on the table. "Do you really have to go back to Boston tomorrow? Can't you stay here and go back to the same time next year?"

"No. All time is local and I would have aged but no one else will have done so, I should think. That creates a problem. This can be very confusing and contradictory."

"Crap. You have an answer for everything."

"I still must, however, execute at least one trial before actually strapping on the Atomotron. Perhaps that will delay the departure."

"Okay… boy did that ever make me shift gears," she said as excitement shot through her. "Am I about to witness a time machine at work?"

"Highly likely." Jones stood the machine on its end. "I do not have my maps but I think I can figure out my coordinates from the range toggled in when I arrived. East?"

"Generally in that direction because that's where the sun comes up."

"That is really not the case. The sun does not come up and go—"

"Not now Jones."

"Right." Jones stood and went out the back door. "I will need to pace off the distance from where I materialized to the kitchen and again to the bedroom. That should give a close enough range so we can send the machine to your bedroom and back."

"Get outta town. Are you serious? This is just waaaay cool. Okay, go ahead. Do whatcha need to do to make this thing fly!"

Jones double-checked his new calculations. He placed the time machine in the middle of the kitchen where he had marked the coordinates on the floor.

"I thought of asking for a hug, but that feels like a bad movie. Okay, I'm ready."

He powered the switch and slowly rotated the knob clockwise, eyes closed, increasing the speed until he recognized the right pitch. He stepped away from the time machine when it began to increase its volume. Once it synchronized with the universe, it disappeared, leaving them in silence.

Darcy shrieked. Jones grabbed her hand and together they

ran down the hallway to her bedroom. They found the machine sitting on the floor right next to the bed.

"Holy crap!" Darcy called out. "This is absolutely mind blowing."

She flumped to the floor and stared at the metal box.

Jones took a seat beside her and toggled in the return coordinates. The machine began to whirl again.

Darcy scooted backwards as it disappeared before her eyes, leaving the space where it sat, empty. "Holy Crap!" Darcy jumped up and ran back to the kitchen. "Oh my god ... oh my god. Here it is! Oh man, I am freakin' right out."

"As am I." Jones stood next to her grinning from ear to ear. "That is if I am correct concerning the usage of *freaking out*."

"Strap that puppy on, I want to go with you."

Darcy danced in a circle with her hands above her head. She halted and the smile left her face as Jones spoke.

"No. Not until I have made the trip back to Boston safely. I will return and we can discuss it then."

"You're already planning on coming back?" Her frown quickly metamorphosed into a full out smile. "That makes me very happy, ecstatic really."

"Yes, but of course. We have bonded much in the same manner as Roark and I. I am looking forward to seeing him in person. It would stand to reason I would feel the same considering you, Miss Darcy Champagne."

"And that's the way you will feel about me once you are gone... the way you feel about Roark?"

"I have not one doubt."

Darcy came close to Jones, wrapped her arms around his waist and whispered, "So how shall we spend our last night together?"

171

"That sounds rather ominous, I should think," Jones muttered. He took Darcy by the shoulders and continued, "However, after some quick thinking on the matter... I *do* have a suggestion. I still owe you a dinner."

"Yes, you do," she said, staring back into Jones's eyes.

"When we get back, if you are amenable, I will teach you something I learned from Wong Fei-hung while in China. It is a Taoist method of increasing intimacy through breathing."

"Breathing... as in meditating and breathing?" Darcy pulled his hand to her lips and gently kissed his palm.

"Yes, well, in a manner of speaking, but this will be an exercise we will perform together. Are you sufficiently intrigued?"

"I'm gettin' there," Darcy said with a sheepish grin.

"I still require time to meditate and execute my katas as I allowed the TV to distract me this morning." Jones stepped out of the embrace. "If you would be so kind as to offer me this time before we prepare our lunch?"

"It's fine. I should go for a run anyway. I haven't gone once since you showed up."

Jones proceeded to his room where he secured the door behind him. He undressed, assumed the lotus position, and began the deep breathing necessary to connect him with his Ch'i.

As he began to relax, he recalled the lesson he hoped to share with Darcy.

Sunday, 17 June 1883, 8:00 pm

Po-ch'i-lam Shaolin Temple at Foshan

Jones rose from his meditation and greeted a small boy bearing a message from Wong. Filled with angst, as he had never been summoned before in that manner, he followed the usual path to the gym as requested. Upon his arrival, he found Ling Lee and Master Wong sitting in the lotus position in the middle of the gym.

"Please join us," Master Fei-hung said.

Jones tiptoed to the center mat, bowed and took a seat across from the two.

"I believe it would be helpful for you to learn a lesson that concerns your self-discipline. I have asked Ling to assist me. I hope this meets with your approval."

"I most definitely approve." Jones smiled at her. "Ling and I are becoming friends, so I should think this could only increase our familiarity with one another."

"Yes. This exercise is from Tao. It will be performed with Ling as your partner."

She smiled at Jones and bowed her head again.

"I will instruct you throughout the practice." The master rose to his feet. "You both have shown me that you have affection for one another. It is subtle; nevertheless, it is a part of your interaction. As warriors, it is imperative that you focus your attentions to the task at hand regardless of how you may otherwise feel about your yokefellow."

Jones followed Master Fei-hung with his eyes while every few moments glancing at Ling to see her reaction to the speech. She stared straight ahead without the slightest indication of what she might be feeling.

"Let us begin. Please face one another with your knees touching. Place your hands on your thighs."

Once in position, both students continued to track his movements while pretending to ignore each other. He surprised them by reaching down and turning their faces toward one another.

"This is where the lesson will take place—between the *two* of you. I am only an observer and instructor. You are the willing pupils, so may you enjoy enlightenment through this teaching."

The pair stared at one another until Ling closed her eyes.

"You each play an appropriate role in the yin and yang of a relationship, of life. Ling open your eyes and look directly into his eyes and tell me what you feel."

She looked intently.

"I feel excitement, an urge to create jing, the joining of our essences."

"And you Jones? What do you feel?"

Master Fei-hung's voice conveyed a silky and nonjudgmental tone.

"I am sure of one thing… I have not understood, until this moment, the charge I have been repressing. I feel a gravitational pull to Ling. I want to merge with her."

"Why are you talking to me? This is an opportunity to relate your truest feelings *to* Ling, not to me."

"I see." He did not take his eyes off Ling. "I feel a pull in your direction. I have an urgent feeling concerning our immediate future, but the master related that you are not a stream I will join to make a river."

"Each of you must take a deep breath, alternating between inhaling and exhaling to create a rhythm between your life forces, allowing you to merge as one. Ling, you breathe in first, deeply, and as you exhale, Jones will inhale her breath, and so on, for ten breaths. On each subsequent breath you move closer without touching lips."

Ling drew in her breath and released it to Jones, then Jones followed suit until they shared the tenth breath. Their lips were but a hair's width apart when Jones could not take it any longer. As he moved to kiss Ling, he felt a sting across his back. The master had removed a small cane from under his sleeve and used it to bring back Jones's attention.

"You must not go further than the directions given. You lost focus and this is exactly the purpose of this lesson."

Ling smiled at Jones.

"We are walking together but we have not walked far enough as yet. We are streams that may join forces before reaching the river but we are but a trickle gathering momentum."

Ling rose, bowed, and walked out of the gym.

"Your nature needs to be curbed that you may be as clear as a mountain stream when you meet the yin to your yang." Master Fei-hung extended his hand to Jones who remained seated on the floor. He pulled him to his feet and patted his shoulder. "Good night."

Jones strolled away lost in his thoughts.

Friday, 22 June 2012, 4:00 pm

Snohomish, WA

"**M**iss Darcy Champagne, may I accompany you on a dinner engagement this very evening?"

"You certainly may, Mr. Whitman. I'm thinking informal though. How 'bout you? Like maybe Sockeyes in Monroe. We can take the bike over."

"Yes. That is a very good idea," Jones said. "I am sure I should know what a 'sockeye' is, but if I may?"

Darcy laughed.

"I guess if you don't know a sockeye salmon is a fish that could be a weird name for a restaurant, right?"

"Ah. A salmon fish restaurant. That should make me feel right at home, I should think."

Friday, 22 June 2012, 5:30 pm

Darcy donned a pair of jeans, an emerald green pullover, a black leather jacket and a pair of boots. She pulled her hair back into a ponytail to make it easier to slip on her helmet.

Jones looked up as Darcy entered the room.

"I am truly stunned. I could never have believed a woman wearing men's clothing could be so... alluring." Jones reached out and thumbed her long silver earring. "No, allow me to be more specific," he whispered and moved closer. "You are beautiful and overflowing with charisma. Your personal magnetism is powerful. And... I think I shall temper any further thoughts."

"Don't feel like I need for you to temper yourself. A girl can never get enough of 'You're beautiful'." She picked up her keys and walked out the side door. "Maybe you can explain my magnetism to me over dinner."

She laughed as she mounted her motorcycle and patted the seat for Jones to join her.

They rode to Monroe before dusk on a warm June evening, lost in their own thoughts of each other and their growing connection. Once Darcy parked and secured the bike, they entered the bustling restaurant filled with lively patrons enjoying their evening meal.

After the host sat them at their table, Darcy said, "So tell me about the Tao."

"It's not *the* Dao, just Dao and it means *the way,* but not in religious terms. It is the turning of the universe, if you will. Taoist experience *De* as the essence supporting the natural world that keeps the universe balanced."

"So what has that to do with us and our play-date?"

"A person practiced in Tao understands their place within the universe. A person who dwells within Tao transcends their self and their impulses to achieve oneness with the source of all that is. The idea is to live honestly without interfering with the course of natural events, most importantly, as a time traveler. I cannot explain the experience and you should not think it comes easily to those who pursue the way of Tao, but I would very much enjoy sharing an experience of Tao with you tonight."

"I don't know what to say."

She thought it probably wasn't the type of merging she had been hoping for.

"Please say yes. I promise you won't regret it."

"Of course, I will. I'm game to try anything… once."

⚙⚙⚙⚙⚙

"If it wasn't so late we could let you drive around the parking lot a couple of times. Hey and if you didn't spill it, maybe you could even drive home."

"That would be delightful. However, I think my legs to be a bit too long for your seating. Not to mention these jeans are rather restrictive."

"You look like one of the guys now. Blue jeans, red sneakers, T-shirt—man, you got it going on."

"I do very much enjoy the sneakers. Why are they called sneakers?"

"Ha. I'm such a nerd. I actually know the answer. They coined the term because they were the first shoes with rubber soles. Meaning you could sneak up on someone without them knowing it."

"For what purpose?"

"I'll show you tonight." Darcy laughed. She cranked the engine, Jones mounted the saddle and off they rode back to Snohomish.

✿✿✿✿✿

They strolled into the house and flipped on a couple of lights. Jones sat on the couch and Darcy went into the bathroom. When she returned she sat on the arm of the sofa.

"So? When do we play?" Darcy asked. "I'm asking not because I Dao-t you would follow through but… did you see what I did there?"

"Sometimes your sense of humor takes me completely by surprise, but you do inspire me to be more spontaneous." Jones rose from the couch. "Okay, we should take a few moments apart to dress in something comfortable and meet back here in three minutes?"

"This is with clothes on? Not as much fun as I thought it was gonna be," she said as she skipped down the hall, holding back a laugh.

"Darcy, trust me. I think you may enjoy this very much."

Jones made his way to his room and changed into boxers and the steampunk T. He brushed his teeth and checked himself in the mirror.

Darcy returned in UW sweatpants, an oversized T-shirt and high-top sneakers. She strolled up to Jones and knelt down across from him.

"So what do I do first?"

"Let me explain. We will face each other, knee to knee, and take in three deep breaths and allow each breath to flow out slowly."

"Wait… you brushed your teeth." She immediately stood. "I'll be right back," she said as she scurried away.

"It is not necessary."

Darcy pivoted around. "Then why did you?"

"You are right. I will wait."

Jones crossed his legs, drew in a breath, and closed his eyes.

Darcy quietly sneaked back to Jones. "Is this better?"

"I have nothing to compare it too." He opened his eyes to find Darcy's face merely inches from his own. "However," he said lightly, "your breath is as sweet as roses in the garden."

"Nice."

Darcy took her position once again.

"Now, we shall take three deep breaths and exhale slowly. Then we will bring our faces close together without touching but our mouths will be in perfect alignment. I will breathe in a deep breath and release it. As I release, you will draw in my exhalation. Once we have accomplished this, we will move a bit closer and this time you will breathe in deeply, release and I shall take in your breath. We will perform this ten times. What do you think?"

"I'm vibrating… seriously, like I'm going to start bouncing around."

Jones laughed.

"So shall we try?" He sat up straight and leaned toward

Darcy. "Are you ready?"

"Yes."

She closed her eyes.

"Oh and one more thing."

"Really?" she said in a small huff with her eyes still tightly shut.

"I will be brief. You cannot close your eyes."

"Uh oh. This should be interesting."

Darcy opened her eyes to see Jones smiling.

They took in three deep breaths and exhaled slowly each time.

"Ready? I'm going to breathe in." Jones stared straight into Darcy's dancing eyes. As he released, Darcy began to inhale his breath. She felt exhilarated as he captured her in his steady stare.

"Now, your turn," he whispered.

Darcy began to exhale. Jones moved closer to her mouth, until his own mouth was no more than an inch away. He allowed her breath to blend with his as he absorbed her exhalation deep into his lungs.

"Oh this is way cool," she whispered. "I'm sorry and why are we doing this?"

"Last night together, depending on when I return. Complicated, too much to think about."

Jones lingered in her gaze and felt the energy between them expand and grow.

"I'm mesmerized," she said as they continued to blend their breath, speaking directly into each other's mouths.

"May I brush my lips against your lips?" Jones whispered.

"I think that would be really nice," she breathed back.

Jones moved closer and while still gazing into her eyes,

he ever so lightly touched his lips to hers.

"You are the yin to my yang," he whispered.

"Holy smokes… what just happened to me," she mouthed, keeping her face next to Jones.

"I feel drunk. I feel energized. I want you … to…"

"I can't, Jones. I want you too, but I can't under these circumstances."

She broke the spell and leaned back on her hands. Abruptly she jumped up and began to pace, wanting to accept this man into her bed but knowing her heart could not withstand the inevitable loss.

"We need to… I need to stop this exercise before I explode."

"Yes indeed," Jones remarked sadly and looked down at the floor. "Tomorrow will be difficult for me to say farewell, no doubt. I shall return to you as soon as I am able."

"May I kiss you this once?" Darcy reached out and touched Jones's face, stroking his cheek.

"I will conjure my entire Ch'i to resist going any further than a kiss, and yes, we shall share a kiss for all time."

Jones rose and took Darcy into his arms. She felt the warmth of his lips on her own and breathed in his scent. She felt the stubble of his beard and the curve of his jaw when she placed a hand to each side of his face. His mouth covered hers with suckling soft caresses and his tongue gently dueled with her own, scarcely inside her lips. His strong hands warmed the small of her back with deliberate massage, drawing her in close, causing their bodies to tingle touching one another. She felt grateful to be in his arms and he in hers. She wanted to remember everything about Jones—just in case.

"Dare I say something wonderful has bechanced me,"

Jones whispered into her ear. "I cannot speak to the enormous ache I feel in my heart. I cannot recall ever experiencing a longing akin to what I am experiencing at this moment, and I can assure you, be it fulfilled, quieted, I would be an extraordinarily happy man."

"I… I want to say… I love… that—we have shared this time together and I will never ever forget it. You have changed me forever." Darcy lowered her head. "Your kiss… amazing," she whispered and looked back into Jones's gray blue eyes. She smiled through the tears now collecting on her cheeks.

"If it is within my power, I will return."

Darcy led Jones to her bed and lay down, pulling him in behind her without saying a word.

Sunday, 6 September 1891, 7:00 am

Boston, MA

Father Carlini rose from his bed, determined to execute his plan for the arrest and confinement of Jones to the Danvers asylum. He quickly dressed in his Sunday cassock and drank a glass of wine to steady his nerves. He paced the floor, formulating his plan to exploit the most politically influential person of his parishioners. He would need someone who had connections and he knew just the man. He threw back the last of the glass of wine and headed into the streets adjacent to the rectory.

"Good'a morning," he said as he encountered two couples out for a Sunday stroll. "It's'a very fine day to thank'a God."

He felt excited to put his plan in motion and felt God walking beside him. He was practically skipping.

The couples stared at him as they passed, looking him up and down.

"Why everybody act like I'm'a crazy?"

He continued up the street, searching for council member Markus.

Saturday, 23 June 2012, 4:00 am

Snohomish, WA

Jones quietly made his way to his room, where he stretched, meditated and revisited his calculations one last time. He had a difficult time rationalizing the need to leave when he knew he could depart at any time and return at the same time he had left, but he felt driven to find out the answers to the mystery of his house burning down and most importantly to check on Roark.

"You didn't come back," she said as she abruptly stormed to the door of the guest room. "I had a dream you didn't come back and I was a lost soul for my entire life. I hate those kinds of dreams."

She slumped against the doorframe.

Jones sprang to his feet and rushed to her side.

"I will do everything in my power to return so we will have a chance to start anew." He touched her face and softly stroked her hair, holding her until he felt her sigh. He then resumed with the business at hand. "Now, I've toggled in the return time of Monday, 7 September 1891, 9:30 am to synchronize departure and return, along with the return location coordinates, and we know the Atomotron will work so I think it is a matter of time… and space." He frowned slightly. "I will explain everything to Roark but to no one else."

"Sounds like a plan. What time is it anyway?"

Darcy came into the room and plopped down on his bed.

"It is precisely 5:37 am our time but three hours later in Boston which is, of course, no matter because I will arrive *last week* at the point of my departure. This certainly can be… what is the expression? Mind blowing?"

"Yeah, that's about right. Well, there's no *time* like the present."

Jones finished dressing, donning his goggles and dustcoat. He stood before Darcy and unbuttoned the shirt enough that she could see he was wearing the steampunk T she had given to him.

It seemed forever ago to her, but really only a few days had passed.

"Oh, that should go over real well back in 1891." Darcy laughed but it pained her as she buttoned up his shirt. "I'm expecting this back… and wash it first." Darcy tried to sound playful but ended up rushing out of the room to cover her eyes that were brimming with tears.

"Yes, I will make sure of it," Jones called out after her.

Darcy fumbled around in the kitchen in a futile attempt to distract her from the heartache and pain of Jones's departure.

He carried the Atomotron to the kitchen table, took a seat and watched as Darcy ceremonially prepared her morning Blue Mountain drip. Every so often, she paused and lowered her head, trying to rid herself of the overwhelming sadness.

"Shall I return on Friday so you won't feel the pain of my leaving?"

"No. Don't you dare take this away from me." She placed her hands on the counter and lowered her head. "This is what being alive is all about."

"In that case, I shall see you back here today when I return. Reluctantly I must say that it is time for me to depart."

Darcy placed her cup of coffee on the counter and dropped her hands to her sides.

Jones reached out for her arm, removed his goggles, and embraced her, lowering his lips to hers one last time. Darcy wrapped her ankle around his calf as if to keep him from flying away. They remained entwined for some time, sharing deep kisses, resolute to merge and become one.

Jones broke the embrace. "Before I take my leave, I wanted to give you a gift. I have observed that you, with the greatest of intentions, have a dismal outcome when displaying your horticultural attributes."

Jones held up a small planter from the sink window where a dried flowering plant lay limp over the side of the green pot.

"Ah, you must mean my black thumb. I have the *greatest of intentions* every time I buy a new plant convinced it won't happen again, but it always does."

"Well, while you were working I did stop by Legends and picked up a few extras so I might create a gift for you. I hope you will not disfavor me for taking the liberty. Certainly a memorabilia piece if I do say so." Jones reached into his coat pocket and withdrew what appeared to be a small plant with a bulb on top. "This is for you. A flower that will never die. Simply rotate the bottom of the stem and voila." Jones held it out to Darcy and she watched the purple painted copper petals slowly open, displaying tiny gears and patina copper for the centerpiece.

"Jones." She dropped her head. "This is beautiful." She took the flower carefully into her hands and cradled it to her chest. "I have nothing for you."

She peered up with tears pooling in her eyes.

"Well then, you must not realize what you have already given to me. I feel as though you have given me the greatest gift possible."

"Really? What would that be?"

"It is you. Pure and simple. You are the most wondrous event of my life."

Jones eyes began to tear.

"This is nuts," Darcy said after a few moments. "We need to be grownups here."

"Yes. Some of my favorite people are grownups although I do not have much to do with the likes of them." He smiled awkwardly. "But we can certainly learn from their mistakes. Do you agree?"

"Maybe." She eased Jones away from their cuddle. "Let's get this party started, dude. The sooner you leave, the sooner you can return."

"Technically speaking—"

"No. Not another word." She pressed a finger to her lips. "You need to get out of here before I start begging you to stay and that would be completely unlike me and totally humiliating. So strap that sucker on and beam outta here Scottie. Besides, I can't take another day off from work anyway, so I need to get ready in a few."

Jones listened with sadness, determined more than ever to settle his affairs in Boston and return to Snohomish. He trudged over to the table and lifted the Atomotron. He wrote the code N47° 54.6372', W122° 5.6156' in his vest pocket journal and placed it on the table. He then swung the time machine over his shoulder and threaded his arm through the second strap, pulling the Atomotron into place. He reinstated his goggles, placed the journal in his vest pocket and turned to Darcy.

"This is it. I am forever in your debt."

Jones reached behind him and turned the switch. He could clearly hear the revolutions as they sped up.

"Oh my god, what's happening?" Darcy screamed. "Jones—wait—oh my god."

The room filled with a forceful hum followed by silence. Darcy recoiled in fear and slid down the edge of the cabinets, still clutching the flower against her chest. The quiet yielded to the pounding of Darcy's heart while her stomach roiled with nausea. She slumped onto the floor and felt comforted by the cold against her cheek. She closed her eyes as the tears flowed over her face.

Sunday, 6 September 1891, 10:00 am

Boston, MA

Father Carlini approached council member Markus outside of his office Sunday morning before mass.

"Councilman Markus, if you would'a be so kind."

"Yes, Father, what can I do for you?"

"I have'a rather unusual request from the powers that be concerning one Jones Whitman."

"I'm familiar with him. He's the inventor."

"Ostensibly, if I do'a say so myself." He stepped in closer. "He has won the favor of one of my favorite parishioners and I'm'a very concerned for her wellbeing. I have'a heard it said that he is working on a time machine, an obvious blasphemy against God Almighty which certainly brings into question his mental faculties."

"And how can I help you?"

"Im'a sure you have'a the power to assist me in expediting a warrant to have'a Jones Whitman arrested for, at the very least, an observation in Danvers. The Church would'a be forever grateful. He is known for being a transcendentalist—which is, in and of itself, complete heresy."

"So I've been told. I can see Mr. Whitman upsets you, however, I'm not sure that I alone can wield that kind of power. I'll contact a friend of mine at Danvers tomorrow and inquire as to the appropriate procedure."

"Today if possible? You'a see the sooner the better because'a Emily, this parishioner, is to marry Whitman at the end of the month."

"I will ring him and let you know."

The councilman continued on his way, greeting people and making small talk as he approached his office.

Once settled, he picked up his phone and dialed Danvers.

"Good morning. Is Dr. Steinberg available? I see. Could you have him call me at my office as soon as he can? This is Councilman Markus. Thank you."

Giovanni Carlini strolled casually up the street with glee bubbling inside. He entered the rectory and lit a cigar to celebrate what he believed inevitable—the incarceration of Jones Whitman before the week's end.

By one thirty in the afternoon, he began to pace the floor of his apartment in fear that his plan had failed. He started when there was a knock on the door.

"Good afternoon, Father," a young man said. "I have a

message for you from Councilman Markus."

He handed over an envelope, turned, and walked away. Father Carlini slid a fingernail under the partially sealed correspondence and read it aloud.

> *Father Carlini,*
>
> *Dr. Harold Steinberg of Danvers Lunatic Asylum has, as a favor to me, issued a warrant for Mr. Whitman to be served tomorrow morning. An officer of the law will attempt to serve the warrant at the earliest possible hour.*
>
> *Good luck in achieving your desired goal,*
> *Hubert Markus*
> *Councilman, Boston Proper*

"Thank'a you, Lord. This is confirmation to me that what I do is in your favor."

He immediately left the rectory to find Drago. He spotted a group of fishermen standing on a corner that he felt sure he had seen Drago and Nicoli cavorting with in the past, so he approached.

"Gentlemen, and I use the term'a loosely, have'a any of you seen Drago?"

"I think he's wit his girl," a man said.

Several of the men moved away, grouped closely together and continued chatting.

"Excus'a me," the priest called out and they stopped. "Im'a not through with this discussion as yet and would be overjoyed to have you return."

The men glanced at one another. A burly man with curly hair and a beard stepped out of the group and started back. The entire group followed.

"Whatta ya want wit us?" he said.

"If you would'a be so kind, I would'a find favor with

anyone who can locate Drago and'a send him to me as soon as possible."

"Yeah, well, ifa we see him, we'll give'em da message. So now, ifa ya don't mind."

"I don't think I like'a your tone, but I'm'a gonna let it go this time."

The men all laughed and turned, leaving Father Carlini glaring in their direction.

Monday, 7 September 1891, 9:30 am

Boston, MA

Jones heard the rush of white noise just before becoming aware of his surroundings. He opened his eyes and saw Roark standing in exactly the same spot he had been standing in before departing.

"Take it off," screamed Roark. He started to reach for Jones but quickly withdrew his hand. A mass of particles re-emerged as his beloved Jones settled into an animated human being once again.

"Help me out of this will you?" Jones said. "I have something extraordinary to share."

" 'at was strange… demons… I dun know… 'is is…." Roark sat heavily in the only chair in the meditation room. "Losing me mind me thinks."

"On the contrary, you have witnessed the first episode of time travel. I will explain, however, you must promise me that you will hear me out without interruption. Give me your word you will keep this between us. I have even brought back my journal from my adventure." Jones produced his leather-bound book from his waistcoat jacket. "This will tell you everything you need to know should anything happen to me."

"I do swear, by da almighty..." Roark mumbled. "I believe whatever ya say."

"No need to swear to the almighty. I know I have not been gone *so* long that you would bring in another entity to gain my trust in you. I trust your word based on your actions and as consistent as they are, it is by no means difficult to believe *your* spoken word."

"I give ya me word then." Roark leaned forward placing his elbows on his knees and his face in his hands. "Go a'ead, tell me yer story but keep 'er simple."

"Yes, well, that may be a bit of an undertaking. Nevertheless, hear me out. I have been to Snohomish, Washington in the year of 2012. And..."

"Dis hurts me head Jones."

"It is really not hard to comprehend. The math and engineering were always there to be uncovered, so—"

"Snohomish?" Roark asked.

"Suffice it to say Roark, time travel is absolutely possible, but how we handle this is of the utmost importance."

The front door flew open to the familiar, "Jones?"

"In here, Emily." Jones opened the door to the meditation room. "Roark and I are in here."

"I needed to see you right away. I've had the most terrible dream that you were missing after a house fire right here in your home. I hate those kinds of dreams. Whatever do you think they mean?"

"Come over here and let me comfort you. I will hold you until you feel better."

"Hold me... until I feel better?" Emily tilted her head

slightly.

"Yes of course."

Jones looked back at Roark and slowly returned his gaze to Emily.

"And you have nothing intellectual to say concerning my experience. Nothing at all? No dreams are silly or you've been eating too many sweets."

"I'm sorry?"

Jones took a step closer.

"Well, it's not exactly like you to express concern," she said, muffling her words at the end. "It's not like you to be so comforting, not that you are a bad man by any means... I'm not saying that. It's a different experience to have you so... so... sensitive and caring."

"I see. Well a man can change, can he not?"

"Not usually," Emily replied with indifference as she adjusted her gloves. "Something *is* different about you today." She looked him up and down. "Oh well, my dream was just that, so I can forget it now. I'll be off. My dear mother and I will be shopping for the honeymoon next and I do not want to be late. Bye, Roark. Bye, my sweet new man. I adore you."

"And I you," he said but quickly realized his feelings had indeed changed.

He waited for the inevitable slamming of the front door and then continued.

"Roark, although time travel is an important feature of this trip, I must tell you an even more important manifestation took place while I was in Snohomish." Jones paced across the room and turned around on one foot to face Roark. Jones took a deep breath. "I think I am in love," he said with a toothy grin on his face. "I want to return to Snohomish, but I must, with much delicacy, dissolve the engagement between Emily and myself."

"Ya dun't sound right. How long was ya in 'at place?"

"A few days, but at the same time an eternity." Jones closed his eyes to remember Darcy's face. "I want you to meet her. You must travel with me. I will toggle in her coordinates... oh and I must share with you the innovative changes to the Atomotron that Cars created."

Jones looked over at Roark who could only hold his head as if to keep it from exploding. "Never mind. The task is to toggle in Darcy's coordinates and the exact time for return which I will set at 6:05 am." He turned away from the Atomotron to Roark. "This is a great example, Roark, of why a man should not endeavor to accomplish difficult tasks when feeling the pain and joy of love. One can lose perspective, make mistakes and we can't afford that now can we?"

"How do I make the trip, I got no machine?"

"I will have to hold you close and you will travel with me."

"But what if we get mixed."

"That should prove to be very interesting." Jones rubbed his chin. "Hmmm... Although it will not happen because our cells belong only to us. They seem to have a homing device. I promise not to keep you out late." Jones chuckled. "Come here for a moment and let me hug you and get an approximate measure."

Roark ambled over and stood before Jones. Jones reached out and attempted to wrap his arms around Roark's chest, sliding his arms down until he could feel a genuine hug.

"This will never work. We are going to need two machines to travel. Unless, of course, you travel by yourself and then return immediately—this is very complicated. What do you—?"

An authoritative voice and loud banging on the front door startled both Jones and Roark.

"Mr. Jones? Officer O'Brian at your service. I've a warrant for your arrest." There was a pause. "You'll be remanded over to The Danvers Lunatic Asylum for observation as informed by Dr. Harold Steinberg."

Roark immediately grabbed the Atomotron and ran upstairs to the third floor, meeting Jones on the second floor landing. "It appears to be a policeman, Carlini and a couple other men."

Jones ascended the stairs to the lab. Roark remained on the second floor landing, awaiting the fated entry of the men downstairs.

"Roark, we will let them in to discover their business with me. I have an attorney who will have me released as fast as they can arrest me," Jones said from the third floor.

"I got a feelin' 'at you won't make the arrest," Roark called up to Jones. "Me thinks it's a set up." He drew his derringers. " 'is would be good time ta load up. Put'em in yer pockets so ya can fire tru the coat if ya got ta."

The front door sprang open, breaking the glass panels. Roark reacted by drawing his weapons.

"He's got a gun," Drago yelled and performed a forward roll to avoid being shot.

"Keep down," Nicoli called out as he ushered the priest to the safety of the parlor.

Drago and the police officer split off in two directions, one to the library and the other to the bottom of the stairs behind a foyer table for cover. Drago eased his gun out and squeezed off a shot in what he presumed to be Roark's general direction, missing him by a wide mark.

"One shot left fer ya Drago," Roark called out.

Drago waved to the constable to take a shot. He stood quickly, service revolver raised, hoping to get a better aim, but Roark had disappeared from the landing. The house fell eerily silent, except for the heavy breathing.

"Where'd he go?" Nicoli whispered loudly.

"Gentlemen, you need'a to press forward quickly to apprehend these criminals. I have'a other undertakings to attend to this afternoon," Father Carlini said in his normal calm voice. He strode around the corner exposing himself fearlessly, and just as quickly ran back into the parlor when Roark slammed the door on the third floor. "Officer O'Brian, you'a go up first. And we will'a follow." He waited until the police officer had ascended the first few steps and whispered to Nicoli, "Let the Irish shoot each other." He winked.

From their hiding place in the parlor, Nicoli said, "I don't trust Jones. He's maybe got Derringers himself. Wouldn't put it past 'im. And fer sure he'd use 'em."

"I ditn't see Roark's guns when me and the father ran into the parlor. Too much time has passed. Sure enough he's reloaded, too."

"Perhaps we should'a call for reinforcements or maybe we should'a just knock'a the door down and take them," Father Carlini said. "Do not hesitate, gentleman. You do not need'a to worry for God is on'a our side in these matters."

Roark listened carefully at the door of the turret and drew his derringers once again. Jones had hurriedly packed his guns and readied himself for a fight he had never imagined.

" 'ey're coming up the stairs," Roark said and stiffened his body. " 'ey plan ta rush us. I got me an idea." He imagined that they were now right outside at the top of the stairs. He jerked the door open. "Who's gonna get ya," he bellowed while rushing all four men crowded between the stair railings. Bullets began to fly in all directions while Drago and the priest tumbled down the stairs. Nicoli had accidently shot the police officer in the leg and suffered a broken nose falling on top of the cop. Drago raised his last shot and hit Roark directly above his heart.

"Woof, 'is ain't no good." He looked down at the blood beginning to stain his shirt. His dazed stumble back into the lab immediately alerted Jones to the life-threatening situation.

Roark slammed the door and placed a chair beneath the doorknob.

" 'is ain't good."

"I shall turn myself in," Jones said. "We can get you medical help."

"No. Ya gotta travel."

"Brilliant! You are brilliant. I will travel and be right back sooner than later."

Roark collapsed to the floor face down. Blood began to flow from his lip.

"Roark, you must not leave otherwise I cannot assist you. Stay with us. I am going to rectify this situation."

"I know 'is about ya," he muttered, trying to lift his head.

Jones decided to buy more time by firing his weapons through the closed door and heard the men scramble down the stairs.

He snatched up the time machine and toggled in the coordinates for Darcy's kitchen— N47° 54.6372', W122° 5.6156'. He quickly strapped on the Atomotron and flipped the switch.

Saturday, 23 June 2012, 6:05 am

Snohomish, WA

He became aware of Darcy screaming as he arrived back in Snohomish.

"Why do you people always scream when I am leaving?" He stood and stared at Darcy and then waved his hand. "My apologies for even uttering such a ridiculous question."

"You were falling apart. What was I supposed to do? Thank you for stopping it. I couldn't take it."

"I did not stop it. I have returned and must go back immediately to number 4 Garden."

He paced back and forth, removed the time machine, and set it on the familiar table. He carefully, but quickly toggled in the time and location for his return.

"Let me think."

Darcy assumed her position by his side.

"Oh my god! Is this blood? Is this your blood?"

"Roark has been shot and is lying on the floor of the lab. I need to get back to him as soon as possible. I do not know what happens when a person dies. I do not know if I can go back in time to bring them to life again, because that would be local time. Maybe they are destined to die over again at the exact same time. I am not familiar with these dynamics as of yet."

"You went to Boston? And now you're back." Darcy let the information sink into her brain. "Roark? What the hell happened back there?"

"A remarkably long story." He rushed to the guest room, extracted the sneakers for Roark and his crazy striped shorts, and brought them over to the Atomotron. "I will toggle in N42° 21.8533', W071° 3.1876' and Monday, 7 September 1891, 9:30 am. I must go back at the same time but with these items in hand, less explanation will be necessary. I wish I could go back earlier in time but I must not cross my own path. That however, should give us ample time to adjust to the forced entry. I must hurry."

"Forced entry?" Darcy's voice went up. "So it's not good. Jones, how can I help?"

Jones wheeled around and kissed her full on the lips.

"I think I am in love with you. No, I know I have fallen in love with you, Miss Darcy Champagne. I shall return as soon as possible. What time is it exactly?"

"It's 6:05."

He picked up his journal from the table and handed it to Darcy.

"Write that down at once while I strap in." He slipped the vibrant sneakers over his shoes tying them tight, rolled the striped shorts, and stuck them down the side of his pants. "I will see you here again at this time." Jones lifted the time machine, swung it over one shoulder and deftly pushed his left arm through the swinging strap. "I will see you again before you have a chance to miss me. Do I have everything? I believe I do." He then turned the knob and waited with his eyes closed, focused wholly on his Ch'i.

"I love you too," Darcy called out over the hum as he began to disappear. She could see Jones smile as the last fragments vanished and she was left in silence once again.

Monday, 7 September 1891, 9:30 am

Boston, MA

"Take it off," yelled Roark. He started to reach for Jones but held back as Jones began to materialize right in front him. "Ya was disappearin' right before me eyes and now yer whole again and what in god's name are ya wearin'."

He stared down at the fluorescent green sneakers.

"Thank god you are alive and I do not even believe in god! Help me out of this will you?" Jones said. "I've something important to share and we have no time to lose. You must trust me implicitly and do everything I tell you. My journal will explain should anything happen to me." Jones rummaged through his coat pockets with increasing speed. "Wait, it is missing. How could that possibly have happened—let me contemplate. I assume I accidentally, in my haste, left the journal with Darcy. I must write down these coordinates."

He spontaneously hugged the big lug of a man in front of him.

"Are ya awright?"

"Just incredibly glad to see you." Jones quickly removed the sneakers and shorts. "Hide these please." He handed the items over to Roark. "In a few moments Emily will walk through that door and we will have a chit chat relating to a dream she has had. Once she has left us there will be a loud knock followed by an assertion that I am to be arrested and confined for observation. My dearest friend, we must do this differently than last time to influence a different outcome."

The front door flew open to a familiar voice, "Jones?"

"In here Emily." Jones opened the door to the meditation room. "Roark and I are in here."

"I needed to see you right away. I've had the most terrible dream that you were missing after a house fire right here in your home. I despise those types of dreams. Whatever do you think they mean?"

"It's a dream. That's all."

"I thought you might say that very thing," Emily huffed.

"Yes of course."

Jones looked back at Roark and slowly returned his gaze to Emily.

"And you have nothing intellectual to say about my experience? Nothing at all? No dreams are silly or you've been eating too many sweets."

"Not silly by any means, but you should not waste your time worrying," Jones said.

"You are so predictable."

"I see. Would I compel your favor by comforting your worrisome state?"

"Not necessary," Emily replied with indifference. "However, something *is* different about you today." Emily stepped in to inspect Jones more closely. "Oh well, my dream was just that, so I can forget it now. I'll be off. My dear mother and I will be shopping for the honeymoon next and I don't want to be late. Bye, Roark. Bye, Jones. I adore you."

"And I you," he said sadly, realizing the task that lay before him. "Emily, one moment please?"

"Jones?"

"Should anything happen to me, please make sure you live a full and happy life."

"Is this because of my dream? How unlike you, my Jones. What is it you always say? You can achieve what you

200

can conceive?"

"Please, promise me this, will you?"

"Now who is the silly one? If it makes you happy then yes, I will most assuredly go on without you."

"Thank you," Jones said as she stalked off down the hall.

He waited for the inevitable slamming of the front door and then continued, "Roark, seize the Atomotron and take it upstairs to the turret. I shall meet you there momentarily. We must prepare ourselves for the events that are about to take place."

✿ ✿ ✿ ✿ ✿

An authoritative voice and loud banging on the front door alerted them both that the repeat scenario was afoot.

"Mr. Jones, Officer O'Brian at your service," he called out loudly. "I have a warrant for your arrest." There was a pause. "You will be remanded over to The Danvers Lunatic Asylum for observation as informed by Dr. Harold Steinberg."

Jones nimbly made use of the stairs toward the third floor. Roark was returning when he met Jones on the second floor landing. "They are here." Jones ascended the rest of the stairs.

Roark remained committed to staying on the landing of the second floor as he waited for the fated entry of the men downstairs.

"Roark, come upstairs with me. We have not a moment to lose. You must strap on the Atomotron as quickly as possible."

"I got a feelin' that ya won't make the arrest. Me thinks it's a set up," Roark called up and drew his derringers. "This would be a good time ta load up. Put'em in yer coat pockets so you kin fire through the coat if you got ta."

"You must trust me Roark. Come with me now. I will strap you in. NOW!"

Roark ascended the stairs to find Jones frantically toggling in the coordinates.

The front door sprang open, breaking the glass panels.

"Where are you two?" Drago yelled and crouched down low.

"Keep down," Nicoli called out as he ushered the priest to the safety of the parlor.

Drago and the constable split in two directions, Drago into the library and the cop to the bottom of the stairs behind a foyer table. Drago eased his gun out and squeezed off a shot in the general direction of where he thought Roark might be.

"One shot left for you Drago," Roark called out from the open turret door.

Drago waved to the constable to take a shot. He stood quickly, service revolver raised, hoping to get a better shot, but Roark was nowhere to be seen. Everything fell eerily silent.

"Where did he go?" Nicoli whispered loudly.

"Gentlemen, you needa to press forward quickly to apprehend these criminals. I hav'a other undertakings to attend to this afternoon," Father Carlini said. He strode around the corner exposing himself fearlessly, and just as quickly ran back into the parlor when Roark slammed the door on the third floor. "Officer O'Brian, you'a go up first. And we will'a follow." He waited until the police officer had ascended the first few steps when he whispered to Nicoli, "Let the Irish shoot each other."

"I don't trust Roark," Nicoli said. "He's maybe got Derringers himself. Wouldn't put it past him. And for sure he'd use'em."

"Ima sure of it," Drago said. "And Jones may have'em to. We need to be clever when we rush them. Maybe throw somethin' at da door to draw their fire."

"Maybe we should'a just knock'a the door down and take'a them," Father Carlini said. "Do not hesitate, gentleman. You need notta fear for God is on'a our side in these matters."

Roark listened carefully at the door of the turret and drew his derringers. "They're comin' up the stairs." Roark stiffened his body. "They plan ta rush us. I gotta an idea."

"Place the back of the chair under the doorknob and back away from the door. We need nine seconds to dematerialize and travel." Jones placed the Atomotron on the table and lengthened the straps. "You will hold me. Being the slighter of the two, your gravitational field will be larger and I can be included in your travels." Jones assisted Roark into the straps and chuckled. "It has the appearance of a child's lunchbox on you." Jones pulled him by the arm to the middle of the room.

"They're at the top of the stairs," Roark whispered. He drew one of his derringers and fired a round through the door. They heard the sound of the men scrambling back down a few steps.

"Do I have everything I need?" Jones asked.

"Are ya ready?"

A boom hit the door twice and the doorknob bent. A crack in one door panel showed the scene outside. They intended to use a large chair in an all-out assault on the door this next time. Jones lifted his pistol, took careful aim at the constable's hat, and fired, knocking it off his head. He fired a second round, to push them back down the steps, in hopes of earning extra time.

"You have one round left," Nicoli called out. "There are

203

four of us."

"There are three," the priest called out.

"I will switch the Atomotron on right now," Jones said, turning the knob to its designated point for travel.

"I think 'at's a good idea." Roark said. "Me thinks the door's gonna come down this time."

"Hold me close," Jones wrapped his arms around Roark and held tight.

In the midst of whirling gears and the tick tock of clocks came the rumble of Drago and Nicoli breaking down the turret door. Father Carlini and the officer followed closely after them coming to halt as they watched in awe as Jones and Roark began to dematerialize.

Father Carlini snatched the officer's weapon and fired repeatedly at Jones and Roark.

"It's'a not possible," he cried out. "May God have mercy on your soul, you demon." He fell to the floor and began to bang his head with closed fists. "It's'a not possible. It's'a *not possible.*" He rocked back and forth mumbling.

The bullets flew into the vortex and disappeared with Jones and Roark. One shot missed them and ignited an oilcan below the giant map that immediately caught fire. Flames engulfed the entire wall spreading rapidly to the ceiling of the old Victorian house at 4 Garden Court Street.

"Drago, you'a must gather all his drawings as quickly as possible." Father Carlini ordered as he began to choke on the bellowing smoke. "Anything that'a explains how this could happen."

"You'a do it. God is on'a *your* side," Drago yelled and ran out.

They watched for a moment, just outside the lab door, as everything began to burn. The constable had accidentally taken a bullet in the leg when Drago's derringer misfired and he lay on the floor at the bottom of the stairs. The fire had taken on a life of its own and traveled up the walls, igniting the ceiling.

"Let's get out of here," Nicoli called out to Drago. The two descended the stairs and lifted O'Brian to his feet.

The fired spread rapidly and soon engulfed number 4 Garden Court Street, burning it completely to the ground before the Boston Fire Department was able to hose it down.

Saturday, 23 June 2012, 7:00 pm

Snohomish, WA

Darcy, home from work and alone once again, paced up and down the hallway of her empty house, feeling desperate to know anything about Jones's whereabouts. She remembered the newspaper still sitting on the toolbox and ran out to retrieve it.

"There must be a clue here."

She read the article several times and began to cry. She staggered to her bed and lay down. Then suddenly it struck her. She grabbed her cell phone and checked to see if Jones's photo was still intact. She sighed in relief. She hit dial from her list of contacts and typed in Car and Caruthers came up. She hit call and waited.

"Hello?"

"Cars?"

"Yeah?"

"What're you doing right now that you can't postpone or cancel?"

"Working. Uh oh, whatta ya need?"

"Hey, don't say it like that."

Cars raised his voice a couple of octaves and repeated, "Uh oh, whatta ya need?"

"Okay, that was funny." Darcy flopped onto the couch. "*And* I do need your help. Jones had to take off for Boston on an emergency concerning his house, so you won't get to see the time machine just yet, but I was thinkin' that maybe you and I could build a more modern version of the same thing. What do you think?"

"What does that mean?" Cars asked.

"Well, it could still appear kind of steampunk but a smaller version using gyros from cell phones and we could generate the vibration using sound to produce the Om of the universe."

"What're you talking about?"

"Okay, forget the Om stuff. Can you imagine what it would be like?"

Cars waited in silence and then slowly said, "Yeah, I think I can."

"So like when do you want to get started?" Darcy asked. "What time do you get off work?"

"Ten. Is that too late?"

"Nope. I do some of my best work at night."

"Sweet, I'll come by your place around ten-fifteen."

"Seriously? Cars this is going to be so cool. Thanks." Darcy stood, ended the call and pressed the button to bring up the main screen on her phone. Jones's smile greeted her, bringing a sigh of relief. "Geeze, I hope to god this means you are still alive."

She flumped down on the couch for the long wait until Cars would be rapping on her door.

Saturday, 23 June 2012, 10:15 pm

The manic knocking alerted Darcy to Cars' arrival. She hustled to the door and jerked it open.

"Thanks again, dude," Darcy said as she led him into the living room. "I'm excited to get this started."

"You seem in a hurry. What's going on?" Cars said as he flopped onto the couch.

"No, just excited. Do you want anything, water, juice, beer? I mean, dude, think about it. We can make up a really cool looking steam time machine between the two of us, don't you think?"

"Nope, nothing. Sure. So, here's what I'm thinkin'. We can modify a GPS unit, which already has the gyros in it and attach that to the body of some kind of sound maker. Maybe generate the sound while gears turn and lights flash and maybe a bit of dry ice to simulate steam as the driving force—a great mix of eighteen hundreds and now."

"Wow, I couldn't have said it better myself. And I just happen to have an older GPS unit but I have no idea about sound machines."

"Doesn't matter what the sound is, so who cares, as long as it makes some kind of whirling noise it really doesn't matter."

"Yeah but wouldn't it be cool if it made the sound of the universe?"

"Sure, but who'd know?" Cars threw his hand up in the air.

"Yeah, you're right." Darcy reached into her back pocket and thumbed the journal she had found on the kitchen table. It contained everything she would need to adjust her machine to synchronize with the Atomotron. She had to wait for the right time.

Sunday, 24 June 2012, 6:05 am

From the couch, where Darcy had finally fallen asleep the night before, she heard the sudden rush of matter materializing to form not one but two people hugging each other. Roark, who towered over Jones, drew her attention immediately. She thought Jones had the appearance of a child held by his father.

Darcy jumped to her feet with excitement and relief and rushed to the kitchen.

"No mistaking you, you've got to be Roark." She reached down and picked up two bullets from the floor. "What are these?"

"I heard what you proclaimed as I was leaving. I can say, without hesitation that leaves me feeling exhilarated, thank you very much." Jones palmed the ammo. "Those are bullets from a police revolver."

"What... who... hey, what the heck happened back there and you're a day late, damn it!"

"A long story, but regarding our arrival, I was under untold pressure to toggle in the date before being shot. Please forgive my error."

"Okay, I've got to hear the whole story and I'll try to be patient."

Roark began to unload the time machine while keeping an eye on Darcy.

"And I meant it. I do love you and you're very welcome." She took two strides forward and took Jones in a warm embrace. "But from now on, you better be home when you say you will."

As they broke apart, Jones wrapped his arm around

Darcy's waist and said, "Roark, please meet Miss Darcy Champaign. Darcy, Roark."

"Darcy," Taylor called out from the front door. "You up and about?"

"Yeah in here."

Darcy stood with her head bowed as Taylor entered the kitchen.

"Holy crap Dar, how in the world are you gonna feed that one."

"Taylor this is Roark. He's a friend of Jones. Say hello."

"Hey man. How's it going?" Taylor circled Roark, looking him up and down. "Where do you buy shoes, dude?" Taylor approached Darcy. "Well I just came by to say that mom needs a couple of things, but I guess I can take care of it."

"Thank you, Taylor," Jones said. "We have a few matters to work out and we may even take a little trip. But we will, I assure you, be back in no time."

"Yeah, okay, whatever. Have you given any more thought to investing?"

"I have. I will bring you the money in the next couple of days." Jones reached out and took Taylor's hand. "I must acquire the funds from my bank back in Boston, but that should not prove to be a problem."

"I can't tell you how excited that makes me, partner."

Taylor turned and walking taller than ever before, strutted out the front door. They could hear a muted *yahoo* once he shut the door behind him.

"How ya gonna do 'at?" Roark asked.

"Yeah, fill me in too."

"Well, it could be, most assuredly, a small problem if everyone believes I am deceased. However, I will return after the fire but prior to the newspaper article. I believe that will give me the opportunity to close my accounts."

"Get as much gold as you can carry. I mean, are the dollars the same?"

"No, they are not and what a remarkable observation. So that is what I shall do."

"Do ya want me ta come wif you?"

"No, not on this trip. I also have the task of breaking off the engagement with Emily. That should prove to be rather interesting."

Roark lowered his head and quietly mumbled, "Tell her me says she is a real lady and me thinks I'm gonna miss her a lot."

Darcy looked over at Roark, reached out, placed her hand on his enormous forearm, and gently squeezed.

"I betcha she will miss you as well."

"I think tomorrow morning is soon enough," Jones said. "Roark, I am certain you are going to enjoy sleeping in the guest bedroom tonight. The room has its own bath and toilet."

Roark smiled.

Darcy glanced in Jones's direction, tilted her head to one side and peered from underneath her hair.

"Does that mean what I think it means?"

"Surely you are jesting? You do not believe, for one instant, I could occupy the same bed as Roark. I am afraid I must make other arrangements with you." He reached out and pulled her in close. He sighed and kissed her fully on her lips. "Do you not have any ideas of your own how best to accommodate me?"

"Oh yeah. I've got plenty of ideas," she said and winked. "And I think you're gonna like them. In the meantime, what do you guys want to do?"

"I'd like ta sit down."

Jones laughed.

"Sure, have a seat," Darcy said. "Can I get you anything?"

Roark pulled out a chair and sat down gingerly. He laid his arms on the table with his hands reaching over halfway. "'is is a nice house. I ain't sure but I think I'm gonna pass out."

"Oh noooo big boy," Darcy said. "You're gonna be fine." She took the chair across from him.

"I feel strange. Maybe somthin' happened to me coming 'ere."

His head hit the table with a flump.

"This will not do." Jones rushed to his side to check his pulse. "I sincerely hope he has not been damaged. I could never forgive myself."

Darcy dipped a cloth into the cool water from the sink and placed it on the back of Roark's neck. When he began to stir, she moved some distance away from the resurrecting giant.

"Nope. Still here," he said looking around.

"I see, my friend. You thought this could be a dream? Welcome to Snohomish, 2012." Jones patted him on the back. "I assure you, this alternative to the other possibilities has borne out in your favor."

"I can vouch for that," Darcy said. "Do you remember being shot?"

"No."

He then grabbed his head in his usual manner when the thoughts were too great for him to comprehend.

"That is due to the time frame of my reappearance. I left you bleeding on the floor the first time I returned." Jones extended his arm showing the bloodstain on his sleeve. "However, your quick assertion that I must travel gave me an instant solution to the crisis. I must decide, here and now, if I violated my commitment to Master Fei-hung. I made a pledge not to change the past but only influence its outcome. That is exactly what I believed I was doing when I returned to make sure that you were not dead, and if not, also to make sure that you did not die... again. It was a most brilliant suggestion on your part. It seems I made the correct decision after all." Jones smiled broadly. "Shall we eat?"

Roark stood and ambled over to the counter. "What do ya want? It's me job."

Darcy smiled. "I like this arrangement. Here, this is the refrigerator with eggs and milk and such and over here is rice and well I can help out since I know where everything is."

"Extraordinary," Jones said. "This has a feeling of family doesn't it, Roark?"

"Me will let ya know as soon as I know," he grumbled. "Me thinks I might still wake up."

Darcy and Jones laughed out loud together.

Jones sat at the table and watched as Darcy and Roark began to prepare their first meal together.

"Suffice it to say, the house must have incinerated after our departure. I will be able to get more details when I return to speak with Emily."

Sunday, 24 June, 2012 10:15 pm

Jones led Roark into the guest room.

"Watch your head," he said as they entered. "This is the bathroom and you can either shower or bathe in the tub."

"Shower?"

"Yes. It is an option where you pull this knob and the water proceeds from this point. All you have to do is stand there, somewhat like a waterfall."

"And it bathes me?"

Jones chortled.

"Now that would be nice. No, you still have to bathe yourself. Here is a washcloth and there are the towels for drying. Should you have any questions, just ask. We will need to get you clothing tomorrow. And here is a toothbrush."

"How are you guys doing in there?" Darcy called out.

"His height could be a problem."

"Perhaps a bath then," Darcy said. "How would you feel about a bubble bath?"

"What, pray tell, is a bubble bath?" Jones stood with his hands on his waist.

"Maybe not. Anyway, I'll let you two figure it out. But the sooner the better." Darcy slowly retreated while she twitched her eyebrows at Jones.

"My dear friend, these control the water and this lever allows the water to accumulate or by flipping it in this manner, the water is turned out. Does that make sense? Here, I will show you."

Roark stood quietly, occupying most of the bathroom space with his sheer size. Jones ran water in the tub and then

214

went to join Darcy who waited in her bedroom.

"How's he doing?"

Darcy hopped off the bed and stood directly before Jones.

"He seems fine," he whispered. "And you, how are you doing?"

"I am vibrating. I can't wait for you to hold me. I want to kiss you and—"

"I do not want to disappoint you in these matters, but I still must break with Emily before we consummate our relationship."

"Jones, I'll not think less of you, but I'm aching for your total embrace right now. I respect what you're saying, but I can't wait any longer and seriously, if you think about it, you shouldn't have suggested we sleep together if you knew you couldn't follow through. You're asking too much of me."

"Let me weigh this for a moment." He turned his back to her. "It is my intention to do what I consider is best for me... and for us." He stood silent for another minute and then continued. "However, I am inclined to forgo my commitment to circumstance and be ... spontaneous. After all, the breakup will take place in the past. " He circled back to her, pulling her in close. His gentle kiss soon morphed into ardent passion as they released their pent up desire.

Jones lifted Darcy off her feet and kissed down her neck, nibbling her earlobe.

"Oh, man that feels good," she moaned, sliding her fingers into his hair.

Lowering her, he drew his hand from her back around to her side and traveled ever so slowly to her breast. She gasped as he caressed her there for the first time. He lifted the sweatshirt that covered her and kissed her soft skin making his way to her peak. When he gently suckled, she writhed under his touch, reaching to unbutton and unzip his jeans. He in turn pulled the sweatshirt over her head. Her hair dropped forward partially covering her nakedness. Jones draped her hair over her shoulders, exposing her to his gaze. She felt timid and wanton at the same time. She lifted his T-shirt slightly and kissed his washboard abs, while running her hands under the shirt over his sinewy chest.

"Should we…?" she whispered, glancing over her shoulder at the bed.

"Yes. I cannot contain myself any longer," he said. "If I may?"

He gently guided her backwards to the side of the bed and onto her back. He tugged the sweat pants from around her hips and kissed her smooth thighs.

She pulled his head toward her stomach and felt the tickle of his tongue. He continued with small bites that had her moaning out. After he removed her panties, he saw, for the first time, the stunning woman he had desired from the day he had arrived. His pulse raced as he began to explore her fully. Darcy adjusted herself onto the bed, drawing Jones toward her. He quickly finished undressing and joined her, hip against hip, torso against breasts, lips against lips in a heat-searing embrace.

Darcy had never felt so free and yet grounded at the same time. They soared together, taking flight in a steamy kiss. She never wanted to spend a day, let alone an hour without him again.

"You are most definitely the yin to my yang," he said. "A stream joining me to make a river."

"I couldn't be happier about that."

The two intertwined body and soul, reaching heights neither could have imagined.

Monday, 25 June 2012 7:00 am

Jones awoke with a start, realizing he needed to prepare for the travel back to Boston. Roark and moments later, Darcy, joined him in the kitchen.

"Good morning," she said, beaming as she sauntered over to Jones for a hug.

"Top of tha mornin' to ya," Roark said.

"Backatcha, big guy," Darcy said over her shoulder.

"And how are you?" Jones said quietly in her ear.

"I've never felt better." She smiled as she traced the jaw line of his face.

"Should me go about makin' breakfast?"

"Not terribly hungry today," Darcy said, gazing at Jones.

"I, on the other hand, would welcome a hardy meal. I feel fully energized and a bit... giddy," he said with boyish glee.

"I can't imagine why," she said with twinkling eyes. "I'll help Roark while you get ready to go."

"I have calculated a location near Emily's home." Jones held out his journal. "I will wait for her to leave and follow. It will be of the utmost importance that I approach with caution, I should think, considering that she may take me for an apparition."

"Really? No way. She's gonna think you're a ghost?"

"In all probability. I, however, plan to darken my eyebrows and wear a t-shirt and these jeans as a disguise."

"Me thought he might be a demon when he first come back."

"And you my lovely friend expressed terror when you saw me dematerializing. Would it be so difficult to imagine what she might think?"

"Yeah, you're right. I was freakin' the hell out. That was way beyond weird."

"He ain't a demon. He's a time traveler."

"Thank you, Roark. You always seem to say the right thing at the right time." He slapped him on the shoulder. "Whatever shall the two of you do while I'm gone?"

"We could go for a walk along the river. Watch some tele or read a book."

"Me dun't read so good."

"So, that's okay. I can read out loud. Don't worry about us, we'll find lots to do."

"So shall I return later, perhaps a few hours or a day later?" Jones thumbed through his journal. "I'm surmising you may want to archive these memories."

"I like that idea. Come back this evening. That should give us enough time to hang out."

"What does that mean to ya?"

"What she is suggesting is that the two of you will spend the day getting acquainted."

" 'at seems nice," Roark said.

"Well then, I will toggle in this evening, seven?"

"This just hit me so funny. Can you be home in time for dinner? Roark and I will make something special for you. A little welcome back party for the three of us."

"That being the case, I shall return in time for the festivities. Should I bring anything? Boston clam chowder maybe?" he laughed.

"Now *that* would be really funny."

"All me clothes would be good."

"Yes. However, we already know the house incinerated and my travel is after. Anyway, clothing is a small problem to resolve when I return. I believe you may enjoy the new style of dress."

After breakfast, the three convened in the kitchen to say their goodbyes. Jones darkened his eyebrows with mascara, toggled in the coordinates for Boston, strapped on the Atomotron and stood silently as he reached behind and turned the knob.

"I'll see you for dinner," Jones said and smiled as he began to disappear.

Darcy ran next to Roark and grabbed his arm.

"I'll never get used to that," she said, looking up and seeing Roark nod.

Tuesday, 8 September 1891, 8:30 am

Boston, MA

Jones materialized in the alley right behind Emily's house. An alley cat flared its furry tail and sped off. Jones removed the Atomotron, goggles and dustcoat, and stashed the items in the bushes. He then poised himself in direct view of the front door in wait for Emily to exit. After ten minutes by his pocket watch, she did leave the house dressed in black. Jones quickly made his way to her side.

"Emily," Jones said calmly. "Do not be startled."

Emily froze in her steps and slowly turned to see Jones standing in front of her.

"I... I... do not know. What is your explanation for this? Are you real? Am I dreaming this as well?"

"It is not a dream and I have a complete explanation. May I walk with you?"

"Of course, but you must hasten to explain these

circumstances as my heart may give way."

"I am sad to say that I am here to break off our engagement. My life would put you in grave danger and this will not do."

"To be perfectly honest, I had also been having second thoughts. I am relieved that we have arrived at the same conclusion."

Jones pulled a sealed envelope from underneath his shirt and held it out to Emily.

"I need you to give this to my solicitor and tell him I gave you this in case anything happened to me."

"Of course, Jones, I will do it as soon as possible. Please promise me, wherever you are going, you will be safe."

He embraced Emily and held her without speaking. After several moments, Jones released her.

"Father Carlini attempted to have me arrested for observation and—"

"Yes, I am aware. Do you not know Father Carlini has been taken to Danvers for an extended rest? He was babbling on about how he witnessed you and Roark vanishing into thin air. Where is Roark?"

"He sends his love. He is out of town, in a safe place where I intend to join him shortly. How ironic concerning Father Carlini and I imagine, he will never recover. I am actually slightly concerned for him."

"It was believed that you died. I was devastated, but honestly, in the recesses of my mind I held hope you had escaped. Now that I know that you have, I can go on with my life intact."

"That pleases me a great deal." Jones pulled her to the side and said. "I am also here to retrieve my money from my accounts, so I will join you on your walk to town, if I may."

"Yes, you may. I dare say no one will recognize you without a hat and your rather odd garments. Perhaps this may be a problem at the bank?"

"I didn't frequent the bank, so I feel certain that I can conduct my business without issue."

They strolled through the streets of Boston to Jones's bank where he, without suspicion, removed two hundred gold pieces from his main account, which he placed in a small satchel provided by the cashier.

"Shall you continue on or will you be joining me for the return walk to your house?"

Emily stopped short on the corner and faced him. "I must depart but I feel compelled to thank you. I feel so much relief that you are alive and I am going to miss you terribly. Please tell me we will always remain close friends."

"Without one doubt. I will steal a visit with you in the future and on as many occasions as I can arrange."

✿✿✿✿✿

Jones, fleet of foot, returned to the Atomotron and excitedly toggled in Monday, 25 June 2012 6:00 pm and N47° 54.6372', W122° 5.6156' for the trip back to Snohomish.

"I shall be home in time for dinner," he said, feeling the relief from the closure with Emily. And with that, he turned on the time machine only to hear nothing. He quickly removed the Atomotron and inspected the switch.

"This just will *not* do." He scolded.

He knocked the side of the frame twice with a clenched fist and turned the knob. The connection had been restored and the whirling of the gears caused Jones to panic as he slung the Atomotron onto his back. At the last second, as the machine settled, Jones could feel his body dematerialize.

Monday, 25 June 2012 6:00 pm

Snohomish, WA

"**I** had this ridiculous thought that maybe you wouldn't make it on time. How stupid is that?" Darcy said as Jones unstrapped the time machine and set it on the table.

"Yes. I will have to admit the question was not well thought out. Good evening, Roark."

"Evenin' Gubna."

"Gubna?"

"He saw it in a movie today. He can't stop saying it. He really likes the word."

"You watched the television together? And he is still in one piece? Interesting."

"So how did Emily take the news? Tell me."

"She actually had a similar sense of our relationship as I do. It was not difficult at all. However, we did commit to a lifelong friendship and visits on occasion."

"Platonic, I'm guessing."

Darcy glanced in his direction as she began to prepare the dinner.

"To be sure." Jones captured her in his arms as she passed. "I would love for you to meet her someday."

"Me thinks I should go back to see her."

"Perhaps it can be a family trip. But we will need to devise a second machine."

"That's okay. I think I've already started working on it. Leaving your journal helped me with some ideas, but having you here, we can knock it out in no time. What's in the little black bag?"

Jones lifted the black leather satchel, unfastened the brass buttons and held it up for Darcy to peek inside.

"Holy smokes! How many are in there?"

"Two hundred eagles. By my calculations they have a market value of three hundred thousand dollars, which, I am assuming, is a fair amount of money by today's standards?"

"Not really. But you can buy a lot coffee with that."

"I would like to cash in several for Taylor's loan. I should think that would make him exceedingly happy indeed."

Jones turned to Darcy.

"We should take Roark shopping tomorrow. Where it may be a bit an issue, but I am sure you can assist us in locating a suitable haberdashery."

Darcy laughed.

"What the heck is a haberdashery?"

"Clothier. Where clothes are made? Really, I trust you are not under the impression we are going to find clothing for Roark at the Goodwill."

"In fact we did, but only sweat pants and Hawaiian shirts."

"Hawaiian shirts? Sweat pants?"

Darcy laughed and slapped her thigh.

"Me likes the Hawaiian shirts," Roark said.

"You should of seen us in the store. He was attracting a lot of attention. He'd be wearing them now but the smell of fabric softener was making his eyes tear. I'm going to throw them in the wash after dinner. Roark, just try on a pair with one shirt so Jones can see."

Roark left the room for a few minutes and returned grinning.

"Very twenty first century, my dear friend. You look fantastic."

"Me likes the shirts," he said as he swiped the sleeves with his massive hands.

"There's still the big and tall store for men in Lynnwood. We can drive there tomorrow. I'll see if I can use Taylor's car again." She pulled her phone and called. "Hey, can we use your car tomorrow to run to Lynnwood to shop for Roark? Yes, of course, I'll fill it up. Okay cool. Thanks."

"Roark, perhaps we should go for a walk so I may ease your mind about the drive into the city."

" 'at dun't sound right. Will me be sickened?"

"Not in the least. Possibly frightened but this could be viewed simply as a new adventure to add to the collection of memories you already enjoy."

A knock at the front door pulled Darcy away from the conversation.

"Hang on. I'm coming," Darcy said as she approached the door. "Cars, what are you doing here. By the way, Jones is back from Boston."

She led him into the kitchen where he froze in the doorway at the sight of Roark.

"Wow. You are a big guy, dude. I mean… I'm sure you already know that and I mean no offense. But damn."

"It's okay Cars. He's harmless."

"Cars, this is a friend of mine from Boston. We shall be traveling together for a while."

"The Steamcon circuit?" Cars asked. "Definitely a blacksmith, right? Dude, you'd make a great metalworker."

"Never dun 'at before, but thinks me can learn."

"Man, that's so cool. You got the voice down and everything."

Darcy placed her hand on Cars shoulder.

"So what brings you here?"

"Okay. Seems like we were working on a time machine. Am I right about that? Did you tell me about using a GPS?"

"Yep… that was one of the ideas. Now that Jones is back we can all work together? Can we reschedule? We have plans for the evening."

"Sure, we can reschedule. Just feels kinda weird, you know whatta mean? Like a dream or something." Cars said. "Anyway, just let me know when you want to punk on."

He waved and immediately took his leave.

Jones approached Darcy.

"I am surmising that while I spent time in Boston you became anxious. Perhaps you decided to build a time machine to join me?"

"Yeah, that must be right. I had no idea what was going on, dude. You know me, I don't have a lot of patience. I thought you might not come back. I think my plan was to come and get you."

"Ya know what me was thinkin? He was gone fer days and I dun't know if I'm dreamin' or if me losing me mind. 'is is a hard friendship sometimes. It was like I'm dreamin but it was real."

"Déjà vu," Jones uttered.

"So does that mean whenever I experience those feelings I'm doing a time warp? A déjà vu?"

"I cannot be sure. However, I feel strongly this could be the case. We have so much to learn regarding time travel."

"I'm excited," Darcy said. "And I have an idea."

"I am sure you do. What pray tell do you have in mind?"

"I was thinking we should travel to Hiva Oa and hang out with Gauguin."

"We would need a second time machine. Alas, the gravitational field is approximately eighteen inches. I do not believe that is not enough for the three of us to travel."

"So let's you and I travel there and come back at the same time and Roark wouldn't miss us, would he?"

"I cannot in good conscience leave Roark behind again. We will endeavor to assemble another machine. Perhaps using your new design?"

"We'll need to bring Cars back in on it."

"Me thinks takin' me is a good idea."

"Yes. I agree. You are the source of our protection should we find ourselves in a life-threatening predicament." Jones turned his attention to Darcy. "Perhaps you could speak to Cars pertaining to your design and we can engineer the product from his description."

"I'll call him."

After a long conversation and the scribbling of the parts needed to manufacture the new time machine, Darcy and Jones went to work. They spent the next two days tinkering and on occasion walking over to Legends to solder shafts for the gears that would duplicate the hum of the universe.

Tuesday, June 26, 2012 5:00 am

Jones awoke ahead of Darcy and Roark, ready to prepare for their first trial of the new time machine. He carefully examined all the joints and the mesh of the gears. He heard Roark stir from a lumbering sleep. He stretched and growled like a bear waking from hibernation.

Darcy stumbled down the hallway, stopped short and asked. "What exactly was that?"

Jones laughed. "That would be our friend upon awakening. Hopefully, you will not find it annoying in the future."

"It wasn't annoying as much as frightening. I think I need a hug."

"In that case, I hope you will always be a little frightened by his roar." He chuckled as he encompassed her with his arms. "This morning I was thinking we need a name for your time machine. The Atomotron is based on Democritus and his theory of atoms, so what shall we call this new one?"

"How about the Adventurer?" She wiggled her eyebrows.

"I think a clever name for sure. Adventurer it is then. And today will be the first trial."

Jones took the smaller machine and placed it in the middle of the floor in the kitchen. Roark joined them, leaning against the doorjamb and yawning.

"Should me wait in the next room?'

"I don't think that will be necessary. However, we should keep a safe distance."

Darcy found her way behind the gentle giant and peered out from around his girth. "Okay, I'm ready."

"That is probably the safest position in the entire house," Jones said. He had toggled in the same coordinates he had used from the first trial of the repaired Atomotron.

"Okay then. I am turning on the unit." He held down the button to bring it to life and moved to a safer place behind the door.

The Adventurer began with a quiet purr, building up to the perfect pitch. The machine vanished followed by a thunderous rumble of the three of them dashing down the hall to Darcy's bedroom. They found the softly humming GPS unit, resting on Darcy's floor.

"I really don't believe this," Darcy screeched. "You are a genius!"

"I must admit to having reservations concerning the functionality of the design."

He touched the screen to set it to the new coordinates and the little time machine began to purr once again, but remained on the bedroom floor.

"Me thinks it ain't workin'," Roark said from his position outside the bedroom.

"Yes," Jones whispered while staring at the contraption. "What could possibly have gone wrong?"

"I don't know, you're the genius," Darcy said.

"And that, my love, has a very different tone as compared to the first assertion of my engineering prowess."

He glanced back at Darcy.

"Well, sorry. No offense intended. I just mean if anyone can figure it out, you can."

Jones smiled.

"I am comforted by your confidence. Now I shall attempt to reflect upon the actual failure by examining the process we have followed."

He gingerly stepped to the machine and with caution turned it off. He carried it to the kitchen table that had become the workspace during his visits.

After several minutes, he grinned at the two who stood close, watching his every move.

"What an incredible dolt I am. It is as simple as not inserting the correct return signature. I do not understand how I missed that."

"Ya din't say everythn' out loud like ya used ta do."

"I dare say you are absolutely correct in your assertion. I must remember this from now on. Thank you, Roark."

"So that's it? You're telling me it will work this time?"

"Only one method of proof."

Jones once again placed the machine on the kitchen floor and turned it on.

"I'll wait in the bedroom."

Darcy skipped her way to the back of the house.

The sound of the whirl began to pick up speed until it reached the correct pitch. The Adventurer disappeared.

"It's here!"

Jones and Roark made their way to her bedroom.

Jones touched the screen to set the return coordinates and the Adventurer dematerialized seconds later. The three crowded back down the hallway to find the machine sitting quietly on the floor.

"Eureka," Jones whispered. "Well, we shall now perform a travel with an organic product. We used an apple last time."

"A banana," Darcy said.

"Why a banana?"

"That's the only fruit I have in the house."

"It makes perfect sense. Roark and I will share the banana when it travels full circle. Then, and only then, shall I make a short trip from this point to the bedroom and back."

"Why can't I make the trip?"

"Because I have traveled through time and space to be with you and I would never forgive myself should something horrific betide you."

"I see, but if you go flying off into space as a bajillion particles, it's okay? That's no better."

"Me. Put tha machine on me. I can travel. Me thinks ya make a good couple. Dun't wanna lose any of the two of yous."

"Roark, my dear friend, I cannot ask so much of you. While I do appreciate the offer, I must decline."

"Me thinks ya should be nicer to me. Me offer is 'cause I

229

feel good about you and you are me best friend."

"How can I say no to that?"

Roark smiled and stuck out his hand for a shake, whereupon Jones pulled him in for a hug.

"You guys are killing me here," Darcy said. "That's so touching."

"As the trial with the banana went extraordinarily well, we should prepare you for your first solo travel. I am fully confident. Here, hold the machine in close to your chest. Do not panic when you arrive in the bedroom. Are you ready?"

"Me thinks I am."

"Okay. I'll be waiting for you in my room big guy. I'll be the one smiling," she said anxiously.

Jones stood in front of Roark and turned on the Adventurer. He felt a lurch of angst as he watched his friend and companion begin to dematerialize.

"Wahoo!" Darcy exclaimed.

Roark stood as still as possible with his eyes closed. He opened one eye and smiled at Darcy.

"He's here and he's fine," she yelled back toward the kitchen.

Jones joined the two and punched in the return coordinates.

Roark reappeared laughing; a first time experience for Jones.

"Success. And may I say your laughter has made this an auspicious occasion. We have but one task left. We should discuss taking a short trip to a destination of our choice."

"Hey, I was only half joking about going to see Gauguin. Can you make that happen?"

"I assumed as much. I will need as much information as I can get in order to calculate his exact location and time frame."

"That should be simple enough. I'll look him up on the wiki." Darcy brought her laptop to the table, booted up, scrolled through her favorites to the wiki website and typed in Paul Gauguin.

"Not sure I want ta know what 'at is." Pointing to the device, he backed out of the kitchen into the living room and sat on the couch.

"Okay, so it seems that in 1892 he spent a lot of time painting on the Hiva Oa Island in French Polynesia." Darcy turned toward Jones.

"This should prove interesting. I speak neither French nor the native language, and I struggled with Chinese but learned enough to get by. "

"So does that put the kibosh on going?" Darcy asked.

"If we are unwelcomed, we can always travel home again."

"Home again? I like the sound of that."

"Shall I calculate?"

"Or Google it."

She googled for the location coordinates and turned the computer to Jones.

"How convenient. These are extraordinary times you live in."

"We should also jump ahead a hundred years and see how we end up."

Darcy penciled Paul Gauguin's location into the journal: S09° 11.5395', W139° 41.4331'

"I should think it prudent for me to make a quick jaunt to the island and return. That way I will be certain of both the new machine and the environment. We shall toggle in the coordinates for the island."

"Okay. And if all is well, can I go?"

Darcy stood close to Jones with her hands on her hips.

"I should think it would be time for all three of us to make the trip."

"Excellent."

" 'at'll be fine with me," Roark said as he entered the kitchen.

Jones placed the journal next to the new unit and punched in the time and location. He put on his goggles and dustcoat, hugged both Darcy and Roark and took his place in the middle of the kitchen. "I will return... now... in one minute. You will most certainly not miss me."

He smiled and booted up the Adventurer. The whirl, matching the universal chord, began to play and Jones slowly disappeared.

"Does that seem slower to you?"

"Yeah. What makes it "at way?"

"Not sure. I just hope it doesn't make a difference in traveling. It would kill me if anything happened to him."

Sunday, 19 June 1892 12:00 pm

Hiva Oa Island, French Polynesia

As Jones materialized, he felt the crush of the lush tropical forest encompassing him.

"This will not do," he said in a strained voice. "Gather your Ch'i and relax."

He flipped the Adventurer in order to press the touch screen for the return location. The machine began to whirl and he was off again.

Tuesday, 26 June 2012 9:01 am

Snohomish, WA

Jones reappeared before the two as they were preparing food for lunch.

"I must recalculate the point of terminus. I arrived in a thicket and was barely able to move. I believe it would be to our advantage to arrive in Atuona since it's located on the bay and there will be beach for us to land on."

"Welcome back," Darcy said. "I have a question for you. Did you feel like everything happened slower with the Adventurer than with the Atomotron?"

"I was not aware of a difference. However, I am only now becoming comfortable with the operations of both machines."

"Oh my god, we do, don't we? We have two working time machines and I can't tell anyone about them."

"This one's best," Roark said. "Me like the lights." The Adventurer was like a toy in his massive hand.

"Yes. I can appreciate that you would find favor with the smaller of the two."

"I like it because it's lighter and you can hold it against your chest," Darcy said.

"Shall we find the coordinates for Atuona?" Jones asked.

"Coming right up, commander." Darcy booted up, went straight to the Wiki, and typed in Atuona, Hiva Oa. She turned the computer around to Jones and said, "Here ya go."

"Let me see." He ran his finger along the screen while writing S09° 48.0', W139° 1.9803' into his journal. "It is imperative that we arrive within a few feet of one another. I will toggle in slightly different degrees."

"Am I riding with you?"

"It would be my pleasure to have you accompany me on our travels to Hiva Oa. Roark can take the Adventurer and we shall travel with the Atomotron."

"What time do we leave?" Darcy asked, practically jumping up and down.

"My preference would be to arrive there at night in order to be less conspicuous."

"Yeah. Particularly with Roark, but you know, come to think of it, with Roark with us, who cares, right?"

"My sentiments exactly, however, we would be hard pressed to fabricate a story of our travel to the island, would you not agree?"

"We should dress as pirates." Darcy laughed.

"You did well naming your time machine," he said with a wave of his hand. "I suspect there are quite a few adventures awaiting us in the future. But, we, I, will not be dressed as a pirate. You may dress however you feel most comfortable."

"Thank you for your permission. When do we leave?"

"If I may, will you be dressed as a pirate?"

"You're remarkable," she said shaking her head. "It would delay the trip to have to get a pirate's costume, so no, I will not be dressing as a pirate. Again, so, when do we leave?"

"There is no *time* like the present. Allow me to toggle in our time and destination coordinates and we are secure to travel."

"Me new clothes?"

"When we return. We will not be absent for very long."

"Should we pack anything?"

"Taking into consideration the amount of time we plan to

spend there would be helpful in answering what we should pack. How long did you plan to stay? My plan was to meet Paul Gauguin and leave."

"What? We can't go to a tropical island and then just leave. We have to explore a bit. Hang out with Paul, meet a couple of his friends and *then* sneak off into the jungle and disappear."

"I have the distinct feeling you are going to make for a wonderful traveling companion."

"Okay then. I'm excited. Let's get this party started!"

Jones strapped on the Atomotron and handed the Adventurer to Roark.

"Hold this close to your chest and push this button when you are ready to travel. Everyone ready?"

Roark turned on his machine at the same time as Jones but panicked when the other two disappeared before he did. He stood rigid with fear as he began to hear the white noise that arrives right before the point of dematerializing.

Sunday, 19 June 1892 9:00 pm

Atuona, Hiva Oa Island,

French Polynesia

Jones and Darcy arrived at Atuona in ankle deep water and driving rain. The chilly droplets began to soak their clothes while they waited for Roark.

"What could be keeping him?" Darcy called out over the storm. "We need to get some place dry."

"I am sure that he will—"

"There he is. Right over there." Darcy pointed in the direction of the beach.

" 'at took me a long time. I dunt like this machine no more. Made me feel like I wasn't gonna make it." He pushed the machine into Jones's hands. The big man stood soberly as the rain pelted them.

"Let us find some type of shelter. I will place the machines behind this tree."

He did exactly that and covered them with his dustcoat.

The three made their way along the beach for around three hundred yards when they spotted a thatched roof hut big enough for a large group to gather. In the center, a large circle of stones held hot coals from what must have been a fire. Roark picked up a log, cradled it in his arms and rolled it over the stones into the pit.

"Perhaps coming in at night was not well thought out. We should return and plan for another day." Jones then raised his finger to his lips. "I believe someone is coming."

"Me thinks we got visitors."

Roark puffed out his chest and stood as tall as he could.

"Serendipitous, surely, if Gauguin," Jones whispered.

They waited impatiently for the voices to arrive and when they did, it was indeed Paul Gauguin followed by several young women and two men. Gauguin held an umbrella over himself while the others carried similar coverings made from palm leaves.

"*Bonsoir*," Paul said as he inspected the three.

"*Bonsoir*," Jones said. "You have me at a disadvantage in that I do not speak French."

"Not everyone is *parfait*, perfect, you know. I do speak enough English to get both out of and into *difficulté*, how you say… trouble." He extended his hand with a toothy grin.

"*Surtout avec les autorités*. The government, yes?"

"Yes. Remarkably, I do understand."

"You are English?"

"American from Boston and these are my friends. This is Darcy Champagne and Roark Fogerty."

"*Comment allez-vous*," Paul said. "How do you do, Darcy Champagne. Oh how I miss the days of champagne and certain French women."

"I'm enthralled. This is amazing." She circled Gauguin.

"Are you by chance French yourself?"

"There must be French somewhere in the gene pool," she said staring at his eyes. "Is my understanding correct that you've made yourself at home among the women here on the island."

"How would...? It is true. They cannot help themselves. As you can see these young women follow me everywhere I go and in return I paint them. *Je capture leur beauté naturelle*. They feel honored? Is that the right word... *honoré*, honered? I love it here. I will die here."

"That's true enough," Darcy mumbled. She glanced in the direction of Jones, whose look gave her a chill. "You're a remarkable painter," she said, trying to deflect from her faux pas.

"Ahhh, you have seen my work?" Paul asked, eyeing her up and down. "Where did you see my work?"

"Darcy. May I have a word with you... in private?"

Jones had a very stern frown on his face.

She winced at the tone of his voice. She knew she had violated some rule but she was not sure which one.

"I cannot be any more explicit in expressing my concern that you do not understand the value of maintaining anonymity when traveling from one time period to another.

These mishaps could well lead to dangerous consequences. Do I make myself clear?"

"Very clear," she said. "And you don't have to speak to me that way."

"I shall endeavor to communicate with a lesser authoritarian tone, but you must keep to the code of silence for the sake of us all."

"I understand, but the way you spoke to me just now, hurt my feelings."

When Darcy finally looked up at Jones, her eyes were teeming with tears.

"Oh, this will never do. I certainly did not intend on hurting you, but rather, to express firmly the importance of trust. May I ask for your forgiveness?"

"You may," she said, wiping away the tears from her cheeks. "Well, go ahead."

"I see. Darcy Champagne, will you forgive me for my overreach in expressing my concerns?"

"Maybe."

She took his hand and pulled him back toward the rest of the group only to find several more women had joined the circle and three of them were huddled around Roark. They pushed at his curly red hair, as if he was a doll. One had climbed onto his lap, stroking his face and chest.

"*Il est si blanc, sa peau*," she said.

"What did she say, Paul?" Darcy asked.

"Ah. She said that his skin is so white and they seem enamored with his red hair. Roark may actually enjoy being here, no?" He sat on a log next to the fire pit.

"That could never happen," Darcy said. "Could it?" She turned to face Jones. "Would Roark leave you?"

"He is a free man. He may pursue any path that he finds

appealing to his interests."

"*Je m'excuse, excusez-moi*? What is your business on this island? I do not mean to intrude."

"We are interested in the cultures of the world. We plan to travel to our favorite destinations and explore the realism of history."

"For what purpose? You have a reason, *oui*? Maybe you are spying on me?"

"Nothing could be further from the truth. Miss Champagne has always dreamed of traveling to the Marquesas. How fortunate to have made your acquaintance. Perhaps tomorrow we could see some of your paintings?"

"*Oui*, tomorrow then. I am looking forward to your *evaluation globale* of my work."

"I can't wait," Darcy said. "Is there somewhere we could crash… I mean sleep for the night?"

"Ah *oui*, please forgive my social deportment. After kava kava, I sometimes forget my *responsabilités*. As travelers, you are most welcome to sleep in the village."

"Me thinks someone has offaed me a sleepin' quarter," Roark said with a broad grin. "She dunt wanna get off me lap."

"Well, it seems we shall be staying for one night then?" Jones asked.

"Yep," Darcy responded. "And I can't wait till tomorrow."

The rain had given way to a starry night sky and a warm ocean breeze as they followed Paul and the others to the village that was not too far from the gathering house. The villagers greeted them with open arms and encouraged them to share in the celebration by drinking kava kava.

"If I may inquire as to the specification of this drink? I

would like to understand the outcome before partaking," Jones said.

"*Oui*. The drink is meant to let your mind rest. You will feel *tranquille* and yet, spirited. Drinking kava always leaves me feeling amorous."

"I see. That being the case, I shall imbibe as well."

" 'his dunt taste right."

"There's no alcohol, Roark. You can buy this anywhere as a tea," Darcy said.

"Me ain't ever heard of 'is. Me thinks it's a good idea ta wait ta see what happens afore drinking anymore."

"Good idea," Darcy said. "We wouldn't want you to start dancing an Irish jig, now would we?"

"Me dunt dance."

The beat of the drumming circle provided the enthusiastic dancers with a powerful enticement of the senses. Everyone laughed and chatted. It was as though the new strangers were meant to visit. The revelry lasted for a few hours until the three could no longer remain awake.

"Paul, can you point out where we are to sleep for the night?" Jones asked.

"*Oui*. Miss Champagne may share my quarters, if she would care to, and you may pick a female companion among the women before you. I believe your friend has made his own arrangements."

He winked as he witnessed Roark surrounded by three women.

"You got that all wrong," Darcy said.

"Yes. Darcy and I will be sleeping together," Jones chimed in.

"Then you should follow *moi*."

Paul led Darcy and Jones to a small thatched-roof hut

with mats on one side, opposite the opening. He handed Jones a lantern.

"Je vous souhaite une bonne nuit… I bid you a good night."

"This is rather cozy, do you agree?" Jones asked as he settled himself down on the mat.

"As long as I don't know what lurks in here, I'll be fine."

Jones watched Darcy's silhouette, against the light of the bonfire, as she got out of her damp clothes. Her toned physique captured his unwavering gaze. He could see the sway of her breasts in the dim light as she came toward him.

"Our excursion to this tropical paradise has left me with a thirst that can only be quenched by the closeness of two bodies."

Darcy lay next to him.

"Your turn," she said and tugged on his shirt buttons.

Jones immediately jumped to his feet and quickly shed his clothing.

"Not so fast there fella. Stand up straight and let me take a good look at you in this light."

Jones stood and began turning in a circle with his arms outstretched.

"Not bad at all." Darcy patted the stacked fern that was to be their bed. He joined her for a night of exploring intimate pleasures.

✿✿✿✿✿

When they awoke, the sun was already high in the blue sky. In the distance, they could hear the ocean waves sloshing the shore with foamy seawater. The temperate weather left the two of them excited to be in Atuona, Hiva Oa Island with Henri Paul Gauguin. The village men were already hard at work fishing and the women had gathered at the meetinghouse to prepare the meals for the day.

"I earnestly can state I do not believe I have ever experienced a happier bunch," Jones said as he dressed.

"I know, right? They just seem to be so carefree and accepting," Darcy said as they stepped out of the hut. "They've taken us in as if they've known us all their lives. That's a little weird for me."

As they watched the activities, Roark approached them from behind.

"Me thinks this is paradise."

He raised his arms toward the sky.

"For sure," Darcy responded. "Nice place... well actually more than a nice place to visit, but I wouldn't want to live here."

"Me thinks I would." Roark stepped from foot to foot. "Jones, you said I'm a free man."

"Yes indeed, Roark, you *are* a free man." Jones turned to stand squarely in front of him. "Am I to surmise that you will not be returning with us to Snohomish?"

"Me was asked, me thinks, to stay."

Roark looked back over his shoulder at the three women he had spent the night with and waved.

"Are you sure?" Darcy asked. "I mean you don't know the language or the culture. And what if you need us? It's not like you can pick up a phone or write us or text. I'm not feeling great about this."

"Your attachment to Roark is admirable. However, I do believe it is time for this young man to strike out on his own. We shall come to visit you in the future—"

"The past," Darcy said.

"Correct, the past, so we may see your progress here and should you ever have the notion to return to us, that can be arranged as well. Perhaps we should leave you an exit possibility and pass on the Adventurer to you."

"Me thinks it aint workin' the way it's supposed ta. It scares me."

"Very well then, I shall return with it in hand and research the issue. When we check back, we will bring the Adventurer or possibly an even better model."

"I don't know how to say good bye to you." Darcy leaned in for a hug, whereupon, Roark lifted her, holding her out in front him like a child. He embraced her and held her close. Darcy's eyes began to brim with tears. "I don't understand why I'm acting this way. This is not the way Darcy Champagne behaves, ya know?" He lowered her to the ground. "Roark, thank you for being you. I'll miss you and I *will* worry about you. That's it, that's all I'm going to say."

"I, too, will miss you. And perhaps I *should* worry but given your physical prowess I am convinced you will do remarkably well here with Paul. And speaking of Paul, Darcy, I thought you wanted to see with your own eyes one of his paintings."

"I do," she said, wiping away a tear. "I can't go back without seeing at least one."

"Follow me," Roark said.

The three made their way through the small village to an overlook at the edge of the bay where Paul sat painting in a makeshift chair.

"*Bonjour*! Miss Champagne I trust you slept tight, no?" Paul adjusted his beret against the morning sun.

"Yes, I guess. I slept fine, *merci*. Hey so this is the burlap…I mean this material seems to be burlap. Right?"

"*Oui*. This came from a cargo ship that was passing through. I have had a *difficile*, eh … difficulty … acquiring

243

canvas, so I now have several burlap sacks I use as a canvas to paint. This is one painting I most like because she is one of my most affectionate companions, my young wife. The title will be *Manao Tupapau, The Spirit of the Dead Watching*."

"…of the Dead Watching," Darcy mumbled. She snapped a glance at Jones. "Jones, eh…never mind, just a thought."

"Very nicely quelled. I have, from the first time of our meeting, believed you to be an astute protégé and a potential long term traveling companion."

"Speaking of traveling. Are we traveling back in time to the moment we left?" she whispered.

"No. My reasoning is this…if we travel back to the exact moment we left, Roark would need to be with us and since he does not want to return, we must make it a minute or more later, I should think. This is all new to me as well, so we must be deliberate in our analysis of the possibilities of what might happen. I understand the math and science but one cannot hope to have wisdom based on an untried experience."

"So Jones." She cupped his hand. "Can we go home now? I'm looking forward to spending time alone with you, dude. Just you and I cuddled up on the couch."

"I believe you have some of the best ideas. I like this about you. Let us say our farewells to Paul and Roark one last time."

They strolled to the beach where they found Roark already learning to mend fishing nets and to tie hooks to a fishing line.

"Roark, if I may? I do not want to interrupt your training but we have come to say our farewells. I do plan to check in on you on occasion. I must confess that I am going to miss you greatly. However, it would seem that you have found your paradise where time is of no consequence."

"I'm hatin' this. I'll miss you so much for having just met you. You are *so* endearing. I can't imagine you'll have anything but wonderful times here with Paul."

"Me gonna miss you. Take care of Jones. He needs someone ta look after him."

Roark lifted Darcy into a bear hug; likewise, he pulled Jones into the two of them and held on with his eyes closed to ingrain this moment into his mind forever.

After bidding everyone *adieu*, they slogged, hand in hand, through the hot sand, the distance to where Jones had hidden the time machines.

"Do you still think Gauguin a scoundrel?"

"Yes. Yes would be the correct answer here."

"That sounds very familiar." Jones laughed.

After strapping on the Atomotron, Jones placed the Adventurer between him and Darcy for the ride back to Snohomish, June 2012.

"Although it would seem impossible, given our circumstances, I wish to ask you to marry me, a civil union of sorts."

"And I would say *Yes!*" Darcy yelped. "*And* you're right—now that I think about it. Coming from two different centuries is a problem, huh? Maybe it'll have to be something we agree on and leave it at that."

"Certainly something to discuss when we get back to Snohomish," he said and embraced her, pulling her up close with the Adventurer between their stomachs.

"Are you ready, Miss Champagne?" he asked, beaming love into her eyes.

"I am indeed, Mr. Whitman."

Tuesday, 26 June 2012 9:12 am

Snohomish, WA

They opened their eyes to see the kitchen they had left behind yesterday, having returned the same day that they had departed.

"I am so in love with you," Jones said. "I have not experienced this type of feeling ever before; exuberant at the thought of spending a lifetime together; traveling anywhere we should choose." He laid the Adventurer on the table and removed the Atomotron from his back. "Come here to me."

He wrapped Darcy in his arms and kissed her with escalating passion.

"I'm stunned—and that's not so easy to do. You said 'I love you'. I'm going to say it, too. I love you, Jones. I would love to be your lawfully wedded wife, even if only by the laws of the universe. Laws of attraction and such."

Jones laughed.

"I have an idea."

"Go on."

"How would you feel about being married in China by Master Wong Fei-hung?" He stroked her cheek. "Suffice it to say it would not meet any criteria for marriage anywhere else in the world but we would enjoy the comfort of knowing we made a public declaration of our love and devotion to one another."

"When do we leave?" Darcy cooed.

"I need to calculate the exact location and it would seem we can get an excellent pin point destination, so we will not have to worry about surprising anyone with the exception of monks who are sworn to a vow of secrecy."

"Then let's do this. Let's shower together, make love, eat some food and then while you figure out where we're going, I will pick out a few items for us to take with us. Nothing too conspicuous, ya know what I mean?"

"We shall not need much as the temple will provide us with a gi that matches everyone else. I am assuming we will be with the Master for two or three days. I am excited to share both you and the Atomotron with Master Fei-hung."

"Alrighty then, let's do it. I'll start the shower."

Jones joined Darcy in the master bathroom and disrobed. He admired her silhouette through the shower doors, realizing that he had to travel across space and time to find the yin to his yang, a timeless love.

"May I join you?" he said, sliding the shower door open.

"If you think you can handle it."

She shot him her best come hither look.

"I shall do my best." He slid the glass closed behind him. "You are amazing." He pulled her into his embrace, allowing the water to run over both of them. They shared a fiery kiss, as he ran his hands over her body.

"I'm in love with you and I never want this to end," Darcy whispered. Her desire took over and she trailed a natural path to his manhood. "I really like the way we fit together."

"I am of the opinion that we are highly suitable. Perhaps we should take a day or two to get to know each other more intimately?"

"Okay by me. And we can stay flexible. If we decide to, we can just fly right on out of here."

"I am fortunate that you are so accommodating. Thank you."

"Last one in the bed is a rotten egg," she squealed and ran out of the bathroom.

Jones followed her closely and dove in next to her, wrapping her up in his arms and entangling their legs. Darcy felt her arousal spike and relaxed into the rhythm of love making with Jones.

When they awoke, the low sun filtered through the windows reflecting the lateness of the day. Jones rose from the bed and made his way down the hall to retrieve his journal. He made a note to remember everything about the day.

"That was a delicious experience that I shall never forget," he said as he snuggled back in bed next to Darcy.

"And it's only gonna get better the more we practice." She pushed her buttocks against him and pulled his arm over her waist. "Are we going to sleep here tonight?"

"Yes. I think it would be to our advantage to sleep now and leave in the morning."

Jones stroked her hair and then began to massage her ear.

"Wow," she said as she squirmed. "That feels awesome. I had no idea."

"Shall I stop?"

"Yeah, but only when I tell you to." She laughed. "Oh my, I just got chills."

"Turn over. You would not want to be unbalanced."

She obliged and rolled over to face him.

As he started to massage her left ear, he leaned in and kissed her closed eyes.

She sighed heavily in relaxation and smiled.

Wednesday, 27 June, 2012, 6:30 am

Snohomish, WA

"Good morning," Darcy said. "Today is the first day of our life together, well, sort of, I mean as a couple."

"Yes indeed," Jones said. He scooted in close and hugged her. "We are about to start a marvelous adventure. I am so looking forward to your introduction to Master Fei-hung."

"Me, too. He has to be an incredible person to have produced you."

"I should think that my parents should garner the greatest portion of your praise."

"For sure, but he is the one that pushed you to your greatest potential. That's all I'm saying."

"And you would be quite correct. Let's prepare shall we?"

"Let's," she said as she threw off the sheets. "I'm excited and a little scared. I have no idea what to expect."

The two dressed and began to gather what they would need for the three-day trip. The Atomotron was on the kitchen table where Jones and Darcy sat to survey the last minute checklist.

"Okay, you've the coordinates written in the journal and I've made sure we have toothbrushes, toothpaste and clean undies. A girl can never be too careful. And several batteries for the Atomotron, just in case."

Jones stood.

"Well then, shall we?"

"I'm definitely ready."

Darcy jumped to her feet and took her place in the middle of the kitchen.

"It is important to note that we will be arriving in the courtyard and there will be activity. However, do not be surprised if no one takes particular notice of our arrival. It would seem that it is difficult to ignite surprise among these monks."

"I think I'm ready for just about anything."

Jones pulled her in close and turned the switch on the Atomotron. As the time machine reached the correct pitch, they dematerialized, leaving Snohomish and the twenty-first century behind for the eighteen hundreds in China.

Friday, 12 June 1884, 6:30 am
Po-ch'i-lam Temple in Foshan,
Guangdong, China

Jones had not taken into account certain logistics, whereupon he found himself, while still embracing Darcy, with his feet in the reflection pool and she just outside.

"So much for not attracting attention," she said watching as monks gathered around.

Jones stepped out of the pool and bowed. Darcy clutched his hand as fear ramped up in her heart.

"They mean us no harm, I assure you." Jones once again bowed slightly. "I am in search of Master Wong Fei-hung."

The group of orange clad monks parted to allow a figure dressed in a black gi to step forward.

"I have been waiting for you, Time Traveler," Master Fei-hung said. "You are on time as usual."

Jones grinned.

"How did you know?"

"You have found the yin to your yang."

"I have, Master. This is Darcy Champagne."

Jones threw his arm over her shoulder and hugged her to him.

"It is an honor to meet you," Master Fei-hung said. "You must be a special woman to have tamed his nature."

"Well I kinda hope not." She felt her face flush. "What I mean to say—"

"I have come to ask you to oversee a ceremony where we may make a declaration of our love and commitment to one another."

Darcy pointed at Jones and then bowed slightly. "That's what I meant to say."

"I would be honored."

A young man approached and whispered into the master's ear.

"For now, I will have you shown to your rooms. I must speak to the Manchu military waiting at the gate. When I return, we shall prepare for your marriage."

Two monks escorted Darcy and Jones to separate sleeping quarters and provided the morning meal. They both anxiously awaited the next step in their journey, beginning with their commitment ceremony and then, a world of new adventures.

Author's Bio

Dana Bennett lived in north central Florida for the first chapter of his life. After high school, he spent the next chapter working with problem teens and their families in Pensacola, Florida and then spent time on the Colorado River Indian Reservation, in Parker, Arizona helping the Native American population. He graduated from Nova Southeastern with a degree in psychology later in life. He has had many eclectic professional experiences in the work arena, always returning to the creativity he finds in building and construction as well as crafting new stories.

He has three wonderful daughters and two adorable grandsons. He is married to his best friend and partner in life, love, and business. They have a strong supportive community of friends and neighbors who encourage them daily to keep writing.

He enjoys each day with Blakely as they work on their never finished project, life. Writing is his bliss and both he and Blakely are chasing the dream of writing full time.

You can find out more by going to:

http://danabennettblog.wordpress.com/

https://www.facebook.com/GearedToThePresent

https://www.facebook.com/fracturedfidelities

COMING SOON

The second novel

in the

Jones Whitman
Time Traveler Series

Geared to the Past